P

M000012769

"WHEN YOU FOUND ME"

"Anna Augustine's stories are not only sweet, but they get to the heart of the matter in a profound way. "When You Found Me" is a timeless collection of short stories about the Princes of Allura and how they overcome trials and find love in the midst of their brokenness. Augustine excels in witty dialogue, and her interweaving of Christian themes is beautiful." – Alissa J. Zavalianos, Author of The Earth-Treader

"Anna Augustine's writing is filled with lovable characters, suspenseful events, redemption, and sweet romance! "When You Found Me" is an enthralling collection of novellas about a marvelous family and their stories as they learn how to love Christ and each other more." – Eve Parnell (Goodreads Review)

"Anna's writing style is beautiful and captivating. She does an amazing job of keeping her reader totally absorbed in the story. I will be reading everything she writes." – Abby (Goodreads Review)

WHEN *You* FOUND *Me*

ISBN – 978-1-7365391-0-1

This novel is a work of fiction. The events and occurrences were invented in the mind and imagination of the author. Similarities to any person, past, present, or future, are coincidental.

Cover by Germancreative

ANNA AUGUSTINE

WHEN

You

FOUND

Me

WHEN *You* FOUND *Me*

ANNA AUGUSTINE

I dedicate this book to my parents: Jim and Cindy. Thank you for showing me what true love looks like.

"Let all you do, be done in love."
1 Corinthians 16:14

WHEN *You* FOUND *Me*

ANNA AUGUSTINE

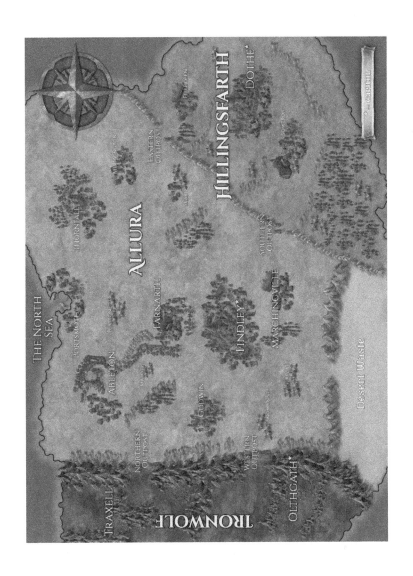

WHEN *You* FOUND *Me*

ANNA AUGUSTINE

BETTER

His

WAY

NICHOLAS AND DELLA'S STORY

WHEN *You* FOUND *Me*

ANNA AUGUSTINE

"...And who knows whether you have not come to the kingdom for such a time as this?"

Esther 4:14b ESV

WHEN *You* FOUND *Me*

1

NICHOLAS

"You what?" Collins practically hollered, throwing his hands up into the air as he started to pace in front of the massive fireplace, a habit we were all used to. He glared at our father. "How could you think that was a wise decision, Father?"

Father coughed for a moment, before catching his breath, "I am not getting any younger, my boy. I want to see you happily settled down before I pass. All of you."

"There are other ways, Father." The low, quiet voice of Benjamin came from the corner where he stood. My eldest brother always seemed to be in complete control of himself, but there was a danger about him that simmered below the surface of his facade, threatening to expose him at any moment.

Father shook his head, looking tired, "I'm sorry, my boys. It's done. The proclamation was sent out yesterday, and they shall be here within the week."

"You've been awfully quiet, Nick." Collins turned his angry brown eyes on me, "What do you think about this?"

I smiled, trying to lighten the tension that seemed to be sucking the very air out of the room, "Fifty of our land's finest ladies? All under our roof? It sounds like heaven."

Father laughed lightly, "Well, you all must behave as gentlemen while they are here."

"Father, you wound me! Who ever heard of a prince who wasn't such?"

Father raised his bushy white brow at me, and I realized that maybe that wasn't the proper jest to make at such a time. He turned to look at Collins, who'd resumed his pacing, "I am sorry, son. But what's done is done. You might as well make the best of the next month."

"Month?" Benjamin growled, pushing off the wall and stalking into the candlelight, "You invited fifty women into our castle – our home – for a *month*?"

"Aye." Father straightened and looked right into the frosty blue eyes that were shooting daggers in his direction, "I did. You will all be betrothed within three months if I have anything to say about it."

"What if none of the ladies meet our requirements?" Benjamin ground out, "What then?"

"Out of fifty ladies, one is bound to catch your eye. And there are tests I've created that they must pass in order to continue."

"What if none of them pass?" Collins asked, stopping his pacing to turn toward our father.

Father sighed, "If that is the case, then you will not have to pick a bride. But I hope and pray, my sons, that one of these young ladies will be yours. That she will catch your heart, pass my tests, and be worthy of the title of princess."

WHEN *You* FOUND *Me*

2

DELLA

I groaned as the cock crowed, signaling that it was time to rise. I pulled my rough blanket up around my nose, trying to ward off the chill that had settled over my room in the wee hours of the morning.

The annoying bird crowed again, and I begrudgingly threw off my covers and padded over to the hook on the wall. Pulling off one of my gowns, I tugged it over my head, smoothing down the front as it fell into place. I quickly brushed my long blonde hair, twisting it into a simple braid that I flung over my shoulder as I moved out the door.

"Good morning, Lady Della!" Ella, our only maid, bobbed a quick curtsy to me as she moved down the hallway toward my mother's door. She raised a knowing brow my way, "Your morning meal is on the table in the kitchen, if you're planning on eating this morning?"

I shook my head, "There's much to be done in the store."

Ella planted her hands on her tiny waist, "You made sure everything was in order last night, m'lady! No one has been in there since, so I'm sure you have time to eat before you open the shop."

"Nay," I laughed, shaking my head again, "I have much I wish to do. But if it will make you happy, I will go eat a small bowl of your porridge."

That seemed to satisfy her, and she continued down the hall. I shoved aside another wave of worry about my mother as Ella knocked lightly on her door. Ever since Father had been lost at sea a few months ago, it was as if she'd lost all her will to continue with life. Indeed, it was amazing that we were being allowed to run the store, as women in our situation often lost everything.

Father had been wise in his business dealing, however, and had made sure we were well taken care of. When my sister, Lydia, had married two years before, Father had made it so her husband would have the land in his name, and I could continue to run the store for him.

I walked toward the front of the large room, breathing in deeply the scent of the spices and leather that swirled around me as I moved forward to unlock the door.

The shelves ran all along the walls, with tables in between filled with goods for the people of the town to view and purchase. I opened the door, stepping out into the early morning light. The street was just starting to move again, with wagons and horses and people moving up and down slowly, as if they too were just awakening.

"Good morning, Della." I turned to see Les, the blacksmith's son, smiling sweetly at me. I blushed, turning away, not wanting him to see the color that was climbing into my cheeks. The last time I'd spoken to Les had been…uncomfortable.

"Good day, Les." I turned, stepping back into the shop, "What can I get for you this morning?"

I had almost made it to the back counter before Les reached out and grabbed my wrist in his rough, calloused hand. "Della, you've been avoiding me for days. What of the question I asked you? Do you have an answer for me?"

I shook my head, trying to pull my hand from his, "Les…I am in no position to marry as of yet."

He grunted, "Because of your mother? I can take care of both of you. My father is the most favored blacksmith in all of Findlay – the favorite of the king. You would lack for nothing!"

"And what of this shop?" I asked, tugging free and moving around the counter to adjust some of the spices

11

that weren't in their precise places, "I love this place, Les. You would have me squirreled away in a little home, having your children and fixing your meals."

"Is that not what every woman dreams of?" He asked in a scoffing manner, as if any other idea was foreign to his imagining.

"Not this woman." I jutted out my chin, "My answer to your proposal is no. I will not marry you, Les. Good day!"

He looked like he wanted to argue, but after a moment he threw up his hands, a vein in his forehead ticking in and out. "You are a stubborn woman, Della. Good day to you, and good riddance!" Les turned on his boot and stormed out the door, slamming it hard enough to make a few of the candles tumble off of the shelf they sat on.

I grabbed the broom that sat in the corner, gently sweeping away the dirt that had fallen off Les' boots. Anger was coursing through my blood, but I dealt with it like I always did, by putting the store into perfect order.

It was a blessedly busy morning, and I had little time to think about Les and my refusal to marry him. Mother had had her hopes hanging on me accepting that proposal, but I just couldn't. Father had never been content to stay home with my mother, and their marriage had been a cold one. Mother was often in bed with depression, and when Father was home, he and mother bickered about her refusal to handle life. When he'd died, Mother's condition worsened to the point where she hardly ever left her room. Nothing within me wanted to marry a man simply for the wealth or convenience. If I was to marry, it was going to be for love.

I was folding a bolt of silk and laying it back on its shelf when a commotion outside the shop drew me to the doorway. A great crowd of ladies moved down the street, following a knight perched atop a white horse. He was dressed in the livery of the royal castle, and he sat straight as a pole.

"What is happening?" I asked a young woman who was bouncing up and down on the balls of her feet.

"The king has declared a contest!"

I raised my eyebrow, "A contest?"

"Aye!" She nodded excitedly, her blonde ringlets bobbing up and down, "The king is choosing fifty young ladies of this town to come to the castle for it!"

"What is it for, this contest?" I asked, confused, "Fifty young ladies at the palace?"

"It's for the princes!" She squealed, "The King is looking for wives for his sons!"

"No! I will not go! You need me here! Who will run the shop?" I argued with my mother and sister after the knight had delivered the summons to me. I was to arrive at the palace the next day. I had been so angry when the young knight had shoved the scroll at me, that I'd almost thrown it back in his face. It wasn't fair that the king could order us around like animals. I glared at the scroll, as if it was somehow its fault that I was in this predicament.

Lydia rubbed her bulging stomach with one hand while waving away my argument with the other, "It's a summons, Della. You cannot ignore this!"

"But –"

"Ella and I can run the shop until you return." Mother chimed in.

I stared at her as she absentmindedly traced the insignia of King Willhelm that was at the bottom of the scroll. She was still in her nightgown, and a thin robe hung around her shoulders.

"Mother, you barely rise in the morning, and Lydia is near her time of delivery. Ella cannot manage the store alone!"

"Yes I can, m'lady!" A voice carried from the kitchen into our sitting room, where Ella was undoubtedly eavesdropping.

I laughed shortly, shaking my head, "This is ridiculous! King Willhelm can't possibly believe that this is a good way for his sons to find wives!"

"At least they get to choose." Lydia argued, "You don't have a choice, Della."

"I do, but we can't afford it," I snapped irritably. The only way to avoid going to the palace was to pay fifty silver shillings when the knights came to collect the women the following day. I rubbed my face, pacing.

"You have to go," Lydia repeated.

"I know!" I nearly hollered at her. She leaned away from me, hurt in her eyes. "I know," I said more gently, "I just … it seems pointless. No prince is going to want to marry me. And I really don't want to marry a prince."

I could see them all in my mind. Prince Benjamin, the eldest son, was aloof and arrogant. He never smiled, that I had seen, and he rode through the streets without glancing at the people around him.

Prince Nicholas seemed more cheerful than his brother. He had just returned a few weeks ago after being away for a couple of years. When he would pass by on the street, he was always smiling and nodding to his people, but in his eyes and his posture there seemed to be a pain, a guardedness that he was hiding from the world.

And then there was Prince Collins. He always seemed to be laughing on the few occasions I'd seen him, but there was something in his demeanor that was always on edge. Almost like he hated where he was and who he was.

"I don't want to marry any of them," I stated, "So I am going to lose."

"Della," Mother patted my hand like I was a child again, "The families of the winners get two hundred gold florins as a dowry. That would help settle me comfortably for the rest of my days."

She raised her eyebrows at me as if to say, *You do want to take care of your mother, correct?*

I groaned, burying my face in my hands. "I am aware of the prize, Mother."

But is that worth my happiness? I wondered as I glanced once again at the dreaded summons.

3

NICHOLAS

I leaned against the balcony railing, watching some of the knights sparring in the training arena. Captain Waylon barked orders and they all jumped to obey, eager to please both him, and eventually my father.

Oh, Father, I thought, shaking my head as I recalled the conversation we'd had that morning. I agreed with my brothers, it wasn't Father's best idea. We were all rather independent, and the thought of having the choice taken from our hands was a rather disheartening one.

But out of all of us, I was most excited at the prospect of dozens of young ladies in our halls. There hadn't been a lady in the halls of Castle Findlay since Collins' mother had passed away four years ago. The idea of women all around sent a strange thrill through me. The thought that one of those ladies could be my future wife nearly sent my heart into a gallop.

"There you are!" Collins stepped over to the railing to join me in gazing out over the kingdom, "So, what do you really think of Father's idea? You're never one to rock the boat, Nick, and I know you had a different opinion than the one you spoke in the library."

I laughed, softly, "I never can hide my thoughts from you, can I, Collins?"

"No, you can't." He crossed his arms, turning to lean his back against the railing. He gazed at me from the corner of his eye, "What do you think, then?"

"Would you be entirely put off with me for admitting I am looking forward to this?"

Collins snorted, "Yes, I would be. It's a foolish notion to think we'll find wives in a … a contest! They'll all be pretending to be better than they are, false facades on every front."

I shook my head, "Surely they won't all be that way."

He laughed humorlessly, "May I remind you that you've been away from court for two years? You have clearly forgotten the nature of women. No, brother, they're fun for a night, maybe two. But then comes the time to move on." He grunted, flinging his hands into the air, "I don't want to settle down, like Father said; I want to be wild and free."

"You are just put off with him, Collins."

He glared at me, "Yes. And I can't believe you're not."

I shook my head, stiffening at his tone. "Maybe I'm just suffering for a woman's presence. Like you said, I've been away at the outpost for a few years."

Collins' face softened slightly, "How was it there?"

I shook my head, snapping, "It was fine."

Collins stared at me for a long moment, as if waiting for something more. When I said nothing, he shrugged. "I've heard that it's horrible there."

I swallowed, nodding once, "Nothing I couldn't handle."

Collins narrowed his eyes before pushing off the railing, heading back through the arched doorway, "I'm going to see if Cook has any of those sweet buns left from breakfast. Would you like one? Nick?"

I blinked, my mind having momentarily been whisked away to the border, and the memories that I had tried so hard to bury. Collins stood by the door with a raised brow, waiting for my response. "Ah, no. Thank you."

I tried to push my normal, happy smile back into place, but I couldn't seem to find it.

My brother shrugged, before disappearing inside.

I felt lost as the quiet settled around me, only disrupted by the shouts and cheers of the knights below. But even that stirred up visions of things that I wanted desperately to forget.

"Oh, God," I whispered, squeezing my hand into a fist that I rested against my lips, "Please, help me to forget."

"What's wrong, Nicholas?"

I glanced up to find my older brother staring at me intently while we ate our afternoon meal. The chaos in the dining hall never seemed to overwhelm Benjamin. In fact, little seemed to upset my steady, confident brother. He hardly ever raised his voice. He had always been soft spoken, but with an intensity that set most people on edge. There were only three men in the world who weren't intimidated by Benjamin, and all three were related to him.

"I am fine, Benjamin." I straightened, trying yet again to push off the thoughts that had been at war with me since my conversation with Collins earlier that morning.

I met Benjamin's icy gaze, determined that I would win against his scrutiny. He continued to stare at me for a long moment, before nodding once and returning to the meat on his trencher. I swallowed, pushing around a piece of potato with my knife, my appetite evaporating.

"Are you ready for the contest, my Prince?" Lucius, one of my most trusted knights asked with a wiggle of his eyebrows as he sat beside me, "I'm eager to meet all these handsome young ladies. Mayhaps one of them will even fall for me!" He clutched at his chest, as if his heart would burst at the thought.

I laughed along with the men, trying to appear normal as I once again felt Benjamin's eyes on me.

"Mayhaps, Lucius, Mayhaps," I agreed with a chuckle. "Although I don't know what my father will have to say about you lads trying to steal a potential bride from one of his sons." I grinned at the somber looks that crossed all the knights' faces, "But take heart! There will certainly be a fair number of dances during the next few months, will there not, Benjamin?"

I turned toward my brother, who simply nodded in agreement, shoving another bite of meat into his mouth.

My eldest brother had never been much of a talker. Content to simply observe and be seen by those around him, he never tried to be the center of attention. I sometimes wondered if he even wanted the title of crown prince. He enjoyed solitude, something a future king wasn't likely to get all that often. Benjamin would frequently slip away to enjoy a book in a remote study or the library. When we had been children, there had been days when I never even saw him.

"Well, I suppose that will have to suffice, will it not, my Prince?" Lucius sighed dramatically, causing me to turn back to him with a small smile.

"Aye." I nodded, thankful for the man at my side. We had been through much together, and he was one of the few knights who I felt a kinship with. The youngest son of one of the northern lords, Lucius had joined us at our castle at ten years of age. We'd been squires, then knights-in-training together. Through every battle, every loss, and every victory, we had pulled through unscathed. Physically, at least.

I clasped him on the shoulder as we rose. Servants moved to clear the tables, and I smiled at my friend, "Are you ready to fetch our ladies, Sir Lucius?"

"Aye, my prince." He laughed as I smoothed my vest, "Are you sure you're ready to meet your ladies?"

I joined in his laughter, following him as he headed for the door, thankful for this distraction from my traitorous mind, "I suppose we shall see!"

4

DELLA

I kissed my mother lightly on the cheek before turning to hug Lydia tightly as the King's knight waited impatiently on the doorstep.

"You send word when you have that babe of yours!" I ordered my sister, subconsciously straightening the shawl around her shoulders.

She batted my hand away with a small laugh, "Of course, sister. You shall be the first to know."

I blinked back the unbidden tears that sprang into my eyes. I nodded, unable to get words past the lump in my throat.

"M'lady, we must go." The knight huffed, and I glared at him.

"All right." I took one last glance at my family, "I shall be home soon."

They waved goodbye as I moved down the cobblestone streets, my mother's hand pressed against her lips. I quickly fell into step beside the soldier, my short stature struggling slightly to keep pace with him. "Do you know anything about this contest, Sir ...?"

"Lucius." He supplied brusquely, "And no, no more than you."

"I don't even want to be going." I admitted with a sigh.

He turned a surprised eye my way, the tension in his shoulders softening, "I thought that should be the dream of every young maiden in this land; marry a prince, become royalty."

I laughed mockingly, "And every young man who lives and works down this road thinks it is our dream to marry them, have their children, and cook their meals. No, good knight, you men do not know what women dream of."

He smiled, appearing slightly taken aback at my outburst, "I beg pardon, m'lady. I did not mean to offend."

I instantly regretted my impassioned speech. I bowed my head, trying to be demure, "And I am sorry for my outburst. I just … well, I have a certain plan in my mind, and it bothers me when it's not just so."

He laughed aloud, his stiff demeanor evaporating completely, "So I've noticed."

We made four more stops down my road. The young ladies who joined us ranged from fifteen to twenty-five years of age. One of the younger girls began to weep as the knight gently pulled her away from her mother's embrace. I felt sorry for her, knowing how she was feeling all too well. I reached out, wrapping an arm around her waist, trying to distract her as we joined another, larger group of young ladies and began making our way along the large road that led up to the castle.

"What's your name?" I asked, unable to miss the appreciative look Sir Lucius was giving me.

"Maybelle," she whispered, sounding strangled.

"That's a lovely name!" I smiled at her, and she blushed, lowering her gaze, "My name is Della. I don't think I've ever met you, and I know almost everyone down my street."

"We have only just moved here from Thornfall," She said, sniffing slightly, "I didn't expect to be chosen because of that."

I stiffened, "That must be hard, arriving in a new city and being chosen for a contest of this kind."

She nodded, unable to get any words out now. Anger simmered in my stomach, and I silently prayed that I wouldn't be forced to speak to any of the royal family until I had had a chance to calm my frustration.

We'd reached the gate, and one of the many knights that now surrounded us hollered up for the guards to open the gate.

Someone wailed behind us, and I glanced behind me to see the massive swell of parents and relatives shouting and crying out, angry that their girls were getting carted away like cattle. They began to push against the knights, who formed a protective barrier at the back of us and continued to push us forward.

We stumbled through the gate and they quickly closed with a decided thud. The bar fell across them, locking out the angry mob and effectively locking all of us in.

I shivered. The sun was blocked by the towering walls, on top of which knights moved back and forth on patrol. I heard the girls around me begin to whisper, and nervous laughter danced around the mammoth courtyard. A wide set of steps on the far end led up to the great arching doors of the castle. As I studied the intricate carvings on them, they slowly opened, and four men stepped out onto the first step. My eyes traveled over them all and I braced myself when King Willhelm raised a hand to silence our whisperings.

"Welcome, ladies of Findley. Thank you for coming to be part of this contest."

As if we had a choice. I bit my tongue to keep from shouting that thought out.

"As you know, fifty of you have been chosen from all the maidens in Findley. And you are all beautiful young ladies at that."

A titter of giggles wafted over us and I rolled my eyes.

"However," King Willhelm continued, "I only have three sons." He gestured to the young men standing a step above him, "So there are some of you who will be sent home in the coming weeks, and some of you who will stay."

He smiled, and I dropped my gaze, refusing to let myself soften toward this man that reminded me of my father.

"I shall meet with each of you, choosing five of you for each of the princes to get to know better. There shall be other contests as well, in the coming weeks. Fail them, and you shall be sent home." He smiled conspiratorially, "But for tonight, we shall celebrate your arrival with a dance and feast! Welcome to the Castle of Findley!" He turned to the side, gesturing us forward and through the doors.

The mass of women surged forward, but I remained on the fringe, thinking through everything that the King had said. If I could fail at the challenges and be sent home, then I could continue to run my father's store. I wouldn't have to continue to be subservient to men, I could forge ahead, and be the first tradeswoman in Findley, perhaps all of Allura!

"Pardon me, m'lady. But the rest of the young ladies have made their way to the dining hall." I blinked, looking up into the dizzyingly blue eyes of Prince Nicholas. "Are you planning on joining them?"

I opened my mouth, but no words seemed to be capable of passing through my lips. That had never happened before in all my nineteen years.

Prince Nicholas laughed, staring at me like I was the most peculiar girl he'd ever met, "Are you alright, m'lady?"

I cleared my throat, forcing the words to form, "Yes, my prince. I beg pardon. It appears as though I was lost in thought."

He pushed a lock of his curly red hair off of his forehead, but the moment he pulled his hand away, it flopped right back down, "Well, might I escort you to the celebration?"

Finding no way to graciously deny him, I accepted the arm he offered me. "What exactly are we celebrating, your highness?" I dared to ask, as we moved up the steep steps.

"Why, your arrival to the castle, and the fun we shall have during the coming weeks." He looked at me curiously when I didn't respond, "Are you not excited for this contest, m'lady?"

"Your highness," I heard the warning in Lucius' tone as he stepped up behind me, "You'd better watch this one! She has a quick wit, and an equally quick tongue."

I was surprised that Lucius had the right to speak to the Prince in the way he had just done, but Nicholas didn't seem offended. He simply smiled at the knight, "Does she now? Well, that would be a refreshing thing, indeed."

"Truly, m'lord?" I raised my brow skeptically, "Speaking my mind tends to scare most men away."

"Does it now?" Prince Nicholas laughed again, and something about it made me smile slightly. "That shall be your challenge then, m'lady," he leaned forward, dropping his voice to a conspiratorial whisper, "Try and scare me away."

WHEN *You* FOUND *Me*

5

NICHOLAS

I wasn't sure what had prompted me to challenge the young lady as we paused before the dining hall doors. Maybe it was the confident way she held herself, or the slight upturn of her mouth when Lucius had warned me about her. Whatever the case, she was the most interesting woman I had ever met.

"Before we enter," I asked, holding her elbow to keep her from moving forward, "I beg your name."

She stared at me for a long moment. Although her face remained void of any emotions, they were clearly noticeable in her eyes. The moment I looked into them, it was as if I was watching the acting troupes that traveled through Allura. I saw a story play out in her hazel eyes. Loss and sorrow, hope and joy. She blinked, gazing up at me, and I was completely lost in the swirling greens and browns that lay before me.

"Prince Nicholas?" A throat cleared, jerking me from my reverie. Lucius stood, hands folded behind his back, and brows raised, "They're waiting for you. Might I escort the lady in?"

"Right. Of course." It was my turn to clear my throat. Turning back to the woman at my side, I bowed over her hand, "But the lady still needs to tell me her name."

A blush turned her cheeks a most becoming hue of pink. "My name is Della, m'lord."

She tugged her hand away quickly, interlocking her fingers and clutching them before her. I smiled again with a laugh, "A beautiful name."

"My prince." Lucius motioned me into the dining hall, pulling Della back so no castle gossip could be started earlier than necessary. As I stepped in, every woman's gaze immediately glued to me as I walked down the center aisle to the royal table. It was elevated on a dais so that we could look out over all who were eating. But that also meant that everyone could see us too, and that was something that had taken me some time to readjust to.

"What took you so long?" Collins grumbled as I approached. He was hunched in his seat, a scowl on his face as his eyes moved back and forth over the women.

He was bound and determined to suffer the whole time they were here. It confused me to no end. Out of all of us, Collins was the ladies' man. A natural born flirt, he was the prince that had caused the most scandal in his twenty years of life.

"I got … detained," I hedged, taking my seat as my father rose.

"Welcome to the evening meal, m'ladies!" He called out, his voice stronger than it had been in years. Father was clearly enjoying being a host again. He smiled, raising his goblets of wine in the air, "May the Lord bless our meal, and all who gather within our walls. Amen."

"Amen." We all echoed, raising our cups in the air before taking a sip.

The meal progressed quickly, carried along by the laughter and high spirits that were all around us.

As the servants began to clear the trenchers, Father rose again. He grasped his hands behind his back, pacing to and fro as he explained to the ladies what they were to expect in the next few weeks.

"You were chosen for a number of reasons. Some of you are quite young, while some of you are reaching the age where you doubt you will ever find love. Some of you are from the wealthiest families in the city and others from the poorest. Some of you have a fair complexion, some dark. So how on earth did I choose whom to summon?"

He raised a finger, "It was simple. I looked at character."

A whisper ran through the crowd; they were clearly as confused as I was.

Father continued, "I sent some of my most trusted knights into town. They had the task of meeting many of you, asking questions, and searching for those of you who seemed … different. Special in some way." He smiled, waving his hand over the girls, "And here you are."

Another hum of whispers wove their way through the group, and Father waited for it to hush again.

"Over the next five days, I shall meet with all of you individually. I shall see if you truly are who my knights saw you to be. But for now," he clapped his hands, and a handful of the knights quickly pushed the tables to the fringe of the dining hall, "'tis time for dancing!"

I stood quickly, making Benjamin glance at me with a slightly upturned brow. I scanned the room for Della and found her standing next to a shorter, younger woman. I moved along the edge of the crowd, politely ignoring all the ladies who were batting their lashes in my direction.

"M'lady." I stated as I finally reached her. Her eyes grew round, and a nervous smile appeared on her face as she bowed her head in acknowledgement. "Might I have this first dance?"

"Oh," She stared at me and then down at the girl at her side, "I will gladly accept, my prince, but you must first do something for me."

"What is that?" I asked, willing to humor her.

"Before you dance with me, you must first dance with my friend, Maybelle."

She gestured to the girl at her side, and I turned to her. Maybelle was shaking from head to foot, her gaze transfixed on the ground in front of her. She looked to be no older than sixteen and was obviously terrified at being pulled from her home and into our palace.

"If Maybelle wishes it, I shall gladly dance the first dance with her." I smiled at Della, who smiled back. My pulse tripped, and I quickly turned back to Maybelle holding out my hand to her as I bowed. "May I have this dance, m'lady?"

She giggled nervously, flicking her eyes up at me before dropping them again and placing her hand into mine, "It would be my pleasure, my prince."

As I guided Maybelle onto the dance floor, I couldn't keep my mind from wandering to Della, and how she'd noticed this young, frightened girl, and quickly befriended her. I found my gaze drifting over to where she stood as Maybelle and I danced. She was watching all the other couples promenade across the floor as laughter mixed with the music floating all around us.

The dance finished, and as we all clapped, I moved to intercept Della.

"Now, may I have this dance?"

She nodded, no trace of the smile that had been on her face mere moments before.

The music started, a waltz, and we began the simple steps across the floor.

"It was very kind of you to find a partner for Maybelle," I commented as I guided her away from another couple. I glanced up at the dais, and noticed that Collins, who was normally the first to begin dancing and last to stop, was sitting with his arms crossed stubbornly across his chest. He was glaring right at Della and me as I spun her under my arm and back to the normal steps.

"It was more self-preservation then mere kindness." Della bluntly stated, drawing me back to our conversation.

I raised a brow, "And what, pray tell, must you be preserved from?"

"Marriage," she stated flatly. "I had no desire to come here, your highness. I have no desire to win a marriage proposal, and I have half a mind to tell your father that when we have our meeting."

I stopped abruptly, letting the other dancers continue to swirl around us. "You don't wish to win?"

She shook her head, a look of stubborn determination on her face, "I wish to continue to do what I've done since I was a child."

"And what is that?" I asked, raising my hands in exasperation, "What could be better than living in a place, with servants waiting on you hand and foot?"

Anger flared in Della's eyes, and she waved her hands in my face, heedless of propriety. "Working is better! Working with your hands and seeing the fruits of your labor on the table each night. I work in a shop, your highness, which my father built from the ground up. He died while at sea, retrieving goods for it. That shop is now one of the most notable establishments in Findley. My apologies if you think that it must be my dream to live in a castle, married to one of you, the princes of the land. I would much prefer to be home in my tiny little room above my father's store. Good evening!"

She had gotten more and more passionate with each word, edging closer and closer to me until we were almost toe to toe. Her hazel eyes flashed with passion, and I found that I was at a loss for words as she turned on her heel and stormed out of the crowded hall.

6

DELLA

I leaned against the hallway wall, breathing hard as I laid my hands against my face, trying to cool my burning cheeks. Had I really just yelled at Prince Nicholas?

The *Prince Nicholas! I am the biggest fool to walk this earth!*

But something inside of me had liked standing up to him, showing him that I wasn't afraid of his title, his position. I pushed off the wall to stand in front of the large windows. The lights of Findley sparkled like dozens of tiny stars across the black town. I wrapped my arms around my middle, feeling very alone in the great big castle with no one I knew.

God, why did you bring me here? I don't even want to be here! All I want to do is share my love of fine goods with others. Now I'm in a contest to be a wife. I am being paraded around like a trophy to be won, or a cow at auction. I bit my lip, allowing the anger to resurface. It was easier to handle anger than sorrow.

"That was quite the show you put on for my brother." A shiver slipped down my spine as I turned to face the voice. Prince Collins leaned against one of the many marble pillars that supported the roof. His sandy blonde hair flopped into his face, similar to Nicholas' except for the curl was looser. His brown eyes looked glazed, and his words were slurred. He'd obviously had one too many glasses of wine.

"I beg your pardon, my prince, but it wasn't a show." I took a step back as Collins pushed off the column and began to advance towards me, "I was quite vexed with your brother."

"He does have that effect on people, doesn't he?" Collins laughed, and the sound sent another chill through me. Collins stepped closer as he continued, "Nicholas often riles people, simply for the fun of it."

"Prince Collins –" I gasped as my back hit the pillar behind me. He reached up, caressing my cheek with the back of his hand, "Please your highness, this is highly improper."

"It's only improper if you get caught," he lowered his face, his warm breath blowing against my cheek. His eyes gazed down my form in a predatory way, "And I, m'lady, rarely get caught."

"Collins!" The prince jerked back at the voice, his eyes narrowing, "Leave the young lady alone."

The voice was cold, emotionless. Collins stepped away, scowling at the imposing figure. "'twas only a bit of fun, Benjamin."

"You know very well that Father disapproves of that sort of *fun*." Prince Benjamin glared back at his brother, danger in his blue eyes. "You're drunk. Go to bed, Collins."

The younger man turned back to me, taking one last lewd look. I was sure he was going to ignore his brother as he took a half step toward me. But then a sneer turned up the corners of his mouth, "Fine. She was far too feisty for my taste anyways." He turned on his heel and sauntered down the hallway, never looking back.

"Thank you, your highness." I breathed, daring to meet Benjamin's gaze.

"You best stay away from my youngest brother." He shook his head as he watched Collins turn the corner.

"Is he … does he …?" I swallowed, unsure how to finish my sentence.

"Yes." Benjamin turned back to me, seeming to read my mind, "He needs a firmer hand than our father wields."

I wasn't sure how to respond to that information. "He seems … unsafe for the young ladies to be around."

"He will be perfectly safe to be around. I shall see to it." He turned, clearly dismissing me, and walked back into the dining hall.

A servant bustled up to me then. "M'lady, may I show you to your room?"

I nodded, numbness beginning to settle over me as I followed the maid into what was to be my room. It was huge, easily the size of my father's store, with a canopy bed sitting right in the center. The walls were covered in the prettiest floral blue paper I'd ever seen, with a gleaming oak wood floor beneath my feet.

"M'lady, I need to get some measurements." The servant bobbed a curtsy, "Every maiden is to get two new dresses for this coming week, and if you make it to the following week of the contest, you shall have three more."

"Five new dresses?" I breathed as she quickly looped a measuring tape around my waist. I only had three dresses at home, the two I wore for work, and my nicer red dress for church and special gatherings. The thought of even one fine dress was enough to make a girl's head spin. But five was too much to even dream of.

The maid finished measuring me, bobbing another curtsy before she left the room. I padded over to the large wardrobe, pulling out a pristine white nightgown.

Quickly shedding my clothes, I stepped into the soft, although slightly too large, gown. As I unbraided my hair, I walked to the one window that my room had, staring out over the castle gardens. Memories of the leering Collins clawed their way into my mind, but I pushed them away, and instead closed my eyes in prayer.

Lord, I don't know why you have me here. But please, show me. I can't do this alone.

The next morning, I awoke with a start, confused as to where I was. The memories of the day before came rushing back. I groaned, flopping back onto the mountains of pillows, and tugged the blanket further up my body.

A maid knocked softly, quickly stepping through the door with a smile, "Your dress is finished, m'lady."

"Already?" I asked in surprise. Feeling the sleepiness fade away, I swung my legs over the side of the bed and followed the maid to the wardrobe.

"Yes, the castle seamstresses have worked all night to have the first ten of you young ladies ready to meet the king today."

"Me?" It came out like a squeak and I swallowed, "I am to meet the king today?"

"Yes, m'lady." She smiled, as I began to tug off my nightgown, "Here, let me help you. We shall have you looking like a princess in no time."

I bit my tongue as she easily pulled new underthings over my head, deciding to not share that I had no intention of winning the silly contest. She made quick work of settling the beautiful dark green gown around my shoulders, tugging the sleeves to their proper length at my wrists. She then sat me down on a low stool and began to brush my blonde tresses with a vengeance.

I placed my hands into my lap, trying to sit straight and still as she braided and twisted and tugged my hair into submission. As she stabbed one last pin into it, she smiled and led me over to the mirror that hung by the door.

"Does it satisfy, m'lady?"

I blinked, my mouth hanging open at the sight. The dress was gorgeous. It had a square neckline, and the tight sleeves and bodice accented my curves in a very flattering way. It flared out at my waist, falling in gentle folds around my legs. The forest green brought out the green in my eyes. And the crowning glory was my hair. The maid had done an exquisite job, piling it up in an elegant, yet secure style.

"Oh, it's perfect!" I breathed. I felt like I was indeed in a fairy tale, that the clock would strike midnight and it would all come crumbling down.

I don't want to be here, though! I berated myself. *Do not let this get to your head!*

The maid bobbed a curtsy, "Well then, if that's all, m'lady?"

I nodded, "Thank you … I don't believe I acquired your name?"

She smiled prettily, "Emmy, my lady."

"Thank you, Emmy. For everything."

"The princes won't be able to take their eyes off of you, m'lady." She lowered her head, "You are beautiful, and I truly hope you win the favor of the king."

I was too shocked to reply as she turned and hurried out the door. I smoothed my sweaty palms over the front of the dress as I stepped out into the hall. It was empty, but I was certain I knew the way back to the dining hall to break my fast.

However, the hallways all looked the same. Tall, vaulted ceilings with large, marble pillars running along the left side of the wall. On the right were portraits of the royal families, past and present. They stared down at me with disapproving eyes, as if they knew I wasn't meant to be there. I hurried down the hall, eager to be away from their gaze.

My footfalls became muted as I turned the corner and stepped onto a plush red carpet. I blinked, halting my progression to gaze at where I found myself. The hallway had ended abruptly, leaving a tiny alcove. The ceiling was lower, and it created a cozy atmosphere. A square window sat in the wall, a window seat below it. Large, colorful pillows sat on either side of the window, and soft yellow curtains hung across the arched doorway, creating a private little hideaway.

A small table sat to my left, a large tome opened on top of it. I stepped toward it, surprised to see that it was a copy of the Scriptures, opened to Proverbs three. I let my fingers glide over the words of the Proverbs, drinking them in as one might water.

Trust in the Lord with all thine heart;

And lean not unto thine own understanding.

In all thy ways acknowledge him, and he shall direct thy paths.

I smiled, taking a deep breath as the words soothed my soul. I still didn't want to be here, and I certainly had no desire to win. But I was willing to trust the Lord, for I knew that He did have a plan in all of this. And I had to believe that it was going to be good.

"Are you lost, m'lady?"

I leapt a few inches in the air, clutching a hand against my chest to keep from screaming. Prince

Nicholas leaned against the doorway, a small smile teasing the corners of his mouth.

"Oh, my prince. You startled me." I turned back to the book, pretending to read but all too aware of Nicholas' presence. Memories of my last encounter with one of the princes made my pulse trip. Could I trust Nicholas any more than Collins?

"Do you read, m'lady?" Nicholas asked as he stepped closer to me.

I straightened, taking a half step back. "Aye, your highness. I was taught by my father."

He nodded in acknowledgement, "It is a rare thing, to find a lady with so many different talents."

I couldn't tell if he was in earnest, so I simply raised a hand to wave off his comment, "'tis nothing, my prince."

"I disagree," He protested, and I dared to look up at his eyes. The rich blueness of them rendered me speechless as Nicholas pointed a finger at the Scriptures. "To read means you are well-versed in the Lord's word, which is indeed no small thing."

I was unsure of what to say. I had caught the intensity in his gaze and in his voice.

"Are you ready for the morning meal?" Nicholas' seemed to gather himself, stepping back from me with a forced smile.

I nodded, finding that my voice was still gone. Nicholas offered me his arm and I took it, letting him guide me back up the hallway. I tried to commit the path to memory, so that I could find my way back once I was alone.

"Were you lost, m'lady?" He asked as we turned a different corner, and I began to recognize the portraits that lined the hall.

"Maybe slightly." I admitted.

Nicholas laughed, and I was struck by the melodic tone of it. "I thought so. Our castle is so sprawling, it is easy to get lost."

I nodded, "Aye, tis quite large."

We fell into silence again, our footfalls the only sound in the hall. I was fully aware of the heat his arm passed to me through his sleeve, the rise and fall of his chest as we walked and the way his eyes kept flicking to the side to stare at me. I wanted to squirm, but I forced myself to stand straight. I wasn't going to show him that he affected me at all.

We soon reached the dining hall, with girls going in and out. Laughter and conversations floated over to us as we stopped by the doors.

"Thank you, my prince." I tugged my hand from his arm, but he grabbed it, his eyes once again capturing mine.

"My lady, I meant what I said. You are … inspiring."

I laughed a little, aware of the other girls around us, and the glares they were sending my way. "I am no different from the other ladies, my prince. Thank you for showing me the way to the dining hall." I managed to wrest my hand from his, "I never would have found it without your help."

Nicholas straightened, his lips pressed into a thin line, "Of course, m'lady."

Dipping into a hasty curtsy, I turned and walked as gracefully as I could away from Prince Nicholas and his intoxicating blue eyes.

"Lady Della, daughter of Lord and Lady Montgomery." The scribe called as the ten of us who had been chosen to meet with the King sat in the empty hall.

I rose, hands shaking as I stepped up to follow the portly scribe into the study. It was the coziest room I'd been in since arriving the day before. A few bookcases stretched from floor to ceiling and covered every inch of the far wall, interrupted only by a large window in the center. A massive fireplace stood along the left wall with a few red upholstered settees positioned in front of it. A desk sat to my right, with papers spread all across the top of it.

"Come in, my dear!" The friendly voice of King Willhelm floated over to me from in front of the fireplace. He was standing, leaning against the mantle with a smile on his face. He motioned me forward, and I obeyed despite my entire being telling me to run.

"Your highness," I curtsied, holding my breath as I rose. His eyes swept over me. Unlike his youngest son, however, they weren't predatory, merely curious.

"Your name?" He asked, motioning to the seat across from the one he claimed.

"I am Della, daughter of the late Lord Montgomery."

"Lord Montgomery? The Merchant Lord?" He asked with a raised brow, "He was one of the finest merchants in the land, and a very good man."

I felt a blush climb into my cheeks as I nodded, "Aye, he was a wonderful man and father. Although his travels kept him rather far from home."

The king studied me again. His kind grey eyes seemed to catch everything, much like Prince Benjamin's, but they were warm and friendly, like Nicholas'. After a long moment he motioned me with his hand, "Why do you think you should win this contest, Della?"

I cleared my throat, dreading this question, "To be honest with you, sire, I do not want to be here."

I heard him shift in his chair, "And why is that, Della?"

I clenched my teeth together, "I want to continue to run my father's shop, my king. I want to work with my hands, instead of having a servant wait on me hand and foot." I dared to meet his eye. No judgement was there, only interest. "I don't know why God brought me here, your highness, but I will not be saddened if I am sent home."

He stroked his beard, and I shifted nervously once more.

"You intrigue me, Della."

I laughed nervously, turning to stare at the empty fireplace, but did not respond.

"You are the young lady that yelled at Nicholas at the evening meal, are you not?"

I bit my lip, "Aye, sire. I do apologize for that."

"Nay," He waved away the apology as one might a fly, "You showed yourself to be … strong."

"I have always been independent, my king. I am …" I rubbed my hands across my dress, habitually smoothing out all the wrinkles, "I am willing to remain, but only if you truly think it wise. I don't wish to marry for convenience, nor comfort. I only want to marry if I truly believe a strong, loving marriage can be foraged from it. My parents," I turned to face King Willhelm again, "their marriage was simply a pretense, sire. I cannot abide the thought of being trapped in a union like that."

The king steepled his fingers, smiling at me, "Trust me, child. My sons do not want that either. In fact," He pushed to his feet and offered me his arm, "They were quite insistent that this was a horrible idea."

"Oh," I thought through my interactions with the young princes, "Is that why they've been acting so …?"

"Angry? Arrogant? Aloof?" The king laughed, and it brought moisture to my eyes, for it sounded so fatherly and loving, "Yes, dear. They are a stubborn lot. I had to promise them that if they found no one to their satisfaction, then they wouldn't have to pick a bride."

I raised a brow at that, "That is not the impression the young ladies are under."

He smiled, "They shall all go home with a gift, and a rather nice one. Anything they're given here is theirs to keep, and twenty gold florins are also to be sent to their parents at the end of this competition, regardless of them being chosen or not."

I smiled back at the king, hoping I didn't look as surprised as I felt, "That is truly generous, King Willhelm. You're a better king than most."

He laughed, before coughing a little at the end, "I am not that wonderful, my dear, but I do thank you for the compliment."

We reached the door, where he patted my hand, "Well, run along now. We shall see what happens. I have a feeling about you, Della," he smiled warmly, "a very good feeling, indeed."

WHEN *You* FOUND *Me*

7

NICHOLAS

I stood on the terrace again, leaning against the rail and staring out over the city. From my viewpoint, the people scurrying up and down the road looked very much like mice, eager to do their work and then return to hearth and home.

Hearth and home, I thought with a small smile. The young ladies had been here for four days now. The last group was meeting with Father that afternoon, and that night he was to announce who would be remaining for another week.

My mind unwillingly drifted to a certain young lady who'd I run into multiple times over the last few days. Something about Della lifted all the melancholy that seemed to float above my head like a storm cloud. She carried in her heart what I was missing from mine. That spark that I had been searching for since I returned from the border.

Laughter from the doorway made me turn. There she was, Lady Della, walking with Maybelle and laughing at something she'd said. They stepped out on the terrace, not noticing that I stood on the other side.

"the rumor is that you're going through?" Maybelle smiled, "There is little wonder in that."

Della shrugged her slim shoulder, "I know not, only that King Willhelm said he had a good feeling about me. I cannot imagine why, after the scene I made the first night here."

Maybelle shook her head, looking more confident than I had ever seen her before, "Nay, m'lady, it wasn't that awful. I think sometimes the princes need to put in their place."

"Shh!" Della hushed her friend, but she was laughing slightly.

"Put in our place?" I asked as I stepped forward, smiling as the ladies jumped and their faces turning redder than tomatoes, "Well, you did indeed do that, m'lady."

I grinned at Della, who scowled in return. "So now you're eavesdropping on us?"

"No, I was here first. You just didn't notice me." I bowed toward her, and she growled under her breath as I chuckled, "And if anyone had to put me in my place, m'lady, I am most thankful 'twas you."

Della rolled her eyes, stubbornly crossing her arms across her chest and lowering her brows. "You are maddening, m'lord."

Maybelle had taken a great interest in the ground, her hands folded behind her back as I laughed at Della's frustration, "I have been told that a time or two."

"Yes. Prince Collins told me you often rile people for fun." She stated casually as she turned and walked to the railing.

"What were you doing with my brother?" I asked, a twinge of trepidation forming in my stomach.

"He caught me outside of the dining hall, after you so rudely scared me away," the look she sent my way dared me to correct her, "He … well he was quite the interesting conversationalist."

Again, unease wormed its way up to my throat, making my next words sound almost like a low growl, "What else did he say to you?"

Della turned to study me for a moment before answering, "Nothing more than that. Prince Benjamin joined us, and then Prince Collins retired to his room. I think he may have been … slightly intoxicated." She cleared her throat, turning to study the knights dueling in the courtyard below.

I felt the tension in my shoulders relax after her admission, and I wondered that I had had a reaction at all. Never before had a woman so completely captivated me. I wondered if it was simply because I had been away from the feminine set for so long. Yet, even when I'd been home and a part of the parties and celebrations at the palace, I'd never been so drawn to a lady as I was with Della.

"May I have a sword?"

I blinked from my reverie, leaning my back against the banister to study Della, "A sword?"

"Aye, my father taught me to sword fight." She grinned at me and it was almost roguish, "I traveled with him once to purchase some imported fabrics we were acquiring for the shop. He thought it wise to teach me to handle a weapon." She looked back at the knights, "Pirates roam the North Sea in droves, after all."

"But …" I shook my head, completely shocked, "A sword?"

She turned to me, frustration evident in every move she made, "And what is wrong with me knowing how to use a sword, Prince Nicholas? I am quite apt at it and am fairly certain I could hold my own with any of your knights."

"What about me? Would you take me on in a duel?" I challenged, pushing off the banister and leaning toward her. I locked eyes with her, daring her to refuse.

"If that is what you wish." She straightened herself, tipping her head to glare back at me. Standing at least a head shorter than myself, she was somehow intimidating.

"Come then," I motioned for her and Maybelle to follow me, "let us go find our swords."

"Wooden training swords?" Della huffed when we met on the courtyard green. Her hazel eyes flashed with indignation as they glared at me, "Do you not trust me, m'lord?"

"Nay, I trust you." I twirled my wooden sword around my wrist and back into my hand, "I simply want to duel with these. Will that be a problem, m'lady? Would you care to plea mercy already?"

Some of the men who had gathered around laughed at my jab and pointed to the young lady who dared to challenge their prince to a duel.

Della's jaw locked at the laughter, and she rolled her shoulders to loosen the muscles in them. "Nay. It shall be you who begs for mercy, my prince."

The men *ho ho*'d at that comment as well, and I sent them a look that silenced most of the jeers. As I turned back to ready myself, Della was already attacking, slashing in quick succession, pushing me back two steps before I could regain my balance and push an offense.

She was strong, parring each of my attacks with grace, and a number of times she even put me on the defense with her quick blows. I was sweating, trying to find an opening to disarm her, but she was fast, spinning to and fro, keeping me moving and using my size against me.

As I blinked away some sweat from my eyes, Della quickly dashed behind me, holding the sword tip at my neck. I paused, breathing hard.

"Drop – your sword – my prince," Della huffed, equally winded, "And ask for mercy, if you please."

A plan quickly formed, and I let the wooden sword fall from my hand. I timed it perfectly, ducking under her blade and grabbing my own before it hit the ground. With a hard, upward arch, I hit her weapon with all my might. The impact startled her, and she lost her grip. The sword flew backwards, rotating end over end before it clattered against the walkway by Lucius' feet. He smiled and nodded at me as I stood, holding my sword against Della's neck.

Her eyes grew round, before narrowing as she turned back at me, "That wasn't fair."

"I had not yet asked for mercy, m'lady." I wiggled my brows, "The duel was still going. Now, if you would be so kind?"

She clenched her jaw, her eyes flicked to her weapon, then back to me. She apparently thought it futile to try and reclaim her sword, for she lowered to her knee with a mumbled, "Mercy."

The men cheered as I offered her my hand. She stared at it for a long moment before accepting.

"Well fought, m'lady."

"Thank you, my prince. You are quite proficient with the sword as well."

I smiled, bobbing my head at the compliment, "I have had my fair amount of fighting." I grimaced as a memory from the border came to mind. I shoved it away, "While I do not like fighting for my life, friendly competition is quite enjoyable."

Della nodded, a small smile on her lips, "I would quite enjoy a rematch, after I've had some time to hone my skill." She grinned, her lower lip caught between her teeth.

"Indeed, that would be … enjoyable." My breath hitched as I stared at her lips, and I forced myself to look away. Since when had lips been quite so enticing?

Lucius approached us, his knowing gaze flicking between me and Della. "The other sword, my lord." He held it out to me, and I took it with a nod, not meeting his eyes.

"Thank you," I cleared my throat, as my words had sounded strangled. "Will you please escort the lady back to her chambers?"

Della raised a brow, "I need no escort."

"You got turned around heading to the dining hall a few days ago." I swallowed my chuckle as she scowled, "Lucius is one of my most loyal knights, m'lady. You shall be in the very best of hands."

"I am not concerned about that, my prince." She snapped, rolling her eyes as she accepted Lucius' arm, "It is what the other ladies will think."

Lucius shrugged, as confused by the statement as I was. He turned and led Della back to the castle as I turned made my way to the armory. As I placed the swords back in their proper place, I puzzled over Della's parting words, wondering why she would fear her fellow contestants.

8

DELLA

As soon as we reached the garden, I tugged my hand away from Lucius' arm, "Thank you, but I'd prefer to stay in the garden for a while."

"Might I walk with you, m'lady?" Lucius asked, offering his arm to me again.

I swallowed my hasty retort of *you most certainly may not,* and instead summoned up every ounce of ladylike behavior that I could. Staunchly ignoring his arm, I began walking again. "If you so desire, Sir Lucius, I cannot stop you."

He laughed slightly, "You are a very different type of lady, aren't you?"

I studied him out of the corner of my eye as we entered the rose garden, "Aye, I have been told that a time or two."

"I'd wager you've been told that a good many times," Lucius locked his hands behind him as we strolled down the stone walkway, "It must be why Prince Nicholas is so taken with you."

I halted, raising a shaking hand to my lips as I stared at Lucius, who hadn't noticed that I stopped moving forward. "He – he's what?"

Lucius turned, with a small smile on his face. "You are surprised by this," he stated with some confusion in his voice. "Do you not fancy Prince Nicholas?"

"It was not … it isn't that I dislike him." I lowered my hand, "It's simply … this is a contest, no? It could turn out any number of ways." I pushed past the knight, feeling a sudden wave of panic. This couldn't be happening, not so soon after I'd talked to the king, after I told him that I didn't even wish to win! I didn't want to hurt anyone, especially the prince!

"My lady! Wait!"

I pulled up short at the call, realizing that I'd been practically running. I smoothed a hand over my hair that Emmy had done for me that morning. Amazingly, it was still mostly intact despite a swordfight and a run through the palace gardens.

Turning, I saw Collins trotting up behind me, a less terrifying smile on his face than had been there my first night at the palace. He was dressed in a red shirt with a leather vest over top of it. Loose fitting breeches were shoved into calf high boots. A sword hung from a belt around his waist and slapped against his legs with each step. His eyes seemed clear, testament to the fact that wine was the true culprit in his actions toward me before.

"Good afternoon, Prince Collins." I smiled as pleasantly as I could, bobbing a curtsy his way, "How are you this day?"

"Quite well. I saw you almost bested my brother. You enjoy showing him up, do you not?" He smiled, offering me his arm. A shiver of uneasiness slid down my back as I took it, for something about this youngest prince set every hair on my body on end.

I glanced at Lucius over my shoulder. His arms were crossed as he watched us together, a small frown tugging on his lips. He was following at a respectable distance, for which I was glad.

"M'lady?" Collins asked with a raised brow, and I realized that I hadn't answered him.

"Oh, no. I do not enjoy it, per say. It is simply a way to pass the time."

Collins laughed, but it set my nerves even more on edge. I couldn't help comparing it to Nicholas' laugh, and found that Collins' was woefully lacking.

"Most women enjoy needle work or reading. But not the Lady Della. Nay, she'd rather draw her sword against the princes of the land, besting them at their own sport." He grinned down at me, "'tis indeed attractive."

"Well, I –" I swallowed down my desire to fidget.

"M'lady." Lucius stepped up, and I saw a wave of fury flit across Collins face at the interruption, although a smile quickly replaced it, "I was to escort you inside to get ready for supper."

"Oh, of course. How … forgetful of me." I smiled at Collins, "Thank you for the walk and the conversation, Prince Collins. I enjoyed it."

Collins inclined his head, his eyes holding mine for a long moment, "I shall expect a dance this eve? After the announcement?"

"If I am to remain." I nodded, slipping my hand into the crook of Lucius' arm, "Remember, sire, they've yet to announce those who are remaining."

"Ah, you shall remain," Collins waved aside my comment, "Since you've seemed to have caught the eye of all three of the princes of Findley, I'm quite sure you have also managed to win over my father. Until the eve, m'lady."

He bowed, before turning and moving back to the courtyard. I was so lost in the horrific thought of dancing with Collins, that it took a moment for my head to catch up to his parting words.

"Wait. Three?"

"M'lady! Please quit fidgeting!" Emmy sighed in exasperation as she unwove a small braid for the fourth time, "It will take a miracle to finish this before dinner!"

"I'm sorry." I sighed, wiping at my forehead with my handkerchief, "It's just … three! Prince Collins said I'd caught the eye of all of them!"

"I wouldn't take much stock into what Prince Collins says." I glanced into the mirror, surprised at the bitter words from my maid.

"And why not?" I asked carefully as Emmy forcefully jabbed another pin into my hair, scraping my scalp.

Emmy's jaw locked in stubborn determination, "It's not my place to say."

"Emmy, if you know something about him that should keep me from … giving my affections to him," I shook my head at the choice of words, for I was most definitely not attracted to Collins, "then I would like to know."

Emmy turned my head so that she could loosen a few strands of hair around my face, "He uses women, m'lady."

She whispered it, but it still sounded loud in the quiet of my room. I twisted the handkerchief tighter. My first impressions of Collins hadn't been far off.

"How many of the maids have fallen for his charm?" I asked, catching my lower lip between my teeth.

"At least ten that I know of." She whispered, looking nervously over her shoulder at the door, "And after he uses them …" she hesitated and I nodded for her to go on, "well, then he tells his father that they're incompetent in their work, and has them removed from the staff."

Anger boiled in my stomach at the injustice of it all, "And King Willhelm –"

"He is not aware of what is happening, m'lady." Emmy shook her head, "Prince Collins is … very careful."

I nodded, "Thank you for telling me."

She curtsied, patting my hair one last time, "You look like a vision, my lady. Red is a very becoming color on you."

I smiled, smoothing the wrinkles from the skirt as I stood and spun in a slow circle. The gown was indeed lovely, with golden trim and tiny red beads sewn in intricate patterns across the bodice. With matching slippers on my feet, I truly did feel like a princess.

I opened the door, and found Lucius standing on the other side. I glowered at the man, "So has Prince Nicholas deemed me so forgetful that I now need a permanent escort?"

Lucius smiled and shook his head, "Nay, m'lady. This was my doing. I didn't care for …" He cleared his throat, "Let me simply say I thought it safer for me to escort you to the dining hall."

I caught what he had left unsaid, that he didn't trust his youngest prince any more than Emmy did. The look in his eyes told me that any argument on my part would be pointless. With a resigned sigh, I took his arm and let him lead me to the dining hall.

The glares sent my way felt like daggers. Word had quickly spread that I had caught the eye of Prince Nicholas. It was seemingly obvious to everyone, although I couldn't imagine why the middle-born prince had taken to me, of all people.

I shivered, worried that maybe one of the princes truly did fancy me. What would happen if they chose me? How could I refuse marriage then?

"Are you chilled, m'lady? Lucius asked, concern on his face.

I shook my head, a blush flaming in my cheeks as he led me to my seat, "Nay, simply nervous is all."

Lucius smiled. As he pushed my chair toward the table, he leaned down and whispered, "Although you made it quite clear that you have no desire to marry, m'lady, I have no fear that you shall be one of the fifteen."

I forced a smile, "And that, my good sir, is why I am nervous."

He raised an eyebrow at me as he moved to one of the many tables of knights. I dared a glance up at the dais, finding both Collins and Nicholas staring at me fixatedly. I shifted my gaze to Benjamin, who was sitting so straight it looked painful. He was gazing ahead, his steely blue eyes unblinking.

He's taken with me? I wondered.

But I quickly shook my head, as the king stood to bless the meal. The thought of three princes fancying me was turning me into one of the giggling, silly maidens all around me. I would not allow it.

As we ate, I was aware of the silence around my end of the table. The ladies were all glaring at me, sizing me up as if they might begin a fight in the middle of the dining room at any moment. I shifted on my chair, wondering if it was too late to leave, to escape the wretched castle with all its finery and angry ladies.

The king rose, his easy smile flashing out at all of us. "Ladies! It has been a wonderful week getting to know all of you, but unfortunately only fifteen of you may remain." He waved a small piece of parchment, slowly unfolding it, "And those who shall remain are …"

I kept my eyes glued to my hands in my lap as he began, before clamping them shut as I counted the names off in my mind.

One, two.

Cheers and giggles sounded on the other side of the table, but I kept my eyes closed.

Five, six, seven.

More laughter, more shifting skirts, a few tears.

Thirteen, fourteen, fifteen?

My eyes flew open as the king rolled up the parchment. I had been sure he was going to choose me as one of the fifteen. Yet he hadn't. I stared fixedly at the king. His eyes met mine, and he … winked at me.

I felt my mouth drop open as Collins words from earlier flew through my mind, *Since you've seemed to have caught the eye of the three princes of Findley, I'm sure you will also win over my father.*

"And now a surprise!" The king laughed as all the noise in the room instantly stilled. "I have been approached by the princes and also a few knights," the king nodded slowly, "that a few of you have captured their attention. That being said, three more of you shall also remain here for any of the men to try and woo." He pulled a small square from his pocket. "Lady Maybelle, Lady Genevieve, and Lady Della. You are to stay at the palace."

A shriek sounded from across my table. Before I knew what was happening, I was sputtering as a cup full of wine was thrown into my face. Shocked rendered me speechless, and as I was trying to wipe the stinging liquid from my eyes, a body slammed into me. The person was furious, clawing at my eyes and uttering a string of words that would have made the worst sailor blush.

My chair tipped back, crashing to the floor. Stars danced before my eyes as the person on top of me continued to thrash me.

God, is this some cruel joke? Because why on earth are you doing this to me?

9

NICHOLAS

Benjamin was the first to react to the fight, leaping over our table in a swift motion and dashing over to the shrieking ladies. He managed to pull the bigger of the two away, practically having to pin her arms behind her back to keep her from attempting another assault.

"You took it from me!" the girl in Benjamin's arms screeched, wrenching against his strong grip.

I moved around the table and approached the woman who was still on the ground. It had all happened so fast that I wasn't sure who the lady was. She was curled into a tight ball on the floor. I knelt beside her and laid a gentle hand on her shoulder.

"Are you hurt, m'lady?" I asked, trying to see her face through her long blonde hair.

She slowly sat up, tucking a strand away from her face. I stared in wide-eyed shock, for the lady looking up at me was Della. She had scratches across one cheek and on her forehead from her attacker, and the wine had stained her dress and a little of her face, too.

"What is your name?" I ground out in displeasure as I turned to glare at the woman Benjamin was still holding. I was shaking as I stood to face her fully.

"Susan," she whispered. She had the decency to look ashamed, keeping her eyes fixed on the floor.

"Why did you attack this maiden?" Collins asked, having stepped up behind me, "Did you think that sort of behavior would be tolerated in the king's court?"

"Nay, I did not. But it doesn't much matter now, does it?" A little bit of fire lit in her eyes again as she glared at Collins and me. "Della is apparently the special one."

The way she said her name made my fists clench at my side.

"What should her punishment be?" Benjamin grunted softly, dangerously, "For it is a very grave offense to attack a person, let alone a lady in the king's protection."

"Beg pardon, but may I please say something?" We all glanced at Della, who had risen to her feet. Despite all she'd been through in the last ten minutes, she looked surprisingly steady on her feet as she turned to face Susan and Benjamin, "While I agree that it's not proper to throw one's self onto another lady, I do understand that we're all under enormous pressures right now." She shifted her gaze to our father, who had remained on the dais, "If it pleases the King, I would like to forgo any punishment that you would normally bestow to an offender such as Susan, and instead have your guards escort her off the castle grounds tonight."

For not being of noble birth, she held herself with a regal air, hands clasped in front of her. Even with blood running down her cheeks, and wine dripping off her chin, she looked lovely, her hazel eyes shining with determination.

I turned to await my father's answer, deciding it was safer to look at him than the young lady beside me. Father was smiling thoughtfully at Della, his chin propped in one of his hands.

"That is most gracious, Lady Della, for such an assault would normally result in a flogging."

I saw Susan's face blanch out of the corner of my eye.

"Mercy is what I wish for her, your majesty."

Father nodded, "Then it shall be done! Guards, escort the lady to her room to gather her things and then have her off the grounds immediately."

Benjamin slowly loosened his grip on Susan's arms, and she stumbled forward, crumpling in front of Della in a puddle of tears. She kept muttering, "Thank you, m'lady," over and over as she knelt by Della's slippered feet.

The guards gently lifted her up and guided her out of the dining hall. A hush settled over all of us, every eye in the room on Della who'd turned a noticeable shade of red.

"Well," Collins cleared his throat, "is it time for dancing now?"

10

DELLA

I gasped as a wave of dizziness made me sway unsteadily on my feet. The adrenaline from the attack was wearing thin, and my hands began to shake as I raised them to tentatively touch my cheek. I winced as the wine on my fingers stung one of the open cuts.

"M'lady, let someone escort you back to your room to change." Nicholas said in a low voice to me as the other maidens moved to follow Collins to the dance floor.

I blinked, staring down at my now ruined dress. The purple of the wine had horribly stained the lovely red fabric of the silk gown. The overwhelming urge to cry washed over me, and I stubbornly sucked in a breath, not allowing that temptation a foothold.

"I suppose I do look a fright." I tried to laugh, but it sounded just as wobbly as my legs.

Nicholas' eyes took on a dangerous look, "This is what you meant earlier. About being worried about the other ladies."

I waved his comment away and he grabbed my elbow as I tipped forward again, "Lady Della you are clearly unwell."

"Nay, I am fine." I wrenched my elbow from his hand, the mere touch of him sending a strange – but not unwelcome – sensation into the pit of my stomach. But in doing so, I stepped backwards and would have fallen to the floor again if another pair of strong hands hadn't caught me.

Lucius shook his head at me, smiling in a brotherly way, "Please, m'lady, listen to Nicholas. We'll have Emmy clean you up and then you can come back here." He lowered his voice, "Show these women that you are strong and fierce. Not easily intimidated."

I laughed at that, the tears bubbling up again at his kind words, "Aye, I suppose I can do that."

Nicholas nodded at Lucius, who turned his arm to me and guided me down the hallway. My hand was trembling, and he covered it with his. "You are in shock." He smiled at me as I began to shake my head, "'tis normal to feel that, m'lady. Most men succumb to it after their first battle. Even Prince Nicholas …" He caught himself, and cleared his throat, "'tis normal." He repeated.

We had reached my room, and Lucius opened the door for me, "I'll wait until you're finished, and escort you back."

"Must I go back?" I asked, sounding completely pitiable even to myself.

Lucius nodded, "You must show your strength." He smiled at me again, "You *are* a strong woman, Della. I know you can do it."

I nodded once, shutting the door and leaning against it. For all his talk about being brave and fierce, I wanted nothing more than to break down and sob after what Susan had done to me. I was thankful she was leaving, for I wasn't sure I could face her in the halls of the castles again.

I took in an uneven breath as I moved to look into the mirror on the vanity. I winced, lightly tracing one of the many scratches against my cheek. I had one across my forehead too, and that one was deeper. I picked up a handkerchief, lightly dabbing at the blood that had trailed its way toward my eyes.

Emmy knocked lightly on the door before slipping in, tsking her tongue as she looked me over, "Well, what is a princess without a few enemies?"

I laughed softly, angrily wiping at the tears that started leaking out of the corners of my eyes, "I'm no princess, Emmy. I don't even want to be. Why–?"

I bit my lip, turning to gaze at my reflection again as Emmy poured some water into a basin. Snatching away the cloth that I was worrying in my hands, she dipped it into the basin before gently wiping away the blood and wine from my face.

"I don't know why you've been called to the palace, m'lady," she said after a moment, "but I do know that you are here for a reason. Whether it's to make known to the king the problems within his court, to help a prince or two find his way, or," she laughed, "to give the servants something to talk about, who knows? All I know is that I am thankful you're here, and I hope that whatever happens, you can find the happiness that God gives."

"He feels so far away some days," I sighed.

"I sometimes feel that way too," she whispered. She finished with my face, and moved to my hair. It was sticky with wine, but she ignored that problem and instead picked up my brush. Tugging it through the mats, she quickly twisted my hair into a simple knot, letting a few loose strands hang down.

I stood, letting her quickly unbutton my gown and tug it carefully over my head. I felt tears welling up again at the stains running down it like purple raindrops. "That was such a lovely gown."

Emmy smiled sympathetically at me, "I have a friend who is wonderful at getting stains out of garments. I'll see what she can do with this one."

"Thank you."

Emmy nodded, pulling a pale green gown over my head. It was plainer than the red one, but it was the best I had for a dance. She stepped back after finishing the buttons. "Well, you do look better."

I ran a hand over my face, annoyed that I had the reminder of my attack there for everyone to see, "Only by your magic, Emmy."

She laughed, opening the door and gesturing me out. Lucius smiled at both of us, bowing regally to me, "You're a vision, as always, m'lady. Emmy did a stunning job."

Emmy blushed, bobbing a curtsy before hurrying down the hallway, but not before I noticed a faint blush on her cheeks. I turned back to Lucius.

"Shall we?" I asked, feeling steadier on my feet as he gave me a nod.

Taking his arm, I narrowed my eyes at Lucius. I was wondering if I should ask him about the question that was weighing on my mind.

"Lucius, the king mentioned some knights approached him about the three extra young ladies." I felt his muscles tense and I pulled him to a stop, "You talked to the king about me. Why?"

"I didn't …" At his protest, I planted my hands on my hips and he sighed. "All right! Perhaps I did."

"Why would you do that?" I growled, "You know that I don't want to be here!"

"Because I see the way Nicholas looks at you!" He countered, "He's never looked at another woman the way he looks at you. And when you're with him, he laughs more. Della, I'm his closest friend. We've been through hell together." My eyes widened at the phrase, but he shook his head unapologetically, "That's what the border war was. Hell."

"You … fought at the border?" I whispered, raising a hand to my lips. The border war had been awful, the talk at many tables across Findley for months while the worst part of the fighting had happened. Many people had died during it, both soldiers and innocents alike. The horror of it had seeped into the towns and villages around Findley, and so had the nightmarish tales.

"Aye," Lucius' voice was gruff, "Something Nicholas saw in the war changed him. I don't know what it was, but it turned him … sorrowful."

I cocked my head, "But he laughs –"

"With you, m'lady." Lucius shrugged, "I don't know why it's only you who seems to break through that wall. He will laugh with others, but it's not the rich, joyful laughter that he has with you."

I shook my head, "I am not marrying a prince!"

Lucius raised a brow, tugging me down the hallway again, "You will if the king commands it, m'lady."

"But he said …" I whispered, with another shake of my head, "I don't wish to marry anyone. Even the king can't force that upon me."

"I suppose we shall see, m'lady." Lucius moved us forward again, "I suppose we shall see."

The music abruptly stopped as we stepped through the doors, and everyone turned to stare at me. I sucked in a slow breath, hating the attention. Slowly, like the start of a rainstorm, someone started to applaud until the whole room was clapping and cheering for me.

A blush stole its way into my cheeks and intensified when all three of the princes stepped forward, bowing.

"You're looking better, m'lady." Collins said with a smile that didn't seem to reach his eyes.

"I do feel better, thank you." I smiled back and curtsied.

"Might I have this dance?" Benjamin's low voice rumbled, sending a nervous shiver down my back. His black-brown hair was pulled back with a leather band, and a few pieces escaped and fell across his temples.

I cleared my throat, nodding as he offered me his arm. I felt both of his brothers staring at our backs as we moved to the dancefloor and the minstrels began to play once more.

A strange silence settled over us, and Benjamin didn't seem eager to break it. He guided me through the steps with confidence. I simply had to follow his lead which gave me plenty of time to think. I struggled with myself, wondering if I should try to start a conversation with the stoic prince or remain silent.

Benjamin decided for me. He spun me around, guiding me into the next step. As he did, he glanced down at me. "Why did you offer her a pardon?"

"Susan?" I asked, staring up into his blue eyes.

"Yes."

"She ... she looked so scared, and I truly wasn't injured gravely."

Benjamin shook his head, "She was still guilty."

"But even the guilty deserve grace."

He stopped moving. We were standing on the edge of the dance floor and he stared at me with hard eyes, "Grace? Excusing wrongdoing only makes us weak."

I shook my head, "Nay, my prince. Grace is what makes us strong. It shows that we care for the person, above the grievance."

"If she had maimed you, broken a bone, or rendered you senseless, would you have offered her grace?" He spat the words, a pulsing anger in his eyes.

I couldn't seem to find the words, his fury rendering me speechless.

"So, there are conditions on grace, then?" Benjamin continued when I did not reply.

I shook my head, my own ire sparking, "If it is in my power to pardon a wrong, I am going to do it, Highness. However, you are correct that some actions have consequences."

He grunted, turning and walking back up to the dais, leaving me at the edge of the dance floor. I wondered at his strange reaction to my statement, but not for long. A hand landed on my arm, and I jerked back almost driving my elbow into Prince Nicholas' stomach.

His eyes widened, "Beg pardon, I didn't mean to frighten you, m'lady."

"Nay, you didn't. I'm just a little on edge, I suppose. You would be too, if someone had just attacked you." A shiver stole over me at the thought, and I turned to watch the dancers.

"Aye, I suppose I would be." A sadness laced Nicholas' words, and I remembered what Lucius had said about him fighting at the border. I glanced up at him from the corner of my eye.

"Are you all right, my prince?" I asked, something inside of me tightening at the thought of him being in pain.

"Aye," he shook his head, gazing down at me with a small smile, "Might I have this dance?"

He bowed, offering me his hand and I laid mine into it. His touch was light, yet it felt like lightning was racing down my arm and into my chest. Nicholas guided me onto the floor, smiling at me as we began the slow waltz. I tried to shake the giddy feeling away. I couldn't fall in love with anyone, especially not a prince.

I stumbled as Nicholas spun me outwards, realization over what I had just thought running through my head.

Am I falling in love with a prince?

86

11

NICHOLAS

Della stepped away quickly when the music ended, looking down at her feet. "Thank you for the dance, your highness," she stated simply.

I cocked my head to the side at the coldness in her tone, "It was quite enjoyable."

"Quite." Her voice sounded tight, as she bobbed a curtsy, "If you'll excuse me, sire, I'm feeling quite tired. I think I shall retire for the evening."

Before I could answer, Della had turned on her heel and hurried out into the hall without a backwards glance.

"Was that Della?" Collins asked as I walked back up to the dais, feeling every one of my twenty-two years as I slumped into my chair.

"Yes."

"She left?" Collins asked angrily, "She promised me a dance."

"She did go through quite the ordeal this evening, Collins." I snapped, irritated with his selfishness.

"She danced with you and Benjamin." He glared at me, "No one ever seems to care about me, nor my feelings."

I shrugged, feeling heat flare in my chest at the thought of Della's hand in mine, "Maybe she prefers our company to yours."

"Ha." He rolled his eyes, "Ladies love me, Nick. Truly …" he leaned in closer, lowering his voice, "they just can't seem to get enough of me."

Something in Collins' tone made a shiver sneak down my spine. He'd changed a lot in the two years I'd been gone. He had, at one time, been more jovial than me, laughing easily. He had always been the first to the dance floor, the first to laugh and smile. He had turned many heads over the years and never knew it. Now he was more withdrawn, surly, and easily angered. The way his gaze would linger on the female servants and the ladies around us was unsettling. I knew he still grieved the death of his mother, who'd passed two years before I had left for the border, yet this new Collins was not to my liking.

I stood abruptly, turning to Father with a bow, "I am not feeling well, Father. Please excuse me."

He nodded, "Of course, my son. I hope you feel better on the morn."

"I'm sure I will." I bowed again before heading through the throng of giggling, flirtatious women.

Once in the hall, though, I found that I had no desire to sequester myself in my room. Shifting my direction, I made my way over to the small alcove in the west wing. I smiled at the cheerful yellow curtains, eager for a moment of privacy and reflection on the Holy Word.

I reverently picked up the Bible, settling onto the window seat with my feet braced against the opposite wall. I gazed out the window to the garden, eerily glowing in the pale moonlight, before flipping to the passage that I wanted to dwell on.

The Lord is my Shepherd; I shall not want.

He maketh me lie down in green pastures: he leadeth me beside the still waters.

He restoreth my soul ...

I sighed, leaning my head back against the wall, and letting the words of the Lord pour over me. I wanted Him to restore my soul. But I had not talked to anyone about that night, not even the priest. It had been awful at the border, but that night was when hell had arrived on earth. I clenched my jaw, not wanting to relive it, but knowing that shoving it back and burying it deep inside were only making things worse.

A startled gasp made me snap my head up off of the wall in surprise. I blinked, trying to make my eyes adjust to the light again, and what I saw made a smile tug to my lips.

Della stood in the doorway, her hair cascading around her head like a veil. She was sporting a most embarrassed look on her face, and she wouldn't meet my eye. "Prince Nicholas! I'm sorry for interrupting you. I'll be going."

"Wait!" I leapt to my feet, carefully laying the book to the side, "Did I do something wrong?"

She had her back to me, but I could still see her shoulders stiffen. "No, your highness, you did not do a thing."

"Then why …?" I shook my head, "Please, come read with me."

She turned only slightly, her eyes shifting from the book on the window seat to me, "Would it be proper, if we're found out?"

I smiled at her question, "There is nothing improper about reading the Holy Writ, Della."

She scowled at the use of her first name, and I was struck again by how very regal and elegant she was. She glided over to the seat, sitting as far away from me as she could, and picked up the Bible. "May I read aloud?"

I nodded, cocking my head toward her as she opened and began to read from the first epistle of John. She read eloquently, her voice rising and falling with unbridled emotion for the Holy Scriptures. I closed my eyes, leaning back against the window, and just soaked in her voice.

After a moment, she paused, rereading a certain verse:

He that loveth not knoweth not God; for God is love.

I opened one eye, glancing at her face. Her brows were lowered and she had her lower lip caught between her teeth.

"Is there a problem?" I asked, straightening up as she sighed.

"I just … I'm not always the most loving person."

I laughed softly but stopped abruptly when Collins' face flashed through my mind, and then a few dozen more faces of people I didn't quite care for. "I'm not either."

Della glanced at me as she closed the book, "How then can we know God?"

I turned to face her more fully, tugging a leg up so I had more room, "I'm no priest, my lady, but I think it's a process. The more we understand God's great love for us, and what He's done because of that love, we begin to realize how special people are to Him. It makes us want to love more."

She scrunched her brows up, thinking through that thought. "Even those who hurt others?"

"You showed Susan a great amount of love today." I cocked my head, "It isn't easy to love someone who has hurt you."

She smiled up at me, a sparkle in her eyes, "I don't think your brother shares your admiration."

"Of which brother are you referring?" I asked, with raised brows, hoping against hope that she wouldn't say Collins.

"Benjamin."

I released a pent-up breath of relief, "Benjamin has a very strong moral compass."

"Aye, I noticed," she furrowed her brows again, tracing the golden letters on the cover of the Bible, "He didn't seem pleased with my definition of grace, either."

I nodded, "He sees the world as black and white. Someday he'll see that the world has a little more color to it."

Della nodded, and smiled at me again. Her hazel eyes made my breath hitch, and I couldn't seem to drag my gaze away from her face, as much as I tried. Her eyes grew wide at my staring, and she dropped them back to the Bible.

"Might I ask you a … question?" She cleared her throat, shifting nervously.

I nodded, "Ask anything, m'lady."

She paused for a long moment, before meeting my gaze again, "What happened at the border?"

It felt like a punch to the gut, and all of the air in my lungs whooshed out of me. I stood and stepped away from her, growing dizzy as I tried to make my eyes focus on the wall. "Who – who told you?"

"It's common knowledge that you were gone for two years, but we didn't realize you were at the border." She hedged, flattening her back against the window as I began to pace agitatedly.

"Who told you I was at the border?" I snapped, my eyes not focusing on anything now.

"Lucius." She whispered, appearing nervous by my outburst.

I ran my hands through my hair, grabbing fistfuls of it as I stared up at the ceiling, "Why did he tell you?"

"Does that truly matter?" Della had a defensive tone in her voice, and I noticed she was obsessively smoothing out every wrinkle in her skirt. "I am still waiting for an answer."

"It's not something to discuss with a proper lady." I countered, resuming my pacing.

"I think we can safely say I'm no proper lady, m'lord," she scoffed.

I laughed a little at that, a small amount of my stress sliding away. "Aye, that you are not."

I warred with myself. On one hand, it would feel so good to finally tell someone of the horrors I had witnessed. Something about Della felt safe, and I knew whatever I told her wouldn't leave the little alcove.

But another part of me, the part that was terrified of the memories, argued that it wasn't something that she needed to know.

I groaned, not knowing which side of my mind to listen to.

I met Della's gaze again and was floored by the compassion there. It was as if she could see into my very soul, the darkest, dirtiest parts, and yet she didn't find me lacking or disgusting.

"Your highness, I know it's not my place. I know that I'm just a merchant's daughter, not worthy to even be here. But –"

"Who said you're not worthy to be here?" I asked indignantly.

She looked taken aback, "No one, your highness." I stared at her long and hard, and she met my gaze without hesitation this time, "I only meant that there are many young ladies more … deserving to be here. But if I can help you, sire, then please let me. I am willing to listen … if you wish to speak." She smiled sadly, "I know grief, sire. 'Tis easier to face when shared."

I sat back down beside Della, rubbing my face with my hands. "'Tis not an easy story, m'lady."

I flinched when her hand touched my shoulder, startled by the contact, "I don't expect it to be, not from the grief you carry on your face."

I glanced at her again, surprised by her perceptions, "Are you sure you're ready?"

She nodded, and I took a deep breath. "It started less than a year ago…"

I stepped out of the old tower, straightening my bright red cape that symbolized my title as general of this contingent of knights. Lucius was by my side, my second in command and closest confidant.

"Are you sure they're not going to attack tonight?" I asked, scanning the small river that marked the border. From the small rise we sat on, we could easily see the army of Ironwolf. One of the largest kingdoms after Allura. They were trying to push into Allura, to claim the villages and people that dared to live closer to the boarder than most.

Lucius slowly shook his head, "It doesn't appear so, but their force seems … small."

"What do you mean?" I jerked my gaze back to him.

"I mean," he gestured out of the couple dozen tents and the men milling around on the opposite shore, "they seem like a small force."

"That's small?" I asked, shaking my head, "I'd hate to see a large army."

"I hope we don't have to. You know the village of Snowynne is only half a mile behind us. These men are relentless. If they attack us and push us to the village …" Lucius's eyes met mine, fear in them even though he kept his face neutral, "They strike down anything that moves."

I stifled a shiver that threatened to run down my sweaty back. "Then we can't let them push us back that far, Lucius."

A cry rang from the center of our camp, and we instantly took off running. My heart picked up its pace the closer we got, and, as the sound of men crying out and steel against steel filled my ears, my muscles tensed.

"They're here, Nicholas!" Lucius cried out as he drew his sword and jumped into the chaos. "They've infiltrated our ranks!"

The enemy fought hard, cutting down a third of our men before we were forced to retreat. We ran, taking up our position just outside of Snowynne. I had never been in a battle like this, and the fear made my heart race like a runaway horse. They came, swarming over the hill like ants bent on a crumb of food. Their war cry shook the ground, shaking our very souls. They came hard and fast.

But the worst part … the worst part was what they did in Snowynne.

We had no warning, no way to alert the people. And the enemy knew it. They fell upon us again, driving us into the city square. We fought, but my men and I were tiring. Their captain, Dodger of Ironwolf, rode into the chaos. He wore a patch over one of his eyes, scars all around it. His greasy black hair glowed in the light of the houses that his men had set ablaze. His black stallion cantered up to me, dragging a little girl by her hair. She could have been no older than ten, her dove grey eyes wide with fear as she cried.

"General Nicholas, prince of Allura." He shouted, swinging his sword above his head, "drop your weapons or the child dies."

I leapt onto the fountain, "Not even you could be so vile, Dodger!"

He laughed coldly. His one good eye drilled into me as he yanked the child up by her blonde hair, holding his sword against her throat. She gagged, crying, as blood dribbled down her neck.

"Try me!" He hissed, his eyes glowing with pure evil.

I glanced around, a feeling of total failure settling in my stomach. "If I give you this village, will you allow me, the villagers, and my remaining men to retreat? We will not attack this land until this time tomorrow, after the innocents are safe away."

He scoffed, "Do you truly care about these people?"

"Aye," My chest constricted as the child whimpered again.

"Fine," he shrugged, "but …"

I gagged as he pressed the sword across the child's throat. Her eyes rolled back into her head, and she fell, lifeless, to the dirt road.

Air wouldn't enter my lungs, my eyes not believing what they were seeing. My head snapped back to Dodger, who was laughing atop his steed, "You can't save them all, Nicholas! You couldn't even save one of them!"

"You monster!" I shouted, charging him with a fury and strength that were not my own. I was at a disadvantage, being on the ground, but Dodger had lit my ire, and nothing could stop me.

"I struck Dodger down that day, pushing his men back across the river. Our reinforcements arrived the following morning, and since the enemy had lost their commander, we soon routed them back to their own land. But that child … she still haunts my dreams." I leaned on my knees, my hands fisted under my chin. I couldn't look at Della, certain that she would think me weak, worthless, and a coward for not protecting that little girl.

"That's …" her voice choked off. I buried my face into my hands, feeling the shame roll over me again. I knew I hadn't made a wise decision that day. I had run dozens of scenarios through my mind of how I could have done it differently. Better. But it was too late, the child lay dead in the ground, taunting me.

"My prince, how have you bore that by yourself?" I glanced at her, seeing the tears on her cheeks and the sorrow in her eyes. She raised her hand, pausing for a moment before laying it against my shoulder, "Do you blame yourself for what happened to that child?"

I dropped my gaze, knowing that if I continued to look her in the eyes, I'd become undone. "It was my fault. I am to blame because I couldn't think wisely. I condemned her to death."

"Look at me," she commanded.

I grunted, standing and stepping to the doorway. I didn't like the tone in her voice, not when I was already hurting. "You'd do well, m'lady, to remember who it is you're speaking to."

I heard the rustle of her skirt as she stepped toward me, "And you would do well to remember, sire, that our God is a God of forgiveness and grace. The grace I gave to Susan is but a dim, poor reflection of the love He gives to you, to me, to everyone. He doesn't blame you, highness, for a mistake. He doesn't blame you for the actions of Dodger, nor does He –"

"Enough!" I turned on her, my agitation making me step closer and closer to her with each word. "I don't need you, a merchant's daughter, telling me about God and His grace! I don't deserve His grace! I deserve to suffer for the mistake that I made. I let a child die, Della. She's dead because of me!"

By the time I had finished, her back was against the wall, and I was standing mere inches from her face. Her green eyes grew big, before a dangerous, angry look crossed her face. She looked fierce, like a warrior poised for battle.

I gasped, taking a half step back, but I couldn't seem to make myself move fully away from her. It seemed like our gazes were fused together, both of us incapable of severing the contact. Something in me made me reach up and tuck a strand of her hair behind her ear. Her expression changed then, from anger to surprise. I watched as she captured her lip with her teeth, and I had the overwhelming urge to lean down and kiss her.

Like someone had poured cold water on my head, I quickly stepped away from Della, turning fully around and moving to the far wall. I braced myself against it, trying to shift my thoughts into order.

I heard a little gasp and the rustle of a skirt. I turned in time to see a flash of green fabric hurrying down the hall.

Della was gone.

WHEN *You* FOUND *Me*

12

DELLA

"But m'lady! You can't leave! They'll never let you out of the gate. And besides, you're one of the final eighteen!"

The morning sun poured into my room as I threw my belongings into a bag. I had tossed and turned all night, replaying Nicholas' conversation with me over and over in my head. I was truly sorry about what happened to him at the border, for the guilt he carried due to something he had no control over. Yet when he'd yelled at me for trying to help … I shook my head, shoving my hairbrush into the small bag with more force than was necessary.

"I can't stay here, Emmy. Not after –" I swallowed back the tears that were on the edge of my vision, determined to be strong. "I can't."

"Did Prince Collins …?" She sank onto my vanity stool.

"Nay!" I nearly shouted before lowering my voice, "Nay, it has nothing to with Prince Collins."

"Then what is it?" Emmy asked. When I simply continued to pack, she stood and laid a gentle hand on my shoulder, "My lady, there's something I need to tell you."

I turned, surprised by the rawness in Emmy's tone. Her blue eyes swam with tears. She swayed on her feet, covering her mouth with a shaking hand, as if that would hold in the sobs.

"What's wrong, Emmy? Are you hurt?" I rushed to help her reclaim her seat on my vanity stool, and she gripped my hand tightly in hers.

"Nay. I'm just so frightened, m'lady." She met my eye, forcing out in a whisper, "It's … Prince Collins."

Anger flared in my stomach, and I stood, "What did he do to you?"

"Sh!" Her wild eyes flicked to the door, "Do you know what could happen if he finds out I told you?"

"What did he do?" I asked again, but in a more level tone.

Emmy's eyes dropped to her lap, "He didn't do anything, he simply tried."

"Was he drunk?"

She slowly shook her head, "No, m'lady."

"You need to tell the king. Or one of the princes. Heaven's sake, even Lucius!"

Emmy's head snapped up, "He will send me away from here, m'lady, if I tell any of those people! Why would the king believe me over his own son?"

I began to pace, "Then what can we do? He can't keep … molesting innocent women and girls!"

"M'lady …" Emmy swallowed, hesitating before taking a deep breath, "Have you thought that maybe they would listen to you?"

I stopped, almost tripping over my own feet, "Why would they listen to me? I'm just a merchant's daughter." I cringed, hearing Nicholas' voice in my mind, as he had said those very words to me the night before.

"No, m'lady." Tears were in Emmy's eyes again and she stood before me now, gripping my arms in her small hands, "You are more than that. You're a woman who is kind and gentle to everyone, who extends mercy and grace. You're strong, and fierce, and you stand up for the innocent. You're a woman who I would gladly serve as my princess until the day I die."

She spoke with such conviction, such power that I felt my knees go weak. I sank to the edge of my bed, head swimming as I stared at Emmy. "Do you truly think the king would listen to me accuse his son?"

"I know not. But what about Prince Nicholas? If you talked to him, told him what is happening, then mayhaps he'd go to the king. He *would* be believed."

The thought of talking to Nicholas at all made my stomach turn, but at the same time, I could not in good conscience allow Collins to continue to hurt the servants.

"What if Nicholas doesn't believe me? What if I'm accused of lying to the court? Emmy, I could be cast out of the castle, or even thrown into jail!"

Emmy's face was filled with fright, but she slowly shook her head, "You've proven yourself to be noble, m'lady. I do not think they would throw you into jail."

I clenched my hands together, staring at them as I thought through what I should do.

"Mayhaps you were brought to the palace for such a time as this."

I glanced up at Emmy, who once again looked like she was about collapse to the floor and sob. I stood, gradually moving to her side, "For you, Emmy, I will do my best. I will speak to the Prince. And if I am thrown out, or imprisoned, then I will believe that it is the Lord's will."

I felt my hands begin to tremble as Emmy clutched them in her own.

"May the Lord be with you, m'lady," Emmy said shakily. I wiped at a tear that was trailing down my cheek, and then I drew my maid into my arms. We stood there for a long moment, both silently crying as we petitioned God to help us.

Please, Lord. I silently begged, *Please be with us.*

I told Emmy to lock the door behind me as I stepped out into the hall. It was empty, but that only made my heart pound harder as I moved to the dining hall. My footfalls sounded like thunder, and I couldn't seem to catch my breath as I stepped through the double doors.

My eyes instantly connected with Nicholas', and I felt a blush rise in my cheeks. I couldn't seem to make my feet move through the door, and the only sound I could hear was the beating of my heart. I seemed incapable of breaking my eyes away from Nicholas, fear rushing through every fiber of my being.

Why should he listen to me? Why should he care? I'm just a peasant girl, a merchant's daughter.

But I thought about Emmy, her frightened, tearstained face, and I knew I had to do it. I looked down at my dress, smoothing the wrinkles out as I took a hesitant step forward. I willed myself to keep moving through the tables. As I neared the dais, I forced my eyes to Nicholas. He wasn't smiling.

Feeling lightheaded, I dropped into a low curtsy. I caught sight of Lucius out of the corner of my eye, sitting with some other knights breaking his fast. He looked surprised to see me, and I knew it was because he'd waited for me that morning, but I had refused to join him.

"Lady Della!" The king smiled at me, and I discreetly wiped my sweaty palms on my dress, "What can I do for you, my dear?"

I stood, trying to look anywhere but at Nicholas, who was sitting to the left of the king. Collins was nowhere to be seen, which relieved and terrified me simultaneously.

"If it pleases the king," I tried to keep my voice as low and as steady as possible, "I was hoping I might have a word with Prince Nicholas and Sir Lucius. There is a matter I need to … discuss with them."

Nicholas snapped his head towards me, and the ladies closest to the throne glared at me. I ignored them all. This was bigger than winning the favor of a prince or the king. It was a matter of morality, of protecting innocent people.

The King raised his shaggy brow, "And what is the matter of this discussion, my dear?"

"It's … delicate, sire." I swallowed, panic bubbling up again, "Something I must first talk about with them before I share it with anyone else, even you."

He studied me for a long moment, and I was all too aware of the bright blue eyes to my left drilling into my skull. Benjamin, on the right of the king, was also staring at me, and somehow I felt like he knew exactly what I was talking about. It was unnerving.

At last the king nodded, "Of course you may meet with them, my dear."

"Father –" Nicholas tried to protest but the King waved away the comment.

"I will hear no argument. After what Lady Della has suffered by being here, the least we can do is hear what she has to say. However, I expect to know about it afterwards." His tone left no room to argue.

I nodded as Nicolas stood and stiffly offered me his arm. I accepted, barely allowing my fingers to make contact with the soft linen of his shirt. I heard Lucius following us as we walked back out into the hallway, the eyes of every person in the room on us.

Nicholas kept a quick pace through the twisting hallways, walking so fast that I was almost jogging to keep up.

As we walked, I glanced at the man by my side, the words we had shared last night crashing through my mind. For the first time, I saw him for what he was: a broken person trying to live the best way he knew how to in a broken world. I was no different from him, because I was just as broken. I was stubborn beyond belief, I was outspoken, and I was sinful. I often thought I knew better than others and looked down on them for their faults. I had done that with Nicholas, blaming him for holding onto the past. True, it was a past that he had no business holding on to. But how was I any different? I was holding onto Father's store, simply because I wanted to prove to a dead man that I was capable of being what he wanted me to be.

But what if God was asking me to let go of my dreams, and listen to His will for me? What if I was grasping at something that wasn't what was best for me? What if God had greater things in store?

I almost started crying as we stepped into what looked very much like the study I had met the king in, only smaller with a few more desks and no seating around the fireplace.

Nicolas let go of my arm, striding a few steps away with his hands on his hips. His head was down, and he looked tense. I stared at his back, unsure of how to say what I needed to say.

"Speak your piece." He finally growled, and I clenched my fists at my side, not liking the tone he was taking with me.

"First of all," I took a deep breath, "I'm sorry for the way I spoke to you last night. It wasn't … I wasn't being sensitive to what you were going through." I watched his shoulders slowly lose some of the tension, and I stepped forward, "I'm sorry for not being respectful to you, my prince. Please forgive me."

He turned, staring down at me as he ran a hand through his wavy red hair. He didn't say a word, just stared back and forth between my eyes. After a moment, he nodded slowly. "Aye. I will forgive you."

I smiled slightly, although the nerves in my stomach made me want to toss up what little was in my stomach.

"Now, the other matter?" Prince Nicholas asked as he motioned Lucius forward, "What is that about?"

I stared down at my navy-blue gown, trying to smooth the wrinkles out of my sleeves to keep from looking at the men in front of me. "It's a delicate matter, sire."

"Obviously, or you wouldn't have brought us in here." Nicholas raised a brow, "Or you would have talked to anyone other than me."

I glared at him, hating that he was right. His blue eyes drilled into me, and the cock of his brows seemed to goad me to tell all. It fueled my frustration towards him, yet I also found it rather endearing.

"Are you aware," I began to pace, trying to phrase it as gently and politely as possible, "that Collins is … molesting the servants?"

There was no delicate way to put it, I realized. By the look on Nicholas' face, I hadn't softened the blow in the least. His voice was dangerously controlled. He clutched the edge of the desk with his fingers as he glared at me.

"Collins? Hurting the servants in such a way?" He shook his head, dropping it so that he stared down between his arms, "Why would you accuse him of such a thing?"

"Because he tried to do it to me the first night I was here." I stated, feeling the fear and anger bubbling up in me again at the memory, "And my maid servant told me that he's done it to many servants and then has them removed from the staff."

Nicholas stared at me hard, his nostrils flaring in his anger, "How can this maid servant be trusted?"

"Beg pardon, my prince, but I can vouch for the maid in question." We both turned to Lucius, who was blushing, "'tis Emmy, m'lord."

Looking startled, Nicholas straightened, "If what you say is true, then we must tell my father."

I shifted, "Therein lies the problem, your highness. Collins … he goes to the king with complaints about those servants. That's how he gets them removed from the staff."

"You're saying my father is a party to this?"

I shook my head quickly as he took a step toward me, anger flashing in his eyes. "Nay, my prince. I'm under the belief that the king is simply … fooled by your brother."

Nicholas began to pace, his shoulders taut and his blue eyes a shade darker under his lowered brows. His steps were agitated, almost as if he didn't want to move forward, but his feet had other ideas.

"Sire." When he didn't turn to look at me, I stepped forward and said, "Nicholas!"

I laid a hand on his arm, trying to get him to look at me. We both jerked back at the contact, for it felt like lightning jumped from his arm to my palm. I let my hand fall to my side as our eyes met. There was a power in his gaze, a strength. I had always been told I was a strong woman, capable of standing my ground no matter what. But I could see that Nicholas had far more power in him.

I felt my back bump into the desk, and I braced my hands against it as I stared up at the prince.

Silence reigned for a long moment in the den, only broken when Lucius shifted, and cleared his throat. "What are you going to do, Nicholas?"

The prince took a step closer to me, his eyes never leaving mine, "I want the word of this lady that what she says is true."

I pushed away, striding around him to face the door, "Why do you doubt my word, highness? Have I given you reason to?" I spun on my heel, glaring at his chest, "I would be in more danger if I was lying to you."

Unable to hold my head up any longer, I dropped my gaze to the ground, waiting for an insurmountably long moment before Nicholas turned to Lucius. "We can't go to my father, so we go to Benjamin."

"What if he doesn't believe us?" Lucius asked, "It takes a lot of evidence to convince him of anything."

"He was the one who stopped Collins when he was … forcing himself on me." I dared to speak, "I think he knows about it. However, I don't know if he realizes how far Collins has been taking it."

Nicholas was staring at me again, and I wanted to fidget. Something about the man gave me energy, a strange thrill that I couldn't name.

"Lucius, please find my brothers and bring them here. Also, fetch Emmy from Lady Della's room."

Lucius nodded, pushing away from the smaller desk he'd been perched on and hurrying out the door. I watched him go with a small amount dread, not wanting to be alone with Nicholas.

If the room had been tense before, it was stifling now. Another long moment passed, before Nicholas turned to me. He ran a hand through his curls and sighed. "I haven't been able to get you out of my head, Della."

I hadn't been able to stop thinking about him either, but I kept my lips firmly pressed together. I smoothed my hands against my skirt, looking past him to the window. I didn't trust my voice to speak, even though I wanted very much to tell him what I had realized on our walk to the study.

"Why do you torture me so?" he whispered, stepping closer to where I stood. "I don't understand why I search for you, when there are dozens of young ladies here. Or why, when I find you, my heart triples in speed."

"I – I do not know, sire." I swallowed, still not willing to meet his gaze, "I am just a merchant's daughter."

"I was wrong to say those things to you. They came from a place of hurt, of anger." He groaned, and I glanced at him from the corner of my eye. He was

115

rubbing his face with his large, callused hand and slowly shaking his head. "Please forgive me, Della. You deserve all the happiness in the world. I …" He visibly swallowed, turning on his heel and striding to the window. Clasping his hands behind his back, he stood gazing out at whatever sight lay below.

"Nicholas," I found myself stepping up to stand behind him. I wasn't sure what I was planning on doing, or what I was thinking of saying. He was hurting, broken by his past. I knew that nothing I could do or say would fix that. I wasn't God. Yet, I wanted desperately to be the one to help him find his way to wholeness.

Tentatively, I stretched my hand out, laying it against his broad back. He tensed, as if the contact hurt him.

"I can't fix you." I whispered, "I'm not great or powerful. I don't bend to the will of others. I'm too outspoken, and I don't like the common things that most women would think proper of a lady. But when I see hurt, I want to fix it. I want to help heal people. I saw hurt in you, my prince. And I – I spoke my piece. Please forgive me if that hurt you more, for that was not my intent."

He turned, and I let my hand fall to my side as his gaze arrested mine. I was amazed at how this man seemed to command my attention, and more shockingly, that I wanted to give it. I wanted to be in the presence of this prince, I wanted to know everything I could about Nicholas of Findley, Prince of Allura.

"Della, I am broken." His voice cracked, and he took a step closer to me, "But when I'm with you, I feel as if that brokenness can be mended."

"I can't fix you, Nicholas." I repeated, in a whisper.

"I know, but you point me to the One who can." I blinked as he reached out and grabbed my hand, raising it to his lips. He gently kissed the back of it, his gaze never wavering. "I know I am unworthy of such an amazing woman as you, Della. I know you did not want to be here, to even do this contest, but I am wondering if ... maybe that has changed?"

I smiled at the hope in his eyes, "Aye. It has."

A smile stretched across his face as his eyes flicked between mine. "Has it changed enough to consider ... mayhaps you're willing to be ... a wife?"

I laughed, strangely feeling tears spring into my eyes. "It depends on whose wife I would be."

Nicholas picked up my other hand, "Would you be *my* wife, Della of Findley?"

"Aye, I'd like that very much." I squeezed both of his hands in mine, "God has shown me that His will for us sometimes looks very different than our plans."

Nicholas smiled, bending his head down so that his forehead rested against mine, "Is that good, m'lady?"

I turned my face up to him, so that our lips were mere inches apart, "Aye, my prince. Tis a very good thing indeed."

13

NICHOLAS

I lowered my lips, letting them brush lightly against Della's.

It was unbelievable that she was here, in front of me, letting me kiss her. After the words we'd exchanged the night before and the way I had scared her away, I was sure she would never want to see me again. That thought had only fueled my anger at her. I was also angry at how I had acted, for I hadn't behaved nobly at all. All that anger had become distrust toward her, and that had not been fair at all.

Della stepped back slightly, her hazel eyes glowing with joy. "I was so afraid …"

When she didn't finish, I reached up to gently trace one of the scratches on her face, "Afraid of what, m'lady?"

"That after what I said ... I was afraid that you wouldn't even speak to me again. I was worried that I had missed out on God's plan for me, because I was too stubborn to let go of what I wanted."

"Your father's store." I whispered, realizing for the first time what she was letting go of in order to marry me. "But that is important to you, m'lady."

"Aye. But this," she reached up and ran one of my red curls through her fingers, "this is better. I know that this is ordained by the Lord. Why else should I have favor in your eyes, in the eyes of your father?"

The door to the library opened before I could respond, and we both stepped away from each other. I couldn't, however, seem to tear my gaze away from the woman at my side.

She glided over the floor to the young lady who had entered. The girl was shaking, her eyes wide as Della wrapped a comforting arm around her waist.

"There's no need to fear, Emmy. Prince Nicholas has agreed to speak to his brother."

"I can't lose this position, m'lady. I can't." Emmy pressed her lips into a fine line, her eyes flicking from me to Della. "It supports my family."

I smiled at her, "I promise, Emmy. You shall not lose your position here. I have a feeling that Della will keep you on as her lady's maid, regardless of what my father may think."

Della nodded, stopping abruptly as Emmy gripped her arms, "You're staying? Are you and Prince Nicholas …?" Her eyes flicked to me and she began to smile.

"Sh!" Della laughed, and I couldn't help but relish the sound of it. "Aye, we are going to marry. But we still have to talk to the King. Right now, there are more important things than my marital status."

We were interrupted in our conversing by an argument coming from the hall. Loud, angry voices were moving toward us and came to a climax as the study doors flew open. In strode Lucius, looking very overwhelmed, followed by Collins and Benjamin.

"Here they are, sire." Lucius rolled his eyes so only I could see, "And they didn't come willingly."

I could tell almost immediately that Collins was drunk, although how he had managed it before noon was a puzzlement. His blond curls hung limply across his forehead and his words were slurred as he argued with Benjamin.

My elder brother actually appeared to have emotion on his face, although it was his most common one. With his jaw clenched and his steely blue eyes boring into Collins, it was obvious that he was barely holding his temper in check. I wondered if he was upset by the fact that Collins was drunk, or if there was another reason entirely.

"Brothers!" I practically had to holler to be heard over their debate.

They both turned to me, closing their mouths mid-sentence.

"Thank you." I smiled, despite the tension in my body. "I think we all know why we are here."

Collins stepped forward, and I frowned as he pushed his face into mine, "I, for one, am not aware of anything."

"That much is obvious." Lucius muttered under his breath.

"Collins, the Lady Della and her maid, Emmy, have accused you of molesting the lady servants." I raised a brow as he turned to Della, venom flashing in his eyes.

"You dare to accuse a prince of Allura of such a crime?" He hissed, moving on feet that were amazingly steady. His hand wrapped around Della's bicep, causing my normally steady temper to flare.

"Unhand her!" I yanked my brother away from the ladies, standing between them and him. Tension made me tremble, my gaze never leaving my brother, "They are both trustworthy witnesses, and I'm sure that if I searched, I would find more than a few willing testimonies from maids you've dismissed."

His face paled, but rage still simmered in his eyes, "You can prove nothing."

"I can testify to you touching Lady Della her first night here, Collins." Benjamin's voice sounded tight, his arms crossed over his chest. His eyes simmered with resentment, "You've shamed the title you've been given, brother." He spat out the last word as if it was sour on his tongue.

Collins began to laugh and it sent a chill through me. "You have no idea what it's like, do you, Ben? No, of course not. You're the crown prince." Spittle flung out of his mouth as he turned on his heel and began to pace, "And you, Nick. Always so happy, so joyful. It's sickening."

If you only knew, I thought sadly. I shook my head at Collins, unable to believe that this was the same brother I'd left two years ago. I no longer recognized this man in front of me. He had changed so much.

"No, neither of you understand." He hissed, his brown eyes going cold, "Father despises me and honors you. I'm the youngest. I'm worthless."

"No, you're not." I turned as Della stepped from around me, standing straight and tall without a trace of fear on her face, "You're not worthless, Collins. You may be lazy, and you may have hurt others, but you can change that. God can change that."

A scoff slipped past Collins' lips, "And how would you know that, m'lady?"

"Because the Lord says so." Della planted her hands on her hips, exasperation escaping in a sigh, "Why are you men so stubborn? God offers grace and forgiveness for mistakes. It doesn't make sense, but He does. Yet you three are determined to not accept it."

Collins ignored her, turning to face me and then Benjamin, "You still cannot prove that I did anything."

"We have witnesses. Father will have to listen to them, Collins." Benjamin narrowed his eyes at him, "I hope he is not lenient with you."

"Let me tell you my judgement, my son."

We all turned to face Father, whose frame filled the doorway. His eyes were lined with sorrow, his lips pressed into a thin line that was mostly hidden by his beard. He moved forward, his shoulders more hunched than they had been, his steps slow and weary.

"Father, I have done nothing!" Collins sank onto the top of the desk, his wobbly legs obviously refusing to hold him up any longer.

Father's sad eyes met mine and I nodded slowly, reading the question that lay in them.

"I have heard from some of the servants, Collins. I did not want to believe it was so, but when Della approached Nicholas, I knew that something was amiss. I heard their accusations of you, Collins. Nicholas and Benjamin believe it to be true." Tears swam in his eyes, turning them glassy, "How could you do this? How could you ruin yourself, your reputation?"

Collins laughed again, "That's all you care about, isn't it? The reputations of the princes of Allura! I wish my mother had never married you, I wish I wasn't your son!"

The bitterness of his words shocked me. I glanced at Benjamin, whose raised brows were the only emotion on his face. Father sagged against one of the small desks, grief filling his voice.

"I loved your mother very much, Collins. Just as I loved Nicholas' mother, and Benjamin's. The fact that you wished for something else …" His voice cut off and he cleared his throat. His face turned as unreadable as Benjamin's, and he straightened his spine, his eyes hard and unfeeling, "As punishment for what you have done, I banish you from the palace."

"What?" Collins asked, shock clearing the drunken fog from his features, "Where shall I go?"

"I know not, that is for you to decide."

"My king, might I make a suggestion?" All heads turned to Lucius, who stood at attention, eyes on my father.

"Of course, Sir Lucius."

"What if Prince Collins came home with me, to Ableton? I am scheduled for a few months of leave, and I could bring him back to my family's estate. He could be Sir Collins, a simple knight of Findley, such as myself. He would learn hard work, serving alongside me and my brother on our estate. I know for a fact that we can keep him in line."

Collins bristled at that, glaring at Lucius, but my friend didn't seem to notice.

"A fine suggestion, Sir Lucius." Father nodded, sorrow still in his eyes, "Very fine. It shall be done. Collins, you shall leave in one month's time. Until that time, you shall be confined to your quarters."

Collins glared around at all of us, before turning to brace his arms against the desk. A long, heavy silence hung over the study.

"Go to the devil, the whole lot of you," Collins finally spat, swiping a stack of books off the desk with the back of his hand before turning on his heel and storming out of the room in a fury.

"Oh, my," Della whispered, lowering herself onto a chair. Her hands were shaking, and she was furiously running them over her skirt. I laid a hand on her shoulder, and she jerked her head up to meet my gaze. A small smile tugged on the corners of her mouth, and the overpowering urge to kiss her stole through me.

"Is there something else I need to be told?" A small trace of humor lit Father's voice, and I glanced up at him with a grin of my own.

"Sir, I have found myself a bride."

Father laughed softly, "That much is obvious, my son!" His grey eyes had lost a little of the sorrow, and he smiled kindly at Della, "Is this what you wish, my dear? You told me, in no uncertain terms, that you did not wish to find a husband during this contest."

"The Lord's will is not our own." Della whispered, her voice sounding a little choked, "There is no one I'd rather spend my life with than your son, my king. He is …" She turned to smile at me, tears making her beautiful hazel eyes shine, "He is good, and kind, and just."

My throat tightened, and I reached out to pull Della to her feet, "I love you, Della."

Her eyes grew wide as she met my gaze. They flicked back and forth between my eyes as if trying to discern the truth of my statement. A tear slipped down her cheek as she embraced me, forgetting all about our audience. "I love you too, Nicholas."

My heart soared, hardly able to believe the blessing that I was holding in my arms. Ignoring propriety, I leaned down to capture my love's lips with my own. I was still broken and working on forgiving myself for the mistakes of my past, but I knew that God had brought this amazing woman into my life for a reason. And I vowed in my heart, then and there, to treasure her like the jewel she was, loving her until my dying day.

Epilogue

DELLA

One month later

The bells of the castle pealed with joy as Nicholas and I stepped out onto the front step of the cathedral. Flower petals floated around us as Nicholas wrapped his strong hand around my waist, tipping me back and stealing a kiss in front of the cheering town's people. Laughter bubbled out of me as he straightened, tightening his grip as he guided me down the steps and through the town. I slipped my arm around his waist as well, glad to have him close to me.

"Have I told you how beautiful you look today, my princess?" Nicholas leaned down to whisper in my ear, waving to the crowd that was being held back by the knights.

"You might have." I smiled up at him, "But I wouldn't mind hearing it again."

His blue eyes twinkled in the setting sun, making my chest tighten at the love shining out of them, "You are the most beautiful maiden in all the land. And I still cannot believe that you are my wife."

We had stepped through the castle gates, and as they closed a smile tugged at my lips. For unlike the last time I had walked through them, excitement was what made my heart pound. I was happier than I had ever been. God had seen fit to bless me beyond what I could ever have hoped. I was Nicholas' wife. He loved me, and I him. Tears of joy threatened to spill down my cheeks, and I sighed in contentment.

Seeming to sense my thoughts, Nicholas somehow managed to pull me even closer as we stepped up the steps of the palace and into the dining hall. All the knights not on duty, as well as the lords and ladies of surrounding lands, cheered when we stepped in, raising their glasses in celebration.

Laughter, dancing, and revelry were the guests of honor, but I could seem to think of little else than my husband, who never left my side for a moment.

"May I have this dance, m'lady?" Nicholas bowed toward me, offering me his hand as the minstrels began to play a folk dance popular among the villagers.

I smiled, slipping my hand into his, and allowing him to pull me onto the dance floor.

We twirled and laughed. Nothing could mar this night. Not Collins' sour glare as he sat, arms crossed, on the dais. Not the fact that my family hadn't been able to attend the ceremony, for Lydia had just had her baby girl. I was Nicholas' wife! I wrapped my arms around his waist as he spun me around, smiling down at me with an intensity that made me lightheaded.

The song ended with cheers and laughter, but Nicholas tugged me away and into a hallway, "I am quite through with that type of celebrating." He growled, lowering his lips to mine. He kissed me more intently than he ever had, stealing my breath as I kissed him back.

Wrapping my arms tightly around his neck, we continued our kiss for another long moment.

I sighed, pulling back slightly to drink in his eyes. "Nicholas?"

His gaze met mine, and he smiled, "What is it, my love?"

"God is so good." Tears misted my eyes as he lowered his forehead to rest it against mine.

"Aye." His voice was husky, "He is very good indeed."

The End

ANNA AUGUSTINE

THROUGH

His

EYES

COLLINS AND SAGE'S STORY

WHEN *You* FOUND *Me*

"Not that I have already obtained this or am already perfect, but I press on to make it my own, because Christ Jesus has made me his own. Brothers, I do not consider that I have made it my own. But one thing I do: forgetting what lies behind, and straining forward to what lies ahead, I press on toward the goal for the prize of the upward call of God in Christ Jesus."

-Philippians 3:12-14-

WHEN *You* FOUND *Me*

1

COLLINS

I whistled a jaunty tune as I swung up onto my horse, ignoring my brothers and father who were standing at the top of the stairs that led to the palace. I tugged on my riding gloves, letting my lazy gaze flick over them all nonchalantly. Each had a different expression on their face that I could read like a book.

Benjamin, my eldest brother, stood with his shoulders thrown back, his gaze boring straight into me. His light blue eyes were cold as ice, and his jaw flexed in and out as he gritted his teeth. Having received that look far too often, I was indifferent to it.

Nicholas' mouth was turned down in a frown, his brow lowered. Della, his new wife, clutched his hand, the sun glistening off of a tear on her cheek. As if they truly cared that I was being banished. They were the very reason for it. They had told Father my secret. They had no right to look grieved, clinging to each other as they watched my departure.

Father, however, was a mystery. Not a feature out of place, he stared at me with cold, unfeeling eyes. I deserved it, I knew, but that didn't change the pit that formed in my stomach. Father had never cared about me, or my feelings. All I had ever wanted was a word of praise from him, but all I had ever received was indifference, even now.

"Are you ready, sire?" I jerked my head round, meeting the calm gaze of Lucius. It was to his miserable home I was being cast, stripped of my titles. I was simply Sir Collins, a penniless, landless knight, and friend of Sir Lucius. But I wouldn't stay that way. I would show them, show them all.

"Aye." I straightened in my saddle, refusing to look back at my family. "Let's go."

"Collins!" I stiffened as Nicholas called out my name, "Go with God, my brother!"

I scowled, ignoring his call as I pushed my horse into a gallop. God hadn't been with me in a very long time. He wouldn't start now.

We rode out of the gate and through the streets of Findley. The people stepped aside, allowing us to pass. However, I wasn't able to ignore the glares and hatred leveled my way. Word of my banishment and what I had done had spread like wildfire. No one gave me respect anymore. I wondered if I had had any to begin with.

Grinding my back teeth, I leaned over my mare, urging her forward at a faster clip. Lucius rode to my left, and another knight to my right. Three more flanked our rear. They would only go halfway with us. Once we reached the crossroads, they'd turn back and return to the palace. It was unlikely that anyone past Fornarth would recognize me, and riding into Ableton with a guard would certainly raise more than a few questions.

And we can't have that, now can we? I thought darkly.

We reached the empty road outside of Findley, slowing our mounts to a trot. I glanced at Lucius, my contempt for him waning slightly. Father had been ready to banish me to the streets, yet this man had spoken up in my defense. Part of me was interested as to why, but the other side simply wanted to nurse my contempt for him for siding with my traitorous family.

Lucius sensed my gaze, turning to me with a small smile on his face, "I suppose you would like to know about Ableton?"

"No." I retorted, but Lucius kept right on talking.

"It's a large village, second only to Findley and Marchingville. We live just outside of it on our estate during the summer; our steward is in charge of the town while we are away. Father likes being around the tenants and working in the field." Lucius laughed, "I must admit, summer was always the best time growing up. We'd work during the mornings and then swim in the creek or explore the woods in the afternoon. My brother and sister would come along and we'd hunt for wild strawberries and blackberries in the woods."

Something about the way Lucius prattled on about his family struck me as odd. He seemed to genuinely care about them, to love them even. I turned to look out over the rolling hills we were riding past, gritting my teeth as heat surged through me. The only member of my family that I had truly loved had been yanked away from me four years ago, and four years ago I had sworn off loving ever again. It was too painful.

"It was hard work, running the estate," I blinked back to what Lucius was saying, "But I enjoyed it."

"What made you become a knight, then, if you were *so* in love with country living?" The sarcasm escaped before I could stop it. I bit my tongue, refusing to look at Lucius.

"I left because I am the youngest son." He shrugged a shoulder, "I had to make my way in the world, and what could be nobler than serving my king?"

"I can think of a great deal," I scoffed.

Lucius didn't reply to my comment. He simply urged his horse into a faster pace, pulling me away from Findley and into a world I wasn't sure how to survive in.

2

SAGE

I crossed my arms, glaring at my mother as she paced in front of the great arched windows of the sitting room, to the fireplace and back.

"Why are you so determined to not marry, Sage?"

"Mayhaps because I haven't met the right man, Mama."

She arched a brow at my common name for her. She had been trying for years to have me call her *mother,* but it sounded too formal to my ears.

"What about James, the steward's son?" She arched her dark brown brow at me, "He seems quite taken with you."

"He always smells of the liniment the healer has him rub on his achy joints." I wrinkled my nose and shivered, "I think not."

"What about Gregory?"

I shook my head. I liked Gregory well enough. We had been friends since we were five, running around Ableton without a care in the world. He had recently been hired by my Papa to be the foreman of our estate, running it in the winter months when we moved into the town. But I thought of him as one of my brothers, not as a woman loved a man.

"Mama, I don't want to talk about this anymore, please?"

She walked toward me, grasping my hands in her own, "I just want to see you happy, my lamb."

"Then let me decide when I've met the right man, Mama. You let Robert do that, and now he and Margie are so happy." I smiled, thinking of my eldest brother doting on his new wife. I often caught him staring at her like she was the most precious jewel in the coffers. The love that existed between them made my heart ache for the same. "Please, Mama. Stop pushing me."

Mama sighed, laying her cool hand against my flushed cheek, "Aye. I'll stop for now. I just want to see you settled, darling. You're eighteen. I had been married for a year and was expecting Robert when I was your age."

"We all are different, Mama. You and Papa say that often."

She smiled and then sighed again, "You're getting too wise for us, Sage."

"You've raised us well," I pecked her on the cheek, before glancing over my shoulder at the door, then back at my mother. My feet shifted back and forth restlessly.

"Shoo," Mama laughed, "I know you are itching to be out of doors."

She waved her hands at me, motioning me toward the doors. I smiled my thanks, before twirling out the door and into the warm afternoon sunshine. I breathed in a deep breath. The world smelt warm, the sun turning the wheat and hay in the fields a golden brown. I closed my eyes, tipping my face up to catch its golden rays on my cheeks. Mama often complained about how freckled and tan my face and arms had become. I hated covering my face, and staunchly refused to apologize for my appearance.

After a long moment of soaking in the sun, I turned toward the stables. I paused by the fence, breathing in a long breath of Cook's herb garden that sat on the other side. The strong aroma of lavender and rosemary swirled through the warm air, and I let the tension I'd been feeling from my conversation with my mother ease out of my shoulders.

She meant well, I knew. Being their only daughter, Papa and Mama wanted me to make a good match, to marry someone that would protect me after they were gone. But I still didn't understand why they couldn't let me marry for love. Whether my future husband was rich or poor, I did not care. Yes, we were wealthy. Papa had a position in the kingdom that many vied for. We had even been invited to attend the wedding of Prince Nicholas, although we had declined since it was the same time as Robert's. But why did I have to marry someone well off? Why did I have to marry at all?

I stepped into the stable and over to my mare's stall, rubbing her velvety nose. The sweet smell of hay mingled with the stale smell of horse and I smiled. This, this is where I was comfortable. Horses always were silent, content to just listen and to love. I turned and snatched up a bridle before slipping into the stall.

"How is my sweet Rose today?" I asked softly as I slipped her bridle over her nose and secured the straps. I stroked her neck as she nickered, nuzzling my shoulder. Opening the stall, I led her out of the stable. Swinging up onto Rose's back, I guided her to the road, leaning in as I let her have her head.

We flew. The wind tugged at my hair, loosening it so that it flowed in disarray down my back. My skirt hitched up, showing my ankles, but I didn't care. I was free!

When we reached Ableton, we skirted the town. Father didn't like it when I raced down the street like the devil himself was on my heels. It frightened the people and the sheriff had even come out to our estate once to complain. So now I avoided the place, carefully going around it before rejoining the road a little ways down.

I slowed to a trot, letting Rose cool down as we continued on. I often rode this way, and knew it well. Oftentimes, I dreamt about what lay beyond my little corner of the world. I wondered about what my brother, a knight in the army of King Wilhelm, had seen and experienced. I wondered about the people, and how different they might be.

I sighed, missing Lucius more than ever. He hadn't seen me as a pesky little sister like Robert had, instead treating me as an equal. He, Gregory, and I had had marvelous times in the woods surrounding Ableton, playing bandits and soldiers until darkness had made it impossible to see. We had gone fishing and riding, and talked about anything and everything.

Now, Gregory was grown, and Lucius was gone. While Gregory was still my friend, something had changed between us. There was a strain that hadn't been there before.

Oh how I miss you, brother. I thought, squeezing my eyes shut as I urged Rose into a gallop, trying to escape from my own wild thoughts.

So focused was I on not crying, that I failed to hear the riders coming toward me until it was too late. Rose reared up on her hind legs, and I scrambled to hold on.

Belatedly, I remembered that I was riding bareback, and I felt myself slipping down my horse's rump as she twisted away from the riders. I watched the earth rush up to meet me before I felt my head connect with it. Then everything slipped into oblivion.

3

COLLINS

I jerked my mount hard to the left as the horse that was charging Lucius and I reared into the air with a frightened whinny. Lucius had pulled to the right, his eyes growing wide as the rider slipped off the horse and landed on the ground in a crumpled heap.

"Sage!" Lucius leapt to the ground, calming the beast that was now pacing around its falling owner with agitated snorts and grunts. I glanced down at the form on the ground, confusion filling me as I noticed the brown dress, the light golden-brown hair, and the beautiful round face of a woman.

"What is a woman doing this far from town, and riding bareback?" I ground out, swinging to the ground as Lucius, cradled the young lady's head onto his lap. "She couldn't control that horse."

The look Lucius sent my way made me take a step back. "This woman, Collins, is my sister. Take care how you speak about her." His expression softened as he gently felt her head, wincing when she groaned. No blood stained his fingertips, and he sighed in relief. "I think she just hit her head when she fell. She'll be sore, but she's dealt with worse." A wiry smile pulled on the corners of his mouth.

"She's your sister? Your mother and father let her run around like a common peasant girl?"

"Just wait," Lucius snorted, "Once you get to know Sage, you'll realize why they allow it."

I shook my head, standing from my crouched position. "How are we to get her back to your home?"

"It's not far." Lucius scooped the unconscious Sage into his arms, holding her out to me. "Hold her while I mount."

I took her from him, surprised by how light she was. She appeared tall, and probably would have been able to almost look me in the eye if she had been standing upon her feet. She groaned when I moved toward Lucius's horse, her eyes fluttering open for a moment. I paused to stare at them, startled by the hue. They were brown, but unlike my own plain dark brown eyes, hers were a warm honey color, with flecks of gold woven through them. They stared up at me for a long moment, before fluttering closed again.

"Whenever you're done gawking, Collins." Lucius's sharp tone made my head jerk away from the girl's, and I handed her gently up to him. His features were hard, something I wasn't used to seeing. I swallowed, a bit of my cockiness ebbing. I had to be careful how I treaded around Ableton. Here, I didn't have my title nor my father's protection. As little as that had meant to me before, I now saw that I had relied on it more than I had realized.

I swung up onto my mare again, clutching the reins of Sage's horse before moving to follow Lucius down the road.

I watched the knight as he gently held his sister. She stirred a little and I heard her mutter something to her brother. My thoughts wandered back to the shock of her eyes, unable to displace that memory from my mind. Never before had a woman captured my attention as this one had, and I was acquainted with a fair number of women. I hadn't even spoken a word to this one, yet she was all I could think about.

As we entered the town, I was surprised at the greetings that Lucius received. It was obvious that his people loved him, from the children chasing after us, to the men and women welcoming him with waves and smiles and cheers. I rubbed my chest, surprised by the tightness in it. I glanced at the straight back of my companion, and tried to identify the emotion that was rolling through me, but found myself unable to.

We soon passed through the town, which I had to agree was a decent size. I wanted to urge the horses from the dawdling pace we were keeping, but knew that Lucius didn't want to jostle his sister. I tried to catch a glimpse of the manor house, but all along the road were trees that blocked the view.

I felt my frustration mounting, along with my weariness from the travel. I just wanted a warm bath and a soft bed. Yet here I was, stuck on the road with an overprotective knight and his wild, brown-eyed sister.

"Here we are." Lucius called over his shoulder as his horse stepped out of the tunnel of trees.

I blinked, surprised by the size of the manor house. Castle may have been a more apt description. The sprawling, two story structure had three windows on each side of the large double doors. Towers sat at each corner. There was no wall, no gate, as if the people living there had no reason to fear enemies. I could just make out the stables at the left, and the servants in the garden that lay between it and the house.

The doors swung open as we approached, a woman in a simple green gown hurrying down the few steps to the ground. Her greying brown hair was tied in a simple knot at the nape of her neck, and the closer we got, the more she resembled the girl in Lucius's arms.

"Lucius!" She had a smile on her face until she noticed the girl, "Sage! What happened to your sister?"

"She was riding through town, startled our horses, and ended up on the ground." Lucius gently handed her down to her mother.

Sage, whose eyes were now open, swayed unsteadily on her feet, a sheepish smile on her lips. "It was only a little fall, Mama. Nothing serious."

I couldn't hold back the snort, "You were unconscious."

Sage sent a glare at me, although it looked like more of a grimace. "Who are you?"

"I'm –"

"This is *Sir* Collins. He is a friend of mine." Lucius's emphasis on the title made me scowl, but I did my best to school my features into a smile.

"Thank you for allowing me to stay here, Lady ..." I realized that Lucius had never mentioned his mother's name.

"Marion." She smiled sweetly. It was a genuine smile, I realized. Not vindictive or calculating. Joy poured out of this family, and I couldn't help the anger that wrapped around me like a heavy blanket. Why did they deserve this happiness? Why did they get to be a family, whole and complete, while I was banished from the one place where I had ever known love?

Someone cleared their throat, and I glanced at Lucius. His mother had disappeared through the front doors with Sage while I had been lost in thought.

"Well?" Lucius raised a brow and I realized he was waiting for an answer to a question I hadn't heard.

"Sorry, what did you ask?"

He snorted, "Food or bed?"

I yawned, weariness already tugging my eyelids half shut. The knight smiled as he dismounted and handed the reins to a stable boy that had run up when we first arrived. "Come. I'll show you to your quarters."

4

SAGE

"I am fine, Mama." I batted her hand away from where she was feeling the lump on my head as I tried to swallow the yelp of pain, "It's just a little bump!"

"But Sir Collins said you were unconscious!" She harrumphed, planting her hands on her slim hips. "Honestly, Sage. What are we going to do with you?"

I rolled my eyes, which made her eyes narrow even more. "You just met the man."

"Yes, well, he seemed quite put out with you."

I shook my head, stopping when the room began to spin, "It was his horse that caused Rose to rear in the first place. If you should be mad at anyone, it should be him, not me."

Mama harrumphed again, turning to the doorway both Sir Collins and Lucius had just entered through. Both men were glaring at me, having heard my comment. I simply smiled back as sweetly as I could, the action causing a splitting pain to form behind my eyes. I ignored it as Mama stepped up to Collins.

"You must be quite tired after your ride. Let me show you to your room. You," she pointed at Lucius, "can deal with your headstrong sister."

Lucius nodded as Mama gestured for Collins to follow her. The knight sent me one more withering glare before following her into the hallway.

"You really need to try making better first impressions, Sage." Lucius flopped into one of the chairs beside my own, his leg dangling over the arm. He only sat that way when Mama was nowhere nearby. Lucius smiled at me, "Sir Collins is going to think you're a forest nymph, wild and untamable."

"Why should I care what he thinks?" I retorted hotly, "He's your friend."

Lucius raised a brow, "Please, keep that attitude. It will be easier for me that way."

I snorted, trying not to wince at the pain that speared through my head. "And to think, I was just missing you a few moments before you nearly ran me down on the road."

Lucius laughed slightly, standing to pull me into a hug, "I missed you too, sister."

I melted a little in my brother's arms. It had been months since I had last seen him. He looked well, broader across the shoulders, with a maturity that hadn't been in him before. "How was it? Serving with Prince Nicholas in the war?"

His brows lowered slightly, sorrow making him appear older than his twenty years. "It was … difficult. A lot of blood spilled on both sides. But Nicholas and I returned. That is more than most."

My heart ached at the grief in his eyes and I hugged him tighter, "I am sorry, Lucius."

He took a deep breath before he pulled away. "It's good to be home."

"Papa is going to be overjoyed when he returns from town!" I bounced a little, my head barely hurting at the thought of a family dinner. "I'm sure Mama will invite Robert and Margie and it will be like old times!"

"Let me go rest first," Lucius laughed, "You should too. It might help with your headache."

"What headache?" I tried to feign innocence but Lucius reached up and poked at the lump, "Ouch! All right! Yes, that headache!"

He laughed, offering me his arm as he guided me down the hall to my room, "Rest. There will be plenty of time for fun at dinner."

I slept well, my headache barely a thought as I glided down the hallway to dinner in my favorite green gown. With a beaded bodice, and sleeves that flared out at my elbow, I felt like a grand lady on her way to a ball at Findley Palace.

Everyone else was already in the dining hall, sipping on the spiced cider that Cook served in the fall. I smiled at Margie, skipping over to hug her. I could feel Sir Collins' gaze following me, and I rolled my eyes while I hugged my sister-in-law.

"How are you and Robert settling into your new home?" I asked.

Margie blushed, "It's been wonderful. Marriage bliss is real, Sage."

"It does seem to suit you." I smiled, my eyes flicking to my eldest brother. He was deep in conversation with Lucius, Papa, and Sir Collins. He was animatedly waving his hands over whatever it was he was discussing. Sir Collins' gaze lazily met mine again and he smirked. I glared, still annoyed with him for his lack of defense about my riding skills.

"Is something wrong?" Margie asked, dragging my attention away from the knight. "You could cut the tension with a knife."

"He's the reason I fell off Rose this afternoon." I stated in a low whisper, "And he didn't bother to tell Mama that, blaming my riding skills instead."

Margie laughed, tucking a strand of her long blonde hair behind her ear. "You have always been fiercely loyal. You never understand when others are not."

"I cannot help that," I shrugged, earning a glare from Mama, who was talking to one of the servants, "Loyalty is something everyone in my family has."

"Aye, I know." Margie got a swoony look in her eye. But she quickly shook it away, smiling at me, "You'll someday find someone as loyal as you. And he will live and breathe and die loving you."

I snorted, "I am holding you to that, Margie."

Papa broke away from the other men, moving to the head of the table. We all followed suit, sitting where Mama instructed. I somehow ended up between Lucius and Sir Collins on the left side of the table.

After the blessing, as we began to eat the cooked vegetables, Mama leaned over and laid her hand on Papa's. "Sage was thrown from her horse today, Erik."

Papa's utensils clattered against his trencher, "What? Are you hurt?"

"Does she appear hurt, Father?" Robert asked, a bemused smile on his face, "She's suffered worse than that before."

"Thank you, Robert." I inclined my head in his direction, "It was just a little bump on the head."

Sir Collins repeated his earlier observation for Papa, "You were knocked unconscious."

"For less than a minute!" I protested in exasperation, "I woke up when you were holding me!"

Lucius cleared his throat, "It was only while I mounted." He sounded like he needed to defend his actions to Papa, who was glaring at Sir Collins most severely.

"Yes, well. I'm glad you are fine, Sage. Don't be racing your horse down the main roads. There are plenty of fields around the manor that will work just as well."

"The road is easier to fly down." I muttered, picking at the vegetables with my knife.

"It's also easier to startle someone, m'lady." Sir Collins had dropped his voice to a whisper so that only I could hear, "We wouldn't want that pretty head knocked around anymore than necessary, now would we?"

My temper simmered, my eyes glaring at Sir Collins from the side. "Well, if someone had better horsemanship, I wouldn't have fallen in the first place."

His jaw ticked in and out as he glared at the food on his trencher. We both lapsed into silence, picking at most of our food until dessert arrived. I was fuming. Who was he, with his perfectly styled hair, arrogant walk, and patronizing smirk, to tell me how to handle my horse? I glanced at him a few more times during the meal, noticing the stiff way he sat, the way his eyes darted to everyone around the table. There was an anger on his face, one I had a feeling was more than just at me and my harsh remarks. It was almost enough to make me feel sorry for him.

Almost. But not quite.

It was with a soft sigh of relief from me that Papa stood, motioning for Lucius and Sir Collins to follow him.

"Come. There is much to discuss."

WHEN *You* FOUND *Me*

5

COLLINS

"Now. Tell me a bit about yourself, son." Lord Ableton sat, lighting a pipe that sat on his desk and puffing a few draws. The room held the lingering scent of vanilla and spice that now swirled around us in the plume of smoke.

I turned to Lucius, gesturing in mock submission to him. Lucius' jaw clicked in and out for a moment, before he turned to his father. "Collins is not a simple knight, Father."

Lord Ableton raised a brow, "I know who he is, Lucius. I knew the moment I laid eyes on him. You look so much like your father did at that age, Collins."

I swallowed, a cascade of emotions rushing through me. I was touched that this man thought I looked like Father, angry that Father had sent me to this hellhole of a town, and ashamed that I deserved to be here in the first place.

"Thank you, m'lord." I cleared my throat. "What are you planning for me, Lord Ableton?"

"Nothing more than what I expect of my sons," he smiled kindly. "Helping in the gardens, cleaning the stables, exercising the horses …" He continued to list off tasks, and with each my teeth clenched tighter and tighter, until I was sure I was going to crack a tooth if I applied any more pressure.

"You're able to handle that, of course." Lord Ableton smiled, and it looked more conniving than friendly now. "There is one more thing you must do, my boy, and there will be grave consequences if this rule is not followed."

I cleared my throat again, shifting in my chair. The man's intense gaze met my own. His eyes, dark brown with Sage's golden flecks throughout, started at me without wavering. It was as if they could see into my very heart.

"What is that rule, sir?"

"Stay away from my daughter."   It was said low, threatening, and my airway closed at the danger laying in Lord Ableton's face. A glance at Lucius showed the same, and I shifted in my chair nervously as the lord of the land continued, "I know you are used to having whatever you want handed to you. Money, food, women." The last part was said more harshly than the rest, "But know this, Collins. If you so much as lay a hand on Sage, I have permission from the king to flog you and place you in the stocks in town."

My face paled, and I looked at Lucius again. The insufferable knight simply raised a brow.

"But you shall not have to worry about that, for you will stay away from Sage unless it is an innocent exchange." It sounded more like a question than a statement, so I nodded quickly. "Good. Good. Now, the hour is getting late, and we have work ahead of us on the morrow."

As if to prove Lord Ableton correct, I yawned loudly, making the man laugh good-naturedly.

"Come," Lucious motioned for me to follow him. "Do you remember the way?"

I shook my head, feeling no glib words spring to mind. Mutely, I followed Lucius down the hall to the wing where the family slept. The guest room was at the very end and I stepped into it wearily.

Leaning against the door, I roughed my hands over my face. I replayed the conversation with Lord Ableton in my mind. I had felt stripped down, exposed, before him. Yet, he had not condemned me. No, he had simply told me the way things were to be here. If I balked, that would be my fault alone and I would suffer the shame and regret that came with that.

My mind unwillingly sprang to Sage. As much as I wanted to get to know her, that would now be impossible. For any interaction with the girl would have to be *innocent*.

Whatever innocent means, I thought as I pulled my shirt over my head and kicked off my boots. I hadn't been innocent in ages.

Half asleep already, I fell onto the bed, reluctantly grateful that I had a place to lay my head at all.

"A stable boy?" I growled the next morning, as I glared at the spade Lucius was holding out to me, "You aren't serious."

"I've never been more serious in my life." Lucius raised his brow at me, "You want to eat? Sleep in a nice bed? Then you work." He waved the tool at me until I snatched it out of his hands, strangling the handle in my grip. "Besides, this is one of the tasks my father has for you. Until we can find an extra lad to tend to the horses, you shall do nicely."

I loathed the smirk Lucius shot my way as I turned to stare at the six stalls on the left side of the stable, and then at the matching set on the right. "All the stalls?"

I ground my teeth as Lucius nodded, smirk still in place as he turned to leave, "When you finish there, the servants need help in the garden. That's where I'll be, turning up the potatoes."

I muttered under my breath as I began the task of raking out the muck in the first stall. It was home to Sage's horse, who seemed to remember me, and not with all that much fondness. Every time I turned, she flicked me with her tail or nipped at me with a whinny. After the sixth attempt at harming my person, I finally turned to glare at the animal.

"Do you mind?" I snapped, planting my fists on my hips, trying to intimidate the beast.

If equines could smile, I was certain that this one was. She tossed her head, her brown eyes daring me to try and stop her.

I had never wanted to murder an animal before, but I was seriously contemplating it at that moment. "Why you little –"

"Careful what you say, Sir Collins. Rose is good at holding grudges."

I turned, my gaze colliding with amber eyes. A growl sound escaped from my throat as Sage smirked at me.

"She's as stubborn as you." I stated as I watched the horse take a mouthful of hay in its teeth.

"I'm stubborn?" Sage raised her brows at me. "How in the world would you know that?"

"Call it intuition." I shoveled another scoop of manure into the wheelbarrow. "Is there a reason you are in here and not slaving like the rest of us?"

She snorted, and it was my turn to raise my brows at her. It was then I noticed how she was dressed. Gone were the plain brown garments she'd worn the day before. Instead she was dressed in a pale purple gown. It hugged her in a most becoming way, showing that Sage was no mere country girl. Her long sleeves tapered over the back of the hand that she was waving in the direction of her horse. Her hair had been done up to look like she was wearing a braided crown, although a few wispy strands had already escaped and were softly curling around her ears.

"Sir Collins? Are you listening?"

I hadn't been, and from the angry look I was getting, Sage knew that already.

"Please saddle my horse. I'm going to be late."

"For what?"

"None of your business," she snapped, her brows lowering in anger, "Apparently you didn't learn how to treat a superior when you trained in the army."

I opened my mouth to retort but quickly snapped it shut again as Sage turned on her heel and stormed out of the stable.

If she only knew … But of course, she had no idea who I was, and that was how it was supposed to be. Oh, but how I wanted to give her a piece of my mind.

I grabbed Rose's lead and guided her into the aisle. I threw the sidesaddle over her back and made quick work of strapping it to her, wanting to hand the ornery beast to Sage and get back to the absolutely *lovely* task of scooping muck out of the stable stalls.

Sage had her arms crossed over her chest as I stepped out with Rose. She huffed; a stray piece of hair that was laying against her temple fluttered from the action.

She stepped up between me and the horse, looking up expectantly. I stared back, not entirely sure what she was waiting for.

"Are you going to help me into the saddle or not?" She finally asked, after a long moment of us just staring at each other.

I rolled my eyes, "Of course, my lady."

I was struck again by how very light Sage was as I lifted her up into her seat. I carefully tucked her feet into the stirrups, pausing when I noticed the long scar that ran across the top of Sage's foot. Grabbing hold of it, I narrowed my eyes as I bent for a closer look.

My head snapped back as Sage's other foot came up, kicking me squarely in the nose. I gasped, rubbing it before I sneezed once, twice, three times. I glared at her. "Do you treat all your stable boys this way?" I asked indignantly.

"Only the rude ones," She replied with a toss of her head, "and the ones who linger over my feet too long when helping me into the saddle."

"You're the one who asked for help, *m'lady*." I snapped. Her eyes narrowed at my tone.

"I won't make that mistake again." She replied as she flicked the reins, spurring Rose into motion, "Good day, Sir Collins!"

"Good day!" I hollered after her, anger simmering in my gut. I went back to work, but my mind wouldn't stop thinking about a certain young lady who had a quick and glib tongue that combated my own so perfectly. She didn't appear to be in awe of me and admiration was something I was used to from young ladies.

It bothered me, for I wanted Sage to bat her long lashes at me and giggle at one of my jokes. But instead, she had turned up her little nose since the day I had arrived, and often she completely ignored me. When she did talk to me, she seemed to push my temper to the breaking point.

She was infuriating.

And I was completely captivated.

WHEN *You* FOUND *Me*

6

SAGE

I fumed the whole ride to town. Who did he think he was? Touching my ankle that way! He'd probably seen the scar and been curious. I would have been. But he had touched my foot, traced it. The chills worked their way down my spine again. I had liked it. Heaven help me, I had liked Collins' attention.

You would think I had never seen a handsome man before. I thought before shaking my head. *Handsome?* Where had that thought come from?

I slipped off of Rose and tied her reins to the post outside the seamstress's shop. Stepping inside, I smiled as Margie stood up and enveloped me in a hug. "I am glad you stopped by! Your dress is coming along nicely."

My smile grew as Margie gestured to the beautiful red dress on the mannequin. The top half had

171

all been sewn together, and the skirt was attached with pins. Margie had started to sew the beads onto the bodice, making intricate patterns and swirls.

"It's lovely!" I gasped, trailing the material of the skirt through my fingers, "Oh, I can't wait to wear this gown!"

"I love how you go from romping in the woods like a ..." Margie waved her hand like she could not think of the correct word, "well, from that to this!" She gestured to the dress.

"I like to be both." I smiled, twirling a needle through the beads Margie had in a dish on her work table. I stared at my sister-in-law as she settled back onto the stool and resumed the quick in and out motion of her needle through the rich red fabric of the skirt.

After a short pause, I asked Margie the question that was poking at my thoughts much like her needle poked the material. "Margie, what attracted you to Robert?"

She stopped sewing for a moment, glancing up at the wall. A small quirk of her lips was the only reaction to my question before she shook her head and glanced at me, "It was his thoughtfulness to your mother."

"My mother?" I asked, raising a brow.

Margie nodded, resuming her stitches, "He was always holding open the chapel door for her, helping her in and out of your carriage, escorting her places when your father wasn't available. It was thoughtful and sweet."

"So, it wasn't his looks?"

Margie laughed, "To be honest, the first time I laid eyes on him he was skinnier than a fence rail. And the hair down to his shoulders …"

"That phase," I winced.

Margie laughed again, "Aye. But he filled out nicely and, once he cut his hair so you could see his eyes, he became quite handsome."

I smiled, remembering the younger Margie and Robert. "Aye. I suppose he did."

"Why do you ask, Sage? A certain someone catch your eye?"

I blushed, but ducked my head so Margie could not see. "No, I was just curious."

"Hm," was Margie's only response. We went back to talking about my dress, and after an hour, I bid her goodbye, promising to stop by again later in the week to view my gown once more.

I rode hard back to the manor house, letting Rose have her head. The wind tugged at my hair and I reached up, pulling my pins free so that it spilled down my back.

I laughed, tipping my head back to the sun, letting it kiss my face again.

All too soon, the stable appeared. I pulled up, swinging off of Rose's back without assistance. Collins was just putting the spade away when he caught sight of me leading Rose back to the stable.

"Would you like me to put her up for you … m'lady?" He swallowed like he was in pain and I cocked my head to the side.

"That was a challenge for you to ask, was it not?"

He cleared his throat, his eyes dropping to the ground, "Do you want help or not?"

"Aye! Here." I thrust the reins at him and he took them. Our fingers brushed, and butterflies took to circling in my stomach, the silly things. I cleared my throat now, my tongue sticking to the roof of my mouth. "Thank you, Sir Collins."

He inclined his head before leading Rose into the stable.

Shaking my head to clear the fog, I turned and hurried inside to change.

When I arrived in the garden, both Lucius and Collins were working on spading up potatoes and adding them to the baskets that the servants were carrying down to the cellar. They both looked bored and were moving slower than the slugs that clung to the leaves of the tomato plants.

"Contest time!" I shouted.

"What kind of contest?" Lucius threw his shoulders back, challenge gleaming in his eyes as he smiled.

Collins also straightened up, but his expression was more wary. I couldn't blame him. After all, I had kicked him in the face a few hours prior.

"You both take a side of the potato field. Cook and I," I motioned her over as she stepped out from the cellar, "will each take a basket and follow. Whoever can turn the most potatoes up by the time they reach that post," I pointed to the center fence post, "wins!"

"Wins what?" Lucius tapped his finger against his chin, "A prize must be awarded."

"An extra scoop of the pudding I made for dinner!" Cook called as she picked up an empty basket and motioned for Lucius to join her. Lucius hesitated, shooting a strange look at Collins before jogging over to Cook's side.

"Ready?" I called and they both nodded. I turned to Collins. An intense look was on his face, and he was holding the spade a few inches above the soil, ready to turn into it the moment I said to.

"Set! Go!"

Collins flung the spade into the earth and shoveled in a frenzy. I crouched, picking up every earth encrusted clump that was a potato and dumping it into the basket.

"Careful not to spear them!" I hollered and Collins grunted in acknowledgement.

We soon fell into a rhythm. He was always a half foot ahead, overturning shovelfuls of dirt as I carefully separated the earth from the potatoes.

We reached the middle first, grinning in joy.

"Let's go back and make sure we did not miss any!" I suggested and Collins nodded without a word. We shift through the moist soil, finding five or six more potatoes that we added to our already overflowing basket.

"Five! Four!" I began chanting in a sing song voice. Lucius glared at me as Collins picked up the countdown with me. "Three, two, one!"

"Times up!" I chirped and Lucius threw a clump of dirt at me.

"You did not say it was timed!" He protested.

"You didn't even reach the post. We gave you more than enough time!" I countered, crossing my arms over my chest, "Did we not, Collins?"

176

"We even went back to make sure we collected all of ours." He agreed, laughing. It was a nice sound.

My brother rolled his eyes, turning to Cook, "See what I put up with day in and day out?"

Cook laughed, patting Lucius' face with her dirt-encrusted fingers, leaving muddy smudges on his sweaty cheek, "You poor dear. And unfortunately, it does look like Sage and Collins collected more potatoes."

I cheered, jumping up and down. I hadn't realized that I had grabbed Collins' arm until I felt it stiffen. I quickly clasped my hands behind my back, a blush rising to my cheeks. "That means an extra helping of pudding for us tonight!"

Collins smiled, although it looked strained. "Aye, I suppose it does."

Lucius was glaring again, whether from me grabbing Collins arm or from losing, I could not tell. "Let's gather up the tools." He gestured to Collins, "Then we can all go clean up before dinner."

"All right." Collins agreed, gathering up his spade and a rake that leaned against the fence. I smiled contentedly, turning to help a servant carry the baskets of potatoes into the cellar. We had a good crop this year. The cellar was nearly bursting from all the potatoes in the bins by the back wall.

"God's been good to us this year, m'lady!" Cook proclaimed when I reemerged. "I have not seen a crop like this in ages."

"Aye," I nodded, my gaze locking on Collins and Lucius as they strode back toward us. "He has been very good indeed."

7

COLLINS

"I thought we told you to stay away from Sage." Lucius growled at me the moment we were out of his sister's earshot. "And yet you let her grab ahold of you!"

"I did not plan that." I hissed back, forcing myself to keep my eyes on the ground. "Besides, I prefer that to her kicking me in the face."

"What?"

Did I just say that aloud? I groaned, leaning the tools against the designated wall in the stable.

"Nothing," I sighed, ignoring Lucius as he raised his brow at me.

Frustrated at my lack of freedom, I turned to head back to the house but Lucius gripped my elbow tightly.

His stormy blue eyes darkened as he whispered, "You may be my prince, and I may have sworn service to Allura and to your father. But if you lay one finger on Sage, that will all mean nothing. Understand?"

I had never seen the normally lighthearted knight quite so serious. His jaw ticked in and out, his gaze never wavering. I swallowed with a slow nod. "Aye, I understand."

Lucius dropped his hand and ran it through his hair. "Let's go get cleaned up for dinner."

"And here are your awards!"

Sage bounced lightly in her seat as the cook placed a large bowl of pudding in front of her, her eyes dancing as they met mine.

"Award? For what?" Lord Ableton chuckled at his daughter as she turned her breath-stealing grin toward him.

"Sir Collins and I beat Lucius and Cook at gathering the most potatoes in the garden today." She laughed, "We were also faster."

"Which, I would like to point out, was not in the original rules." Lucius waved his spoon at his sister after he had licked the desert off of it. His much smaller bowl was already half gone. I glanced down at mine. I had never had this type of pudding before. It had a hard crust across the top, with what looked to be almost a brown, thick goo underneath.

"Are you not going to try it, Sir Collins?" I blinked, shifting under Sage's gaze.

I shrugged, "I've never tried this type of pudding before."

"Oh, it is scrumptious!" She laughed, "If you do not care for it, I am sure Papa and Lucius will eat it for you."

I raised a hand to pause her cascade of words, "I have not even tried it yet."

"Well, go on!" She waved her hand toward my bowl, and I smirked, liking this happy, laughing Sage much more than the angry one who had whapped me in the nose earlier that morning. Picking up my spoon, I scooped up a helping of the crust and pudding underneath. It was smoother than it had first appeared, the creamy chocolate flavor exploding on my tongue.

"This is delicious!" I exclaimed, shoveling another spoonful into my mouth.

Sage and Lucius both began laughing as I glanced up at them. Lucius's was more controlled and he tried to hide it with a hand over his mouth. Sage, however, was holding her sides, laughing unabashedly at me.

"What?"

Sage motioned to her face, tears trailing down her cheeks, and gasped, "You have – pudding – on your chin."

Swiping at my face, I discovered I did indeed have a large glob of pudding trailing down my chin. Embarrassment turned my face red and I cleared my throat. "I think I am finished."

Sage stopped laughing, a half-smile twisting her lips. "I'm sorry for laughing. It was just … comical."

Lord and Lady Ableton had been silent through the whole exchange, but both of them were glancing between their daughter and me. Lady Ableton had a quizzical, calculating expression as she gazed at her daughter. Lord Ableton, however, had a stern, unmoving glare leveled at me. I suppressed as sigh as I pushed to my feet.

"If you'll excuse me, I think I shall retire." *At least my room is one place I cannot ruin anything.*

"Goodnight, Sir Collins!" Sage's voice drifted over to me as I hurried out the door, taunting me.

How could she go from hating me one moment to having fun with me the next? And why was the one person I wanted to get to know better the one who was completely off limits?

"No!" I sat up, sweat coating my chest as I heaved in and out from my nightmare. Although, a month ago, it would have been a fantasy.

I groaned, burying my face in my hands. I had been in Ableton for two weeks, but I could not shake free of my past. Whenever Sage and I shared a phrase or a smile, Lucius was always right on her heels, glaring or snapping at me to help him with some menial task. It took everything in me not to snarl back at him.

I had been able to hide most of me, most of my brokenness. But at night … night was the real test. Nighttime brought all the sins I had tried to bury back into the light, parading them through my sleeping mind to show me all my failures.

I suppressed the shudder that shook my shoulders, swinging out of bed and stumbling to pull my clothes on in a haste. I needed to escape the confines of my room. Carrying my boots, I slipped out the door and down the hall to the front doors. Easing one open just enough for me to slip through, I hurried down to the stables and saddled a mare.

There was only one thing that dulled my mind enough to return to sleep.

I rode hard, pulling up to the first inn I came across. Lashing the horse's reins to the post out front, I stepped inside.

It was busier than I expected for the middle of the night in Ableton, but then, there were probably plenty of men like me. Men who were trying to drown themselves in drink to forget.

Forget war.

Forget sorrow.

Forget regret.

"What'll it be?" The gruff barkeeper asked as I sank onto the stool.

"Whatever is strongest." I muttered, slapping a gold florin onto the counter, "And a lot of it."

He raised a brow, but nodded as he turned to fill a tankard and slide it down to me.

Sage's face flashed in my mind as I downed the ale, but I pushed it away. She was unattainable, the one person I could not have. Yet another reason to sink into a drunken stupor.

I slapped the counter, letting the barkeeper fill my mug again.

The nightmare and Sage both warred for acknowledgement, clawing at my mind with enough strength to make me want to scream. I clutched my temples, feeling them pound beneath my fingertips. I grabbed the ale, downing it in five large gulps. The edges of my mind numbed, but not enough.

I just want to forget. I groaned, holding my face in my hands as a curse slipped between my lips, *That is all I want to do.*

WHEN *You* FOUND *Me*

8

SAGE

I stretched, breathing in the crisp morning air that wafted in through my open window. The leaves from the oak tree rustled against the outside wall as the sunshine poured through its boughs.

It had been two weeks since Collins had arrived with Lucius. We had harvested most of the vegetables from the garden, and had just started the harvest of the hay in the far fields. Lucius and Collins had been out there most of the week, although it was nearly done. I smiled. We were planning a feast for that evening, all of the servants would eat with us in the dining room and there would be dancing after the meal. It was the best day of the year, even better than Christmas for me.

"Good morning, Lady Sage!" Tillie, my maid, bustled in as I hopped from my bed and settled on the stool. "Are you ready for the final harvest day?"

She laughed as I enthusiastically nodded, "Aye! It'll be great fun!"

Tillie quickly helped me dress in my plain brown work dress, and had just finished tying back my braid when a knock sounded on the door.

We both raised our brows toward each other as Lucius pushed open the door and glanced around my room, "Is he in here?"

"Why would any man ever be in my room?" I shook my head at my brother.

He had the decency to blush as he cleared his throat, "Sorry. Never mind."

I jumped to my feet, grabbing his arm. "What is going on?"

"Nothing. Just ..." He sighed, "You haven't seen Collins yet this morning, have you?"

I shook my head. Lucius sighed again as he stepped out the door and down the hall. I trailed behind him.

"Where do you think he is?"

"I have an idea. And I am *not* going after him." Lucius picked up his pace and I was practically trotting to keep up with him as he stormed into the barn. He picked up a spade, stomped to a stall, and began to shovel up the manure. His shoulders were tense, and his jaw clicked audibly as he worked.

"Where did he go, Lucius?" I sighed, crossing my arms over my chest as I leaned against the stall door.

"I'm not his keeper, Sage."

"Let me get this straight." I glared at him, memories of the past two weeks fueling my frustration. "You won't go after your missing friend, who may or may not be in trouble, but you will jump between me and him when I am simply trying to talk to him? You are not his keeper, but you *are* mine?" I threw my hands up in the air, "Unbelievable!"

Lucius sighed, rubbing his hands over his face. "If you knew who he was, you would understand. I am protecting you, Sage."

I snorted, stomping over to ready Rose for my ride into town.

"Where are you going?"

"To find him. I am assuming you've already looked around the manor. That means he must be in town."

It was Lucius's turn to cross his arms, "I am not sure that's such a good idea, Sage."

"Why not?" I turned from Rose, my nose almost brushing my brother's as I did. He had moved to stand right behind me, "What are you not telling me about Collins, Lucius?"

I could see the war in my brother's eyes. The greys and blues seemed to darken, and his brows lowered, "I can't tell you anything, Sage. I swore an oath."

"To who? Who are you protecting by not –?" I stopped abruptly, pieces beginning to click into place. The few things that Collins had said when we had spoken. His attitude when he had arrived. His entitlement and general arrogance.

"He's *Prince* Collins, isn't he?" I whispered, interlocking my fingers behind my head as I turned and walked further into the stall, "Why is he here?"

"I can't tell you that. If Collins wants to tell you the truth, then he can. I can't betray him, nor the king in that way. Please don't ask me again, Sage." He stepped out of the stall and strode toward the door, "Feel free to drag the drunkard home, though. I'm not going to fetch him."

I lowered my hands to my cheeks, feeling the heat radiating off of them.

Yes, I will. I will go fetch his sorry, good for nothing – I swallowed the unladylike words that were begging to be used, and instead mounted my horse. I was breathing hard, trying to calm my racing mind and heart before I made it to town. If the rumors about our younger prince were true, then there were four possible places he could be.

And all of them served ale.

That line of thinking did not serve to calm me any as I thundered into town. I decided to try the popular ale house first, which was surprisingly crowded for eleven o'clock in the morning. Every head turned when I stepped through the door, their leers sending chills down my arms. I straightened my shoulders however, and marched right up to the counter.

"Excuse me, but I'm looking for a friend of mine. Goes by the name of Collins."

The bartender snorted, "Oh I know 'im. Certainly paid well for his drink, 'e did." The man held up three gold florins, and I could only imagine how much drink Collins had consumed here, "I kicked 'im out about an hour ago. I think 'e stumbled his way down to Macintyre's down the road, there."

I smiled with a nod, "Thank you for the information."

"Don't know what the fool is thinkin' miss. Iffin' I 'ad a lady like you waitin' for me at 'ome, I sure wouldn't be wastin' my time 'ere."

A blush infused my cheeks and I managed a simple nod before fleeing the ale house. I grabbed Rose's reins, hurrying down the road to the best inn in town, Macintyre's. I was friends with the innkeeper and his wife, so I was surprised at the pandemonium that I was greeted by when I stepped through the door. Tables were overturned with smashed glasses, trenchers and serving utensils scattered all along the floor. The strong smell of ale burned my nose as I moved further into the dining room, my eyes widening even further as I pushed through the ring of men.

There was Collins, sporting a very large black eye. Blood dribbled from a cut on his lip as well as from his nose. His hair was wild, and the look in his eyes even more so. On top of him was Gregory, his grey eyes and black hair a stark contrast to the man he had pinned to the ground. But Collins didn't stay pinned for long. With a strange kick of his legs, he flung Gregory over his head, causing the bigger, stronger man to gasp for air as he landed on his back. Collins was on top of him before I could blink, wailing on my friend with his fists. I had now seen more than enough.

"What in the name of all that is holy are you two doing?" I had to scream to be heard over the commotion, but the moment my voice was caught, the chaos froze. I planted my fists on my hips, glaring at the guilty looking Gregory and the obviously annoyed Collins.

"You two. Outside. Now." I turned on my heels, slightly ashamed of the tone I had taken with the men. But my frustration won out over my embarrassment, and it was only by biting my tongue that I was keeping the verbal assault at bay.

The moment their boots scratched the cobblestones I turned, my hands shaking as I balled them into fists at my side. "What was that?"

"He called you a name." Gregory supplied, his eyes dropping to his boots. "He is drunk out of his mind."

My eyes flicked to Collins. He was swaying, leaning his hand against the side of the building. His brown eyes swept over me for a moment. They were glazed, distant, and unfeeling. A shutter shook my frame. "Well, let's get him sober, Gregory."

"Why?"

I gaped at my friend. The normal care and compassion that always seemed to radiate from him was gone. He glared at Collins with more hatred than I had ever witnessed in anyone before. I shook my head, "I don't care what he said about me while he was inebriated. He can't stay this way and I have to get him home."

Gregory growled under his breath, before grabbing Collins's arm, "Let's get this over with."

After thoroughly drenching Collins in the bucket of water from the well, I sent Gregory off to find some bread and cheese for a meal before he threw another punch at Collins. The prince was slumped by the well, his knees drawn up with his elbows resting on them. His head was buried in his hands, and he groaned slightly as he shifted his position.

"Having a brawl in an inn will do that." I bit my tongue to keep from saying more as he slowly raised his head to glance at me.

Collins' shoulders slumped even more as a small sigh slipped past his lips. "I thought I was past this."

My throat felt tight as Collins rested his head in his hands again, and a strange urge to comfort him pulled at me.

"Has this happened before?" I scooted a little closer, leaning back against the well, trying to catch a glimpse of his face out of the corner of my eye.

"Yes," he leaned back too, our shoulders brushing ever so slightly. He stretched his long legs out in front of him and closed his eyes, "I have memories I would rather forget. The only thing that dulls them is strong drink. I am…a horrible person, Sage."

He said it with such resignation in his tone, like he truly believed it and that it was too late to change. I shook my head, a small laugh slipping past my lips. "We are all bad people, Collins."

He shook his head, "I'm the worst. You don't know what I have done."

I snorted, "Then tell me. It will not change the fact that we all make mistakes, we all mess up, we all –"

"Have you used women, Sage? Used them to feel loved, until they no longer satisfy and then simply throw them out of your home and out of your life?" He pushed to his feet, swaying slightly from the sudden assent, "Have you drunken yourself into a stupor more times than you can count to try to numb the guilt of what you have done? To simply try and forget everything you have lost? Have you…" his voice cracked, "Have you ever felt like the scum of the earth, and wondered if God even hears you anymore?"

I was speechless. Not because of his confession, although that opened up many questions for me. But I realized that the first time since I had met him, I was truly seeing Collins. The real him, not some mask of himself that he wanted me to perceive. This was the real, raw, hurting human behind the facade.

My heart ached, sensing the pain he was carrying. I reached out and grabbed his hand. He stiffened, his eyes flicking between my hand and my face.

"No, I have never done any of that, but I want to help you through this. You are not alone, Collins."

It was his turn to snort. He crossed his arms over his chest, pulling my hand away from his as he slid back down against the well. "Then you don't know me very well."

"I know more than you think, your highness," I dropped my voice to a whisper, pulling a handkerchief out of my pocket as I knelt beside him.

"Lucius told you?" His eyes locked with mine and his brows lowered dangerously.

"No, I figured it out on my own." I turned away dipping the small piece of cloth in the bucket before turning back to Collins, "Let me clean your lip."

"I'm fine." He tried to turn away, but I smacked him on the arm. His head snapped back and he groaned at the sudden motion. "What was that for?"

"Let me wipe the blood up." I sighed, "Honestly, Collins, let me help you."

"Fine!" He huffed, turning his face to me. I scooted closer, dabbing at his split lip first.

I shook my head as I washed out the handkerchief and went to work on the rest of his face. After a moment, I asked, "What on earth did you say about me to have Gregory get so angry?"

Collins had just started to relax, but at my question he went ridged again. "I…It wasn't polite."

I sat back on my heels, "I think I gathered as much from the state of your face, m'lord."

"Sh!" He hissed, his eyes darting around before they settled on me again, "I don't want anyone to know."

"Why?" I asked as I dabbed at a cut above his eyebrow.

"I'm safer that way. So is everyone else in the town." He dropped his eyes to his hands, which were almost as black and blue as his eye.

"From enemies, m'lord? Or from … other temptations?" I whispered. I stilled as he finally dragged his eyes up to mine. They were beautiful eyes. Dark brown, almost black around the outside edges. They had an intensity in them that I had rarely seen from men in my town. I got lost in them for a moment, unable to think of anything else.

Collins must have been under a similar spell for when he answered, his voice sounded strangled.

"Both." He quickly sat back, turning his face away as he asked, "Are you done, m'lady?"

"Aye." I blinked, trembling slightly as I stood to dump the now dirty bucket of water. I tried to gather my composure, for I could see Gregory stomping back toward us with some cheese and bread in his hands.

"What?" He asked, as I glared at him.

"Be nice." I practically hissed as I yanked the food away, turning my back on Gregory as he rolled his eyes at my request. My hands curled into fists at his surly attitude, my nails cutting into my palms. I did not care what Collins had said about me. The last thing he needed was our disdain. What he needed was support and love, something I was determined to give him. I was going to help this broken man.

No matter the cost.

9

COLLINS

The food rolled in my stomach, but I forced myself to eat. Sage kept looking at me out of the corner of her eye, oblivious to Gregory's glares.

I stifled the groan that was in the back of my throat as I pushed myself to my feet. I steadied myself against the well, my head spinning. "I need to go get the horse."

Sage stood, "I need to go get Rose, too. And I don't think it is wise to let you wander about by yourself."

I inclined my head in agreement, even with the heat of Gregory's gaze searing into me, "If that's what you think is best, m'lady."

Sage quirked her brow, but turned back to Gregory. "Thank you for your help." Her voice sounded clipped and short. I was glad I that I wasn't on the receiving end of it.

"Just be careful," Gregory grunted.

"Thank you for the warning Gregory, but I can take care of myself."

Sage turned and slipped her hand into the crook of my arm. Her fingers tightened, and her posture straightened. She gently tugged me forward, and since her hand was firmly clamped around my elbow, I had no choice but to follow. We headed back toward the inn, and I winced.

"I made a fool of myself," I whispered, shame pressing down on my shoulders.

Sage nodded, "Aye, you did. But we all tend to do that now and again."

I was unable stop the scoff that escaped, "I tend to do it far more often than *now and again*. It seems like a weekly occurrence, at least."

She laughed, and I felt a slight smile tug on my lips. I liked this. The feel of her hand on my arm, the smell of apple blossoms that danced around her, and the sound of her laugh slipping off her lips. I bit the inside of my cheek, cursing my stupidity. She was off limits, she was Lucius's sister, and she deserved someone much better than me.

The horses were still tied to the post and Sage let go of my arm to untie them. I swayed, still feeling the effects of the ale that was coursing through my body.

"You shouldn't ride like that." Sage pursed her lips at me.

"Well, I most certainly cannot walk back to the manor." I shook my head, my words slurring slightly from the dizziness.

A smirk pulled up one side of Sage's mouth. "No, but you could ride behind me."

All the reasons why that was a bad idea poured through my mind, but the glaring faces of her brother and father were at the forefront of that list. "I don't think that a wise idea, m'lady."

"Call me Sage." She cocked her head to the left, "And why isn't it wise?"

"Your brother –"

She snorted, "I have had just about enough of Lucius and his meddling ways. I know about you and your past, and I'm not afraid of you. I can handle myself." She straightened up, raising a brow my way, "And I don't think that you would tell me everything you did, just to try and do something to me now."

I swallowed, stumbling when Rose shifted. Sage caught me by the shoulders, easing me back up to my full height but not moving her hands. "There. See?"

"See what?" My voice sounded higher than normal. I tried to breathe but found it quite impossible with Sage that close.

"You need to ride with me." She stepped back, shaking her head once, before grabbing my horse's reins and swinging up into the saddle. Offering me her hand, I allowed her to heft me up behind her. I hesitated only a moment before wrapping my arms around her waist. My cheek was almost level to hers and I felt her body stiffen.

"Are you sure you're all right with this?" I asked lowly, my breath making the stray hairs around her temple dance, "I can ride the other horse."

"No. No, it's fine." Her voice sounded tight. "Let's go."

She nudged Rose into a slow canter, and I tightened my grip around her waist. My heart was pounding much too fast, Sage's proximity far more intoxicating than any of the ale I had drank the night before. I swallowed, realizing how far I had fallen. She had seen me at my worst, throwing punches at someone she considered a friend. Yet she had pulled me up, brushed me off, and dragged me back to her home. I had told her my deepest secret, my worst shame, but she hadn't turn up her nose and flounced away. She had stayed.

I sighed, squeezing my eyes shut. *Why? Why are you doing this to me?* I wasn't sure who I was talking to. I reopened my eyes, wondering what would be waiting for me when we returned to Sage's family.

Sage pulled up on the reins once we reached the tree lined path that led to her home. "Are you going to be able to face Papa and Lucius? Or do you want some time?"

"Might as well get it over with." I sucked in a breath between my clenched teeth, "I don't want them thinking the worst about us."

The tips of Sage's ears turned red at that, and I smiled at the thought of her blushing.

"I do know a place where you can be alone, if you need some time before going back. I can drop you there, if you wish."

I released a breath, "That would be nice, yes."

With a nod, Sage turned Rose off of the road and into a thicket of trees. The horses walked slowly, and I allowed my grip to slacken slightly from Sage's waist. It did not seem right, after all the threats I had received from her family, to cling to her like that. It may have been invigorating, but it was a high I could not afford. I wanted to go about this the right way for once. To be allowed her hand, to have her family's approval of us being together.

Where did that thought come from? I thought, panic clawing at my throat. Marriage, especially to someone as good as Sage, had never even been a passing fancy before. Yet now …

Sage stopped Rose and gestured ahead of us, "This was a tree Lucius, Gregory, and I used to play in. The branches are enormous, and it was always a fun place for a game of robbers and royals. The scar on my foot?"

She paused, waiting for my acknowledgement.

"Yes?" It sounded strangled and I cleared my throat.

"I got it the day I slipped from that branch there." She pointed and I followed her finger to a branch that was a good fifteen feet from the forest floor. "The healer said I was lucky I hadn't broken my foot. Or worse, my neck." She laughed, but her body shivered, as if the memory was still painful, "Anyhow, I thought you might like it here. It's quiet and peaceful and will give you a chance to collect yourself."

I practically leapt from the saddle. "Thank you, Sage."

She inclined her head, "Collins?"

I forced my gaze to hers, and what I saw there almost undid me. She had compassion and kindness swirling in her eyes, and I had to force myself to hold my own emotions in check.

"I am praying for you."

I nodded, not trusting my voice. She smiled and turned the horses back toward the path. With a shuddery breath, I turned and climbed up into the comforting solitude of the tree branches. And in the solitude of those creaking boughs, I tried to pray. But the words simply seemed to bounce around the forest, only to fall back to earth, just as dead as the leaves that littered the ground beneath me.

WHEN *You* FOUND *Me*

10

SAGE

I cantered up to the stables. Lucius came out, looking marginally calmer than he had when I had left. He glanced at the empty horse behind me and grunted as he took my reins. "Can I hope he fell off and broke his neck?"

"Oh, stop it!" I glared at my brother, "When you're perfect, then you can belittle him to your heart's content!"

Lucius's eyes rounded at my outburst. "I knew it! He has bewitched you! You did find him drunk out of his mind, yes?"

"Yes," I grunted as I swung off of Rose. "And he was in a brawl with Gregory, but -"

Lucius raised a hand to stop me, "He was fighting with Gregory?"

I sighed, "Yes. Apparently, Collins said something that Gregory didn't like." I decided right then that Lucius didn't need to know that the comment in question had been about me. That would only make him angrier than he already was. "And before you ask any more questions, I know about his past."

"And yet you're still protecting him?" Lucius scoffed.

"Yes!" I yanked my horse's reins from his hands and stomped toward the barn, "He's hurting."

"He brought it on himself." Lucius protested, and I clenched my fists at my side. Were all the men in my life so heartless?

"He needs mercy, compassion." I raised my brow at my brother. "You do remember what those are, yes?"

Lucius glared at me, "He tried to hurt someone I care very much about, Sage. I have nothing good to say about him."

"You care about someone?" This was news to me. I reached out and gently laid a hand against Lucius's crossed arms, "Who?"

"Her name is Emmy." He cleared his throat, "She's Princess Della's lady's maid."

I smiled, "She must be quite special for you to take notice of her."

Lucius smiled, "She is." The smile disappeared, "And Collins tried to hurt her a few months back. That's why he's here, Sage. He was banished by the king until he can prove himself worthy."

I sighed, "I know. But he's so …"

"Broken. Hurting. Sad." Lucius sighed, roughing a hand over his face. "I know you have a hard time turning away when someone needs help. Your loyalty to those you care about is admirable. But please, Sage. Be careful with Collins, all right?"

I nodded, "I will, Lucius. I promise. But I'm not going to abandon him. He needs to see the love of Jesus in us in order to change."

Lucius sighed again, gripping my shoulders tightly. "I'm not going to change your mind, am I?"

I laughed and shook my head, "I am quite stubborn. It is a trait I learned that from you."

"I know." He tweaked my nose with a sigh, "All right, I will do my best not to interfere. But if he tries anything, he is gone. I'll send him to live on the streets of Ableton."

"You can do that?" I raised a brow.

Lucius nodded, "So he better tread carefully."

I swallowed the lump in my throat as I unhitched the two horses and brushed them down. Collins was hurting, that much was certain. And there was only one person who could heal him.

God, show me how to help Collins. He needs you, even if he does not see it. Help me to show him love. Help me to show him You.

"One day." Lucius stated, glancing between Collins and me, "We'll be back by nightfall. You two can be trusted that long, yes?"

"Do shut up, Lucius." I growled under my breath, embarrassment warming my cheeks.

He smirked at me as he clasped Collins's shoulder and all but dragged him into the sitting room. I sighed and stepped out the front doors to Papa, who was double checking the wagon.

"Sage, are you sure you'll be all right alone today?"

I smiled, "I shall be fine, Papa. Cook and the maids will be here." *And Collins*. I swallowed the last part, deciding I didn't need another overprotective family member threatening my friend.

It had been a week since the incident at the inn, and since then Collins had behaved like a perfect gentleman. We'd taken some walks together in the woods, worked together in the barn, and even played some chess in the evenings. He smiled more, though sorrow still lined his face.

The door opened and Lucius came down the steps, a strange smile that didn't go to his eyes plastered on his face.

"What did you do?" I asked hesitantly.

"Nothing." He kissed the top of my head and jumped up into the wagon beside Papa. "Remember, one day!" He held up his first finger, wagging it at me like he was reprimanding me.

I rolled my eyes, "I know! We're not children, Lucius."

Papa laughed, "I'm not concerned, son. You're being a tad -"

"Stifling!" I huffed, "Go! Sell the wheat and hurry home if you're so worried about us."

Papa laughed again, flicking the reins across the team's backsides. I waved until they disappeared in the trees.

I let out a breath of relief as I turned to smile at Collins, who was leaning against the doorframe. "I thought they'd never leave."

He didn't smile back at me, as he had begun to do over the last week. Instead, hurt lined his face as he stared at me.

"Are you ready to clean the stable today?" I forced my smile to remain, even as confusion crashed through me.

He shook his head, dropping his eyes to the ground, "Why should I help the girl who told my secret to her brother?"

My mouth dropped open, "But I wouldn't. I didn't!"

His gaze snapped up, blazing in anger, "Lucius said he heard about what I told you at the inn. I wasn't aware that I had to watch what I said around you. Apparently, it all gets back to your brother."

I barked a laugh at his irrational thoughts. "You do realize that there were plenty of other people who could have told Lucius what happened, yes? I was not the only person around. We were sitting at the public well when you practically shouted your guilt to me."

His jaw popped in and out, his gaze dropping to the ground once more.

But I wasn't done. My temper had been set off, and it usually took a lot of pulling to rein it back in. "If you're so angry that Lucius knows, then why did you do it in the first place? Mayhaps you should start looking at the one Person you might be able to help you, Collins! Or you can keep hurting those you care about and who care about you!"

"Stop!" He held out a hand as he pushed off the doorframe. He refused to raise his head as he shoved past me, heading down the steps and towards the woods.

"Where are you going?" I hollered, "We're not done here."

His harsh laugh reached me, "Oh yes, we are!"

"Collins!"

But he didn't turn around, just stormed into the woods with his shoulders hunched and head down.

Did I just make a horrible mistake? I wondered as I slammed the door shut, sliding against it as I pulled my knees up to my chest. It hurt, having him accuse me of breaking his trust. I hadn't done it, yet he thought I had. I was trying to think the best of him, yet he was seeing the worst in me.

I sighed, leaning my head against my knees as I did the only thing I could think to do.

I prayed.

WHEN *You* FOUND *Me*

11

COLLINS

I stormed into the woods, anger propelling each of my steps forward. She had no right! No right at all to tell me how to live my life. Heaven knew enough people had told me how to live since I'd come to this back-wood hell hole. But hadn't I done everything they asked of me? Who was she to reprimand me?

Stars danced in front of my eyes, and I forced my jaw to unclench as I leaned my arm up against a tree and tried to slow my thundering pulse. My chest heaved and my eyes burned.

Ever so slowly my temper waned, replaced by an emotion I had long thought dead. Tears blurred my vision as I turned and slid my back down the rough trunk of the tree. My heart ached, so much so that I thought it might split in two.

"I am a wretch." I whispered into the woods. I wasn't sure who I was talking to, if it was a confession to the nature around me or another pointless prayer to God. But I needed to get the weight off my chest before it suffocated me. "I'm angry at Sage. Angry because she's right. I fill my days with drink and women and revelry because I feel so empty. I try to ease this ache, but it only grows bigger." I leaned my forehead against my forearms, pulling my legs up to rest my arms against them, "How do I escape from a past that seems to pounce every time I think I've outran it? How do I fix it?"

"You don't."

I jerked my head up at the voice. A man stood leaning against a tree a few paces from me. He was dressed in a brown tunic that fell to the ground and was cinched at the waist with a leather belt. His bald head gleamed in the afternoon sunlight as he smiled at me, making his bushy grey beard twitch.

"What do you mean *I don't*?" I asked incredulously, "Of course I must fix my mess."

"No. *You*, Prince Collins, can't *do* anything." He moved to crouch down at my side, "Sage told me what you're struggling with."

I stiffened, part of me wanting to trust him. He had kind eyes. But another, stronger part of me wanted to run further into the forest and not deal with this guilt. "Who are you, sir?"

"A friend." He smiled again, his eyes sparkling.

My gaze dropped to my lap, "What has Sage told you, sir?"

"That you're hurting. That you're broken and lost. She's very worried about you, son."

A tear slipped down my cheek, for I wasn't worthy of that kind of compassion. "Why should she care?" I rasped, "I deserve to hang for what I've done."

"Doesn't all mankind!" The man laughed, shaking his head in awe, "Everyone deserves that, my boy. But God …" He paused, his eyes growing distant.

I pushed to my feet, his words agitating me into motion. It was like I had an itch on my back that I couldn't quite scratch, the notion that I could be forgiven taunting me. An argument burst from my lips before I could fully process the words, "No one could have done anything worse than me."

"You think that, do you?" The man stood, stepping toward me as he stroked his beard. "The apostle Paul, before he was redeemed by Christ, murdered hundreds of Christians. King David slept with another man's wife. Peter *denied* his Savior three times." His face blazed with intensity. "No, Collins of Findley, nothing you have done is beyond God's forgiveness. You can be redeemed by Him."

He clamped his hand on my shoulder as I shook, half in hope and half in fear. "How?" I interlocked my fingers behind my neck, tipping my head up to stare at the canopy of colored leaves above me. "Why would He want me?"

The man stepped back, flinging his arms wide, "Because He loves you, my boy! He. Loves. You!"

My knees felt wobbly, like I had just run miles in the heat of summer. I crumpled to the forest floor, my chest heaving again as I tugged my legs to my chest. "I'm not worthy," I muttered over and over again, tears trailing down my cheek as I struggled to breathe.

"Collins." The man knelt beside me, his hand landing lightly on my shoulder once more, "He will make you worthy. He is waiting. Waiting for you to call out to Him for rescue. He wants to redeem you, Collins."

A sob shook my frame, unable to be held at bay any longer. The man rubbed my back, like a father comforting his child. I felt like a vase, being smashed into hundreds of tiny pieces. I felt useless, used and spent. But then, I had once seen a man turn broken pieces of glass into a beautiful colored window. Could my broken pieces be turned into something beautiful again, in the hands of a Master Artist?

My tears exhausted, I pushed to my knees. My puffy eyes met those of the kind man. I took a couple of deep, shaky breaths before I was able to ask, "Can He fix me, sir?"

"You know He can, Collins. He promises that in His word. But … it is a process." He raised his bushy white brow at me, "But you know that too."

"How do I let go of this guilt?" I ran a hand through my hair, dislodging some of the leaves that clung to it, "How do I give Him these broken bits of me that I can't seem to grasp?"

He smiled, his eyes shining with joy, "You ask, my boy. You simply have to ask, and He will clean up the mess and turn it into something beautiful."

"I just have to ask?"

He nodded, "'Ask and it will be given to ye, seek and ye shall find, knock and it shall be open unto ye.'"

I nodded, bowing my head, "All right. I'll ask."

I closed my eyes and poured my heart out to the Lord, confessing things I had long buried. My sin was laid bare at the feet of my Savior. I was sobbing again by the time I had finished, yet I felt lighter, freer.

"Thank you, sir." I whispered as I raised my head from where I had been cradling it in my hands.

But the man was gone.

12

SAGE

I paced agitatedly in the hall. My big mouth had gotten me into trouble. Again. Collins had been gone all morning and into the afternoon. I groaned, forcing myself to lean against the wall. I pressed my hands against the cool stones before turning my cheek against it in hopes of alieving the burning in them as well.

Did I mess this up? Did I push too far? I wondered, squeezing my eyes shut as I prayed what I had been praying all day, *Oh God don't let him do something foolish! Protect Collins, Lord. Show Him your truth.*

A loud pounding jerked me from my thoughts. I stepped to the doors, a strange hesitancy causing me to pause with my hand on the latch. I had the strangest urge to flee and hide. Shaking my head at my foolishness, I pulled open the door.

The moment I did, I wished I had listened to my intuition.

A man, dressed in leather armor, stood there, a long knife clutched in his hand. The dark stains of blood were splattered across his green cloak, and his brown hair was plastered to his forehead with sweat. His eyes kept scanning all around, like a cornered beast.

"Let me enter." He commanded, pushing past me without a glance. "You must hide me."

"Who are you to command anything of me?" I snapped, my temper already thin from my fight with Collins. My gaze landed on the crest that adorned the back of the cape. A large black wolf.

I swallowed my gasp, meeting the hard green eyes of the man in front of me as he sneered. All the fear that had been on his face moments before was gone now that he had entered my home, replaced entirely by an oozing arrogance.

"I, dear girl, am Prince Effelwood of Ironwolf. You will protect me or …" He spun the dagger around his wrist, "I shall slay everyone you care about before your very eyes."

I jutted out my chin, my eyes narrowing, "You are in enemy territory, Effelwood. Why would you expect anyone to want to help you?"

He snorted, "Surely you people don't have *that* strong of loyalty to your pathetic king and his sniveling sons?" He laughed, harsh and cold, "Nay. That most certainly is impossible."

My mind flashed to Collins and worry knotted my stomach. If he came back while Effelwood was still here, the man would surely slay Collins. He was the son of his enemy, after all. But ... would Effelwood even recognize Collins?

"Have you ever met our king?" I asked, not daring to move as the prince leveled his knife at my neck.

"Not that it's any of your business *woman* but I have. My father and I were invited to court four years ago to try to settle the war peacefully." He sneered, "Which was ludicrous. Your bumpkin king was laughable, at best, with diplomatic relations. Why do you think this war is still going on?"

I bit my tongue to hold back the rude comment on the tip of it. I had to be rid of this man before Collins came back.

If he comes back at all. I pushed away the sorrow that that thought stirred to the back of my mind to contemplate later. Right now I had a bigger problem to deal with.

"Show me to a room. I'm tired."

Effelwood began to stalk down the hall, and I had no choice but to follow him. He opened every door we passed, peering in before moving on. My hands tightened into fists when he opened the door to my room, as he had done all the rest. Only this time, instead of moving on, he stepped in.

"This shall be my room while I remain under your roof." He unclasped his cape, throwing it over one of my favorite sitting chairs before tugging his soiled shirt over his head, "Bring me some food. Soup sounds lovely."

Mayhaps I'll add little something to it, your arrogance. Deathcaps give soup a nice flavor, I hear. I turned on my heel, marching out of the room with every intention of poisoning the arrogant prince before he hurt anyone I loved. As I neared the door, he grabbed hold of my arm, his grip tightening like a vice. Fear clawed at my throat as I turned back to face him.

His green eyes were hard, and I felt the point of a blade at my back. "You will bring back my food, and you will eat a bite of everything before I even touch it. Just in case you get any ideas about …" He smiled coolly and didn't finish his sentence. Stepping back to the bed, he sat on the edge and tugged off his boots.

Hurrying out into the hall, I leaned against the wall and clutched at my stomach. The look on the man's face sent terror into my limbs, making me start to shake uncontrollably. He would kill us all. There was no doubt in my mind that after I fed and housed him, everyone I loved would die before he turned his blade on me. I had heard rumors of the army of Ironwolf doing such things. My father was beyond loyal to the king. King Donogan of Ironwolf had to know who we were.

His son is going to kill my family. He could kill Collins. I straightened up, my eyes flicking to the door of my bedchambers before I practically ran to the kitchen. I knew what I had to do.

I just hoped I had the strength to see it through.

"Here's your soup, highness." I balanced the tray on my hand, sliding it easily onto the stand beside my bed. Effelwood was sprawled out on it, the only article of clothing still on him being his hose. I turned, feeling my cheeks warm slightly. My hand landed on my hip. I could feel the cool metal of the dagger Cook had helped my strap under my overskirt. She had managed to cut a slit into it that allowed my hand to slip through and grip the dagger when the moment came. I just needed Effelwood to fall into slumber.

He sat up now, glaring at me as he sniffed the food on the tray. "Took you long enough."

I bit my tongue again, tasting blood.

"Take a sip." He motioned to the bowl.

I bowed my head as meekly as I could before sipping a spoonful of broth into my mouth. I smiled sweetly, although it felt more like a grimace, as I held the spoon out to him. "It's delicious."

Effelwood glared at me as he took the spoon from my hand. His fingers brushed mine, feeling cold and clammy. I dropped my hand, stepping backwards as quickly as I could as his predatory eyes slid over me.

"What's wrong lass?" He sneered and I felt like I might be ill. "Do I scare you?"

I straightened my shoulders, forgetting my plan to be demure. Being timid only made me more of a target. My mind raced. Should I just do it? Not wait for him to fall into slumber and attempt to stab him? The thought of murdering him in cold blood turned my stomach, but he was stronger and larger than me. There was no way I could overpower the man.

"No, Prince Effelwood." I managed as I smoothed my sweaty hands over my skirt, "I was just going to stir up the fire."

He raised a brow, standing and stalking toward me. "No. No, I think you're intimidated by me. Attracted, mayhaps?"

You barge into my home, take over my bedchambers, and you expect me to find you attractive?

It took everything in me not to gag. He was too close. His fingers brushed across my cheek, and I imagined that a dozen spiders would have felt more pleasant. He pulled the strap off my braid, causing my hair to cascade down my back, as he stepped even closer. He pinned me up against the fireplace, bracing his hands against it on either side of my body. His breath brushed my cheek, and I thought I very well might be sick.

His eyes scanned my face, like a hawk zoning in on its prey. "You are quite the beautiful woman. And I don't even know your name."

I swallowed. My hand found the slit in my skirt but I paused as a plan formed in my mind. Smiling up as beguiling as I could, I whispered, "It's Sage, m'lord."

I stepped smoothly under his arm, grabbing his hand and pulling him to the edge of the bed. His smile grew wicked as he laid down, waiting for what he thought would be a show. My heart was thundering harder than Rose's feet on the hard packed road as I turned my back to him, pretending to fiddle with the buttons of my gown. My hand closed around the hilt of the dagger drawing it out. Holding it so he couldn't glimpse it, I sashayed over to the edge of the bed, smiling as I lowered my face down to his. As I had hoped, he closed his eyes.

I acted on instinct. Raising the dagger, I slammed it straight into Effelwood's chest. His eyes snapped open, but I twisted the dagger deeper. He raised his hands to mine, trying weakly to pull the weapon from his chest even as I pressed in harder. Blood oozed around the dagger, coating my hands, but I was focused on one thing. Effelwood. It was only a moment before his eyes glazed and his body went limp even as blood continued to spread across his bare chest and onto my bedspread.

I stepped back, shaking. I wiped my blood coated fingers onto my skirt, the metallic smell churning my gut as stared at the dead man on my bed. The man whose life I had just watched leave his body. I stared down at my dress, seeing the red stains coating the front. My mind kept replaying the scene over and over. The dagger, the blood, and the lifeless eyes.

I gagged, turning to throw open the door and fly down the stairs. The little bit of food in my stomach wanted out, and I barely made it out of the doors before I crumpled into a heap and heaved. My body wouldn't stop shaking as I kept seeing Effelwood's eyes in my mind. Those green eyes whose life was snuffed out by me. Me.

"I'm sorry." I whispered, tears pouring down my cheeks. A sob broke free, turning into a wail as I tried to wipe the blood from my fingers onto the grass. "Oh God, why did I do that?"

The sound of footsteps came up behind me and I leapt to my feet, my brain telling me someone was coming for me. For I had just murdered a man.

Murderer. Murderer. My mind chanted over and over.

"Sage?"

I gasped, turning to see Collins. He looked like an angel, the sun shining behind him as he stood there with concern on his face. His eyes swept over me, growing wide at the blood all over the front of me.

"What happened?" He asked, but that was all he was able to say before I launched myself into his arms. I was sobbing again, and for a moment he didn't seem to know what to do with his hands. But my grip only tightened, my breathing short and erratic.

"Breathe, Sage. Breathe."

He softened against me, his muscles relaxing as he cradled me into his arms. Rubbing my back, he slowly began to guide me to the steps at the front of my home. But the thought of him leading me inside...

I pulled away, my head whipping to and fro, "I can't go in there. I can't. Oh, he's in there."

"Who?" Collins's brows lowered and he snapped his head to the door for a moment before glancing back at me. "Who is in there, Sage?"

My head felt light, my breathing choppy again. I swayed on my feet. "Effelwood," slipped off of my tongue before I felt myself falling. But I never felt myself hit the ground as blessed blackness enveloped me in its inky arms.

WHEN *You* FOUND *Me*

13

COLLINS

Never had fear gripped my heart as tightly as it did while watching Sage crumple to the ground. I dashed to her side, dropping to my knees as I gathered her up in my arms. Blood coated her hands and the front of her dress, but she did not appear to be in pain.

She's unconscious, you dolt. She's not feeling much of anything right now. I brushed back the strands of her loose hair, trying to remain calm.

"Sage." I whispered, my voice strangled, "Sage, please wake up. You need to tell me what happened, love."

I wasn't sure where the term of endearment had come from, but I found that I meant it. I loved her. I loved the way she challenged me, stood up to me, saw me as more than the title of prince and rogue. I loved her sparkling amber eyes, her cockeyed smile, and her freckles. The thought of losing her now made my airway close and my vision blur.

"Collins?" I huffed a sigh of relief as Sage groaned and brushed her forehead with her fingers. A trail of blood streaked acorss it, and she blanched at the smell. "I killed a man."

"Effelwood." I raised a brow, "What happened? Why did you kill him?"

I knew I had phrased the question poorly when violent shudder shook her frame. "He threatened those I loved. I was … he would recognize you. I was afraid that he wouldd kill everyone and I couldn't live with myself if that happened. I took care of the threat."

Tears poured down her cheeks now, and I reached up and gently wiped them away with the pad of my thumb. "You were afraid for me?"

Sage nodded, burying her nose into my chest, "I'm sorry."

I shook my head, "For what?"

"I-I shouldn't have killed him." She clutched my shirt in her fists, a wild glint in her eyes again, "I shouldn't have done it. I should have waited for you or Lucius or Father. I was just scared. He said he would kill you all. I couldn't lose you, Collins. I couldn't bear it."

"You're not going to lose me, Sage." I whispered, my voice thick with emotion. She was sobbing again, shaking so badly I was afraid she would shatter, "Come. Let's go warm you up."

Her wild eyes landed on the doors, "He's in there."

"Do you want me to take care of it?" I brushed my thumb across her cheek again, "I'll clean up the mess. Why don't you go sit in the sitting room? I'll send Cook in to clean you up and then we can talk some more. Or you can rest."

She nodded slowly, but her grip didn't loosen on my shirt. "How am I going to tell Papa and Lucius?"

I ran my hand down the back of her head and lightly held her neck, "We'll face that when we come to it, Sage. Let's just worry about you right now. Are you all right to go back inside?"

With a shaky nod, Sage began to rise. I slowly stood and gripped her elbow tightly as we began the slow walk back into the manor house.

Effelwood. I thought as we slowly climbed the steps. *Surly not* that *Effelwood.*

I glanced at Sage, wondering if I should ask. Effelwood of Ironwolf was a worse rogue than me when it came to women, or so the stories said. He was also ruthless, killing dozens at the border war. I remembered him and his father coming to Findley when we were trying to settle things peacefully. I had been a boy then, sixteen years of age. But I remembered how cocky Effelwood had been, how arrogant. He had thought him and his father better than us, and I had hated him for that.

Did Sage just kill the most ruthless warrior of Ironwolf's army? I wondered, half in awe and half in fear. For if she had, her very life was in danger. Donogan would stop at nothing to avenge his son's killer, even if that killer was a woman.

I swallowed my fear, deciding to follow my own advice and cross that bridge when we came to it. Sage was shaking all over again, and barely able to move by the time we reached the top steps. I didn't hesitate, choosing to sweep her up into my arms and carry her through the doors and down the hall. She buried her nose against my neck, and I could feel the moisture of her tears trailing down it as she softly whimpered.

"How bad was it, love?" I whispered, as we stepped into the room. "Did he touch you?"

If he did, it's a good thing he's already dead, I thought darkly as I lowered myself onto the settee.

"No, but he tried." Sage hiccupped, "It's just … it's terrifying to see the life go out of someone's eyes. And to know … to know that I did that?" She shivered.

I had never felt such fierce protection over a woman before, but in that moment I knew I would move heaven and earth to fix the pain Sage was feeling. I wrapped both of my arms around her, kissing the top of her head as her fist clenched the fabric of my shirt again.

"I'm here, Sage. I won't leave you."

"I … I want to wash." She whispered, but she didn't move away from me, "And I want that man out of my house."

"Aye." I tugged her closer to me, "Whenever you're ready."

We sat like that for another long moment before she groaned and sat up, "We should take care of it before Papa and Lucius get back."

I nodded slowly, "I want him gone, too. But I don't know if it's wise to move the body. The sheriff of Ableton may want to look at it."

"Will I be tried for murder?" I didn't think it was possible for her to turn any paler, but she did.

I grabbed her hands, ignoring the blood on them as I stared her straight in the eye, "No. I won't let that happen."

"But you're not a prince anymore." She whispered, her eyes flicking to the door. She was worried about me, about keeping my secret. I shook my head in awe. She could be in trouble for murder, and she was protecting me. I fell a little more in love at that very moment.

"Just because I don't currently have my title doesn't mean I don't still have brothers," I smiled slightly, "It will all work out, Sage. I promise. I will defend you until this is all over."

Her amber eyes flicked back and forth between my own before she leaned in and kissed me squarely on the lips. I stiffened, unsure if it was her trauma or my declaration causing this reaction. But as her arms wrapped around my neck, I decided I didn't care. I tighten my arms around her waist, turning my head to kiss her back. I had dreamt of this moment, and I was going to enjoy it.

A voice cleared by the door, making Sage sit back. But it wasn't a jerk of shock or embarrassment. It was slow, her eyes gazing into mine before she turned to face the voice.

It was Cook, her eyes wide even as a small scowl was on her lips, "I was worried sick, I was. Did you do it?"

I glanced at Sage, who nodded slowly at Cook. She had paled again, but her cheeks still had a rosy glow from our kiss. "Aye. Col-Sir Collins was just going to see to the mess."

I inclined my head, helping Sage to her feet as I rose. "I think Lady Sage could use some help ... cleaning up." I cleared my throat, not daring to look over at the woman whose hand was still in mine.

"Hurry back." She whispered softly as I stepped toward the door. I smiled at her and winked as I walked around Cook and out into the hallway.

WHEN *You* FOUND *Me*

14

SAGE

I had never been so thankful for clean clothes. I stared down at my hands, which were raw from the amount of scrubbing it had taken to get the blood off of them. The very thought of blood made me gag and I turned my gaze to my pale green skirt instead as Cook buttoned up the back of my dress, trying to make myself breathe evenly.

After she had finished, she leaned close to my ear and whispered, "I know it's none of my business, but Sir Collins seems … different."

"Different how?" I whispered back. My eyes flicked to the door, but Collins hadn't returned yet.

Cook raised a brow, her ample stomach shaking as she laughed, "Well, for one thing he let you kiss him."

I blushed, "I'm sure he has kissed lots of women." *I know he has. He practically admitted that to me.*

"Aye, but I wasn't sure he was going to let you at first. He looked about ready to pull you off of him."

A pang of hurt speared me. "Truly?"

Cook smiled knowingly, "But I also know, Sage, that you don't go giving your heart to just anyone. And I think he knows that, too. He must have done something to … earn it. And he accepted it quite willingly."

I shook my head, "But he doesn't have to *do* anything. I … I see who he is on the inside, Cook. He's hurt, but he's trying. I made a fool of myself in front of him earlier." I placed my hands against my cheeks, the memories of throwing myself at him reappearing all too willing in my mind, "And I yelled at him quite badly before that."

"Yes, and thank you for that."

I yelped at the voice, my hand laying against my chest in fright as Collins stepped into the room. His mouth was twisted up in a smirk as he came and sat down beside me. Cook eased out the door, leaving it open a crack as her footsteps receded down the hall.

"You're thanking me for yelling at you?"

He laughed slightly and nodded, "Aye. Thank you."

"I … I don't understand."

Collins turned to face me, "I have been holding on to a lot of guilt. I've been hurt, Sage, as you know. When my mother died, my brothers were busy with their lives, my father as king. I felt very alone and angry and … I turned to people and things to satisfy, even though I knew there was only One who could truly fill me."

I nodded slowly, reaching out to take his trembling hand in mine.

He stared at it for a long moment, tracing his thumb around my knuckles, "I wanted to do this later, once you were feeling better."

"What happened, Collins?" I pressed after a long pause, raising my brows at him.

"A man came while I was in the woods. He said you had been talking to him about me, and that he knew what I needed to do."

"But I didn't talk to anyone." I protested, "I would never betray your trust that way."

"I believe you. Truly. But …" Collins raised a brow at me, "Are you sure you didn't tell *anyone* at all about me?"

"No." I shook my head, "After you left, I simply …" My free hand landed over my mouth. "I was praying."

"Praying?" Collins repeated, his eyes going wide, "You think that man was …"

"It could be, couldn't it?"

Collins shook his head in disbelief, "I suppose it's possible."

"But what happened to you while you were out there? Cook said you seemed different, and I see it now, too. You're happier, Collins. More … peaceful."

He nodded slowly, "I let it go. All my anger and hurt and bitterness, I don't want to be that man anymore, Sage. I want to change, not just to be worthy of you, but because I *want* to be better. I hate the man that I was. I hate what he did and said and how he acted. I want to be … I want to be good and patient and … are you crying?"

I blinked, my hand reaching up to wipe at my cheek. "I guess I am." I laughed, then. "I guess I don't quite know how to feel."

"You're still in shock." Collins pulled me closer, "I'm sorry for what you went through. That room …" He shivered himself, "You shouldn't have had to deal with that alone."

He pulled me back into his lap, his arms wrapped tightly around me. I was crying again, letting the memory of what had happened finally replay in my mind. I felt like I could handle it, with Collins holding me and willing to listen.

"It was horrible." I whispered. Collins began rubbing small circles against my back, "I wish I could just erase it from my mind. I know he's going to haunt me for forever."

"Not forever. You will eventually begin to recall it less and less. And then one day you'll realize how little you truly think about it."

"Do you really believe that?" I asked, laying my hand over his heart to feel its steady rhythm beneath my palm.

"Yes. I do."

My eyes drooped and my breathing slowed. I focused on Collins heartbeat, on the steady feeling of his hand rubbing my back.

"Rest, Sage. I'm not going anywhere."

I sighed, breathing in the fresh, clean smell of Collins as I drifted off into a dreamless sleep.

"What are you doing?"

I sat up sharply, breathing hard as I stood. I swayed unsteadily and was only saved from falling by Collins' hand gripping my elbow.

I blinked the remainder of sleep from my eyes as I tried to figure out who was talking.

"What were you doing to my sister?" Lucius stood in the doorway, his arms crossed over his chest. His eyes were narrowed and I swallowed the panic of him kicking Collins out of our home. Or worse.

"I asked him to, Lucius." I stepped forward. "A lot happened while you were gone to market."

"Like what?" He didn't wait for my answer, whirling on Collins instead, "You couldn't keep your hands to yourself for one day?"

I began to protest but Collins gripped my shoulder. "It wasn't anything like that, Lucius."

Lucius paused, and I wondered what about Collins' words surprised my brother.

"What happened?"

I swayed again and Collins helped me to sit back down. Lucius' eyed us as he sank down into one of the overstuffed chairs. I opened my mouth to start, but just shuddered.

Collins took my hand in his again, ignoring the glare Lucius sent his way as he began to explain everything. He started with our fight, then him in the woods, then what happened to me. I filled in a few details, but as Collins continued to explain everything to my brother, the weight of what I had done began to make me panic again.

It didn't help that once Collins finished, Lucius simply shook his head and whispered, "Oh, Sage."

I doubled over, burying my face in my hands as I tried to take a deep breath.

"It's all right, Sage." I felt Collins's warm hand rubbing circles against my back again. "Breathe, love."

"*Love?*" Lucius asked, disbelief clouding his words. "What –?"

"Can I talk to you in the hall, Lucius?" Collins voice sounded like venom, and I sat up to grip his hand as he walked past.

"Be … nice?" I managed through the constricting of my chest.

He nodded, squeezing my hand in his, "Try to think of happy things."

"Happy things." I whispered as the door to the sitting room closed. "Collins's smile, Collins's smell, Collins's kiss."

My breathing slowed, and a smile of my own tugged on my lips as I leaned back against the settee. I pushed the horror from my thoughts, letting memories of Collins play in my mind instead.

WHEN *You* FOUND *Me*

15

COLLINS

"One rule. One! And you couldn't follow even that!" Lucius paced back and forth in front of me in the hall. I crossed my arms over my chest, propping my foot up against the wall, waiting for his tirade to finish. He paused to suck in air, and I took the moment to interject.

"Lucius, I followed that rule every day up until today. If you had seen her, covered in blood and shaking like a leaf…" I roughed a hand over my face, "She's truly an amazing woman."

"Girl." He growled at me, but I shook my head.

"She's eighteen, Lucius."

"And naïve enough to fall for you and your charms."

I had known deep down that people wouldn't believe that I had changed, but I had hoped Lucius would be one of the few. He had always seen the best in people back in Findley. I had hoped that mayhaps he would see that in me now.

"I think we have a larger problem that that, Lucius."

"Larger than you and my sister?" He snorted, crossing my arms. "What would that be?"

I licked my lips with the tip of my tongue. "Have you thought about what the kingdom of Ironwolf will do when they find out that their *prince* is dead? Killed by a woman, no less?"

Some of the fight seemed to leave Lucius and he ran a hand through his hair, "No, I hadn't actually."

"I have a solution, but you're not going to like it." Lucius raised a brow in my direction and I sighed, "I take her back to Findley. As my wife."

Lucius shook his head vehemently, "No! Absolutely not!"

"What is going on?" Lord Ableton stepped into the door, his eyebrows raised when he saw the furious look on his son's face and me backed up against the wall. "Lucius, is there a problem?"

"We leave for one day, *one day*, and Sage goes and kills a man."

"She was defending her family," I supplied.

"Like that makes it better!" Lucius laughed harshly, "My sister had to kill a man because you were off *not* doing what you were meant to be doing, which was protecting her!"

"I didn't think she was in any danger. You don't have any gates around your home, after all."

"And then you come back and hold her like … like she's your wife, which apparently you want to make her!"

"*What*?" Lord Ableton raised his hands in the air, making both of us turn to face him, "I am quite confused. Will someone please explain what is going on?"

"Papa?"

All three of us turned to see Sage step out of the door. Her bare feet slapped against the stone floor as she flung her arms around her father. Tears were yet again sliding down her cheeks as she clung to him, much like she had with me a few hours before.

"Sage. Are you all right?"

"I'm … as well as can be expected." He set her back on her feet and she glanced at me, "Collins helped me, Papa. I … I don't think I could have kept my head without him here."

I smiled slightly, that smile quickly disappearing with the scowl Lucius sent my way. I turned back to Lord Ableton, "Let's go sit and I will explain it all, sir. You have my word."

"Aye." He glanced between his children and myself. "I want to hear this story. Every last detail, if you please."

Lord Ableton's mouth was hanging open by the time we finished our explanation. His eyes flicked between Sage and me. She had scooted closer to me through the whole story, trying to sit straight and tall, but the shaking had started again by the time I'd finished.

I reached out, claiming her hand in mine, "I was simply trying to calm her, m'lord. But-"

"I love him, Father."

She whispered it, so softly I almost talked right over her. I stopped, midsentence, and turned to look at Sage, "You ... you what?"

She blinked, "I love you."

Lucius scoffed, "You barely know him, Sage. He's been here a month!"

Sage shook her head, her gaze never leaving mine, "I love him. He stayed by me when I was falling apart. He held me while I cried. He promised to stand by

250

me. I have seen his mess, and it doesn't scare me. I'm not sure how much I can help, but I want to stand by him, support him, love him. The only thing I hope for in tomorrow is that I get to spend it with Collins."

I couldn't seem to get my lips to form words as I stared at her. I shook my head, my fingers squeezing Sage's tightly.

"Is that a no, you don't feel the same way about my daughter, or a no of disbelief?" Lord Ableton asked. I cleared my throat, turning to face him. He had a bemused smile on his face.

"It's disbelief, m'lord." I turned back to Sage, "Are you sure?"

"Yes." Tears pooled in her eyes, "I knew before Effelwood came, when I yelled at you. I was hurt, because you didn't trust me."

"No, I -" I sighed, "I already told you. You were correct. I left because … I love you too, Sage. And to hear what you truly were thinking hurt."

My eyes unwillingly flicked to Lucius. He had an unreadable expression on his face as he gazed at the two of us, "So you truly care about her?"

I nodded.

"And you care about Collins, Sage?"

She laughed, wrapping her arm around mine, "Aye, Lucius. More than I ever thought possible."

Lord Ableton laughed, "Well, despite the rest of the day, this helps solve one problem."

"What problem is that?" Sage asked, her brows lowering slightly.

"Sage," I cleared my throat, unsure how to proceed, "You do know who Effelwood was, yes?"

"The Prince of Ironwolf." She glanced between the three of us, "Why is that important? Beyond the war, that is."

"When King Donogan hears about his son's death, he will want the person who did it slain." Lucius glanced at me, "And Collins thought the best way to protect you is for you to marry him."

She turned to me, a look of hurt in her eyes. She pulled her hand away, crossing her arms over her chest. "Are you marrying me to protect me, or because you love me?"

"I love you, Sage." I pulled her to her feet. "And because of that love, I want to protect you. I can't imagine a world where you're not with me."

Tears swam in her eyes as she launched herself at me, wrapping her arms around my neck as I spun her in a circle to keep from stumbling back into her father.

I laughed as I sat Sage back on her feet, "So, is that a yes? Will you marry me?"

"If Father will bless us."

We turned to Lord Ableton, who was smiling as he stood from his seat, "You promise to protect her?"

"I shall, m'lord. Until my dying day."

He clasped my shoulder, "Then, aye. You have my blessing."

Sage flung her arms around me again, only instead of tightening into a hug, she pulled my face down and claimed my lips with hers. A gagging noise made her smile and step back.

Lucius grinned, winking at his sister, "What? It's what brothers do."

He stepped up and pulled Sage into a hug. He whispered something into her ear, before turning to me. I tensed, waiting for a glare or a harsh warning. But Lucius pulled me into a hug. I stiffened, unsure what I was supposed to do.

"Take care of her. Love her. And if you do anything to hurt her, I will hurt you."

I laughed, "I promise I will love her and care for her. And, with God's help, I shall do my very best to never hurt her."

Lucius stepped away and nodded, "I shall go with Father to get the sheriff. Then I shall ride with you to Findley."

I nodded, "Aye. We should leave soon."

"Why?" Sage gripped my hand in hers, her gaze darting between us, "Why must we leave so quickly?"

"To make sure Donogan can't get to you, love."

"But what about my family?" Sage shook her head, "Won't they be in danger if Donogan attacks?"

"We're riding to Findley to bring guards back." Lucius stated, "The king will protect those who've protected his lands."

Sage hesitated a second longer before she nodded, "All right. I'll go."

"And then you shall have help in planning your wedding." Lucius rolled his eyes. "I'm sure Princess Della will love that."

I laughed and Sage's eyes sparkled as she gazed up at me. I stared back, barely hearing Lord Ableton and Lucius leave.

"Thank you, Sage." I whispered, my voice husky.

She wrapped her arms around my waist, her gaze never leaving my face, "For what?"

"For not giving up on me. For seeing me through heaven's eyes."

She smiled up at me, "You're most welcome."

I sighed, leaning down and letting my lips brush hers as I thanked God for forgiveness, grace, and indescribable love.

WHEN *You* FOUND *Me*

Epilogue

SAGE

One month later ...

I shifted on the front steps of the cathedral, waiting for the moment the priest would say *husband and wife* and I could kiss my dashingly handsome prince. Collins kept glancing at me out of the corner of his eye, smirking at my fidgets.

I smiled, trying to redirect my thoughts. I let my mind wander to everything that had happened in the last month. When Collins and I had arrived in Findley, King Willhelm had immediately sent twenty-five knights to defend Ableton. They had even started building a wall around the manor house to protect it from further threats that might come across the border.

I had been pardoned for the death of Effelwood, the king calling it self-defense. My nightmares had lessened,

257

after much prayer and talking it out with my future brother-in-law, Nicholas. He had struggled after coming home from the boarder, and had helped me process the death I had caused. Though they still haunted me, they were no longer an every night occurrence.

Collins had apologized to his father, as well. King Willhelm had allowed him to return to the castle and his title. Della had told me how upset the family had been by what Collins had done, and how thankful they were for the change that was now so obvious in their brother and son.

And now my husband.

I glanced down at my red gown, smiling at the handiwork of Margie. Had it really only been six weeks since I had been watching her work on it? I still couldn't believe that I was here, getting married. When Margie had heard about Collins and me, she had sent the dress with Mama, who had come two weeks early to help me see to the little details I often forgot about. *Red is the perfect color for a mid-autumn wedding,* Margie had insisted and I had to agree. I felt every inch the princess I now was. My hand grazed the slim golden circlet on my head, my wedding gift from Collins. I smiled, thanking God again for his wonderful blessings.

"And now, Prince Collins," the priest paused, clearing his throat before smiling at us, "you may kiss your bride."

"Finally." Collins sighed, making me laugh as he tugged me closer and whispered, "That took forever."

"Well, then. Hurry up and kiss me."

He raised his eyebrows, a smirk turning up one side of his mouth, "As you wish, my princess."

Collins tipped me down, his kiss lingering and sweet. The crowd cheered as he straightened us, his arm firmly around my waist as we turned and waved at the massive crowd. I spotted Margie and Robert, and Mother and Father. Lucius stood with his fellow knights, looking incredibly proud as he saluted me. King Willhelm, Prince Benjamin, Prince Nicholas, and Princess Della all stood to the side of the cathedral steps. All but Benjamin were smiling, tears making their eyes shine.

"Have I mentioned how thankful I am for you?" Collins asked as the knights began to push through the crowd toward the castle gates.

"Hmm, possibly," I grinned up at him as we hurried along the path and through the gate, "But I'd love to hear it again."

"Thank you, Sage. For pointing me back to God, for loving me at my lowest, and for never giving up on me." He pulled me to a stop at the side of castle gates. As his strong arms around my waist, I wrapped my arms around his neck, "I know I still have a lot to learn, and a lot to overcome but-"

I pressed my finger against his lips, "We'll cross that bridge when we come to it. And we'll cross it together."

He gazed down at me, "I love you, my princess."

"I love you more, my prince."

Collins smiled as he leaned down to brush his lips lightly over mine. "Are you ready to go dance with me?"

I sighed, my arms still around his neck. "Do we have to stay long?"

"Only if you want to." His smile somehow grew larger, "Although, I'd very much like to be alone with you."

"Dinner and three dances," I pecked his cheek, "and then we can go be alone together."

He laughed as I led him up the steps to the palace door. I didn't know what the future might hold, but with Collins by my side, and God at the center, we could face whatever it might bring. Together.

The End

ANNA AUGUSTINE

THEN

There

WAS

Grace

BENJAMIN AND AURORA'S STORY

WHEN *You* FOUND *Me*

"But Ruth said, 'Do not urge me to leave you or to return from following you. For where you go I will go, and where you lodge I will lodge. Your people shall be my people, and your God my God. Where you die I will die, and there I will be buried. May the Lord do so to me and more also if anything but death parts me from you."

-Ruth 1:16-17-

WHEN *You* FOUND *Me*

1

BENJAMIN

"No." I stated lowly, anger churning in my stomach at the idea my father had just suggested to me, "We are not in that desperate of a situation, Father."

"You know I'm weak, my son." As if to prove him correct, a racking cough shook my father's slim frame leaving him gasping for breath at the end, "I want to know the kingdom is at peace before I die. I do not like the thought of you taking the throne, alone, with a war before you."

"So you invite our enemy, the sister of the man Collins' wife slain mere months ago, into our home to try and form a *peace* marriage?" I laughed, but it sounded cold and bitter even to myself, "Really, Father. This plan is worse than the marriage contest."

"Benjamin." Father's grey eyes looked tired, defeated, "Please. She is already coming. I fear what will happen if we cannot form an agreeable alliance. And from what I hear, the princess is a nice girl. She was married to Willa's eldest."

"She was Alfred's bride?" I asked, my level tone masking my surprise. My aunt Willa had moved to Ironwolf with her husband when I was eighteen. Her sons, Alfred and Derek, had been a few years older than I and had married the princesses of Ironwolf a year after their relocation. From his letters, my cousin was happy with his wife, Aurora. But when a plague had passed through the land three years later, both of my cousins and uncle had died. We hadn't heard anything from Aunt Willa in the two years following.

"Yes, Willa was the one who talked to the king about it, and he is the one who approached us." Father coughed again, and when he pulled his handkerchief away, I couldn't help but see the splattering of blood in it. I met his eyes and he sighed, "Please, Benjamin. For the kingdom."

"She's the enemy." I stood, holding my hands behind my back as I began to pace in front of the fire, "Why should I marry her when there are dozens of ladies from whom I could choose? Girls whose fathers and brothers haven't slain thousands of our own soldiers?"

"But what if this could stop that?" Father leaned forward, his elbows on his knees. "What if you could be the catalyst to stop this bloody, horrid war?"

I had always prided myself on my decision making. I always knew the right thing to do, I always knew the answers. But the choice before me had no right answer that I could see. I either married a woman whom I knew I would despise, or I continued to lead my nation in a war that was costing us so many lives. My life, or theirs.

"Please, my son. Pray about it." Father leaned back in his chair, his eyes dropping closed, "We shall talk more later. Let me rest now."

I nodded, turning and walking out the door. My brain was muddled, something else I wasn't used to, as I strode down the hallway. I paused once I reached the large windows in front of the Great Hall. They looked out over the castle gardens, which were covered in an early snow. A few stray flakes floated down from the grey skies, bringing a blessed silence over the world.

Movement drew my eye to the path that the servants had cleared. Nicholas' bright red hair stood out against the pale earth. Della, his wife, was tucked under his arm as they strolled down the walkways. Even from where I stood, I could see the smile on my brother's face, the joy that being with Della brought him.

If I marry this girl, a complete stranger, will I miss out on such joy? Will my marriage be a happy one?

I swallowed, fear and disgust leaving a sour taste on my tongue. I had never thought about wanting – or rather, needing a union of love. I had often thought that if I did marry, it may very well be for political gain. But when Nicholas found Della at the contest Father had set up for us, I realized I wouldn't be satisfied with a marriage of convenience. I wanted what Della and Nicholas had. I wanted love.

God, what are you asking me to do? I growled, frustrated when an immediate answer wasn't given. Shaking my head, I stormed into my room, slamming the door hard enough to make the tapestries on my wall shake. Slumping into an overstuffed chair, I poured myself a glass of the brandy that sat on the table to my left. I took a quick swallow before I leaned on my elbows in my knees and allowed myself to do something I rarely did in front of others.

I let myself feel.

A few hours later, a knock sounded on my door. Pushing to my feet, I schooled my features into my typical hard expression as I turned the knob.

Nicholas stood on the other side, his brows pinched together in frustration.

"I just heard." He pushed past me into my room. His eyes swept over the half empty bottle of brandy before turning to me. "So ... drink, is it?"

I growled, "None of this is your concern."

"You're my brother," Nicholas laughed, but it had a hallow ring to it. "That makes it my concern."

I huffed, lowering myself back into my chair. Nicholas took the one across from me, running his hands through his curly mop. The curls fell right back into his blue eyes as he met my gaze.

"So?"

"So what?"

"What are you planning on doing, Benjamin?"

I shook my head, "I don't have much of a choice, now do I? It's either marry an enemy daughter, or continue a war we both know is …" I waved my hand at the stricken look on my brother's face, "Yes, that."

Shaking his head as if to rid himself of the memories, Nicholas sighed, "But do *you* want this?"

I shrugged, "Father didn't leave me much of a choice."

"From the letters Alfred used to send, Aurora sounds like a sweet girl."

I grunted, "She's …"

She's what? I thought darkly. *Used goods? A hand-me-down bride?* Those thoughts felt crass, rude, and inappropriate. So why was I thinking them?

I buried my face in my hands, hating that Nicholas was seeing this struggle in me. His large hand landed on my shoulder, "Della and I will pray for you tonight, brother. You never know what God has planned."

I glanced up at him, and he had a funny smile on his face. "Not everyone is you and Della, brother."

He shrugged, still smiling, "But I like to think everyone can be as happy and content as us."

I grunted again as Nicholas stepped back out into the hall.

Pushing to my feet, I stepped over to my window. This one looked out over the hills that rolled all around Findley, a green sea where our kingdom was the ship. I gazed down at the houses, the lights flickering in the waning light. I thought of all the children whose fathers were dead or wounded because of the border war. How many fathers would come home, whole and healthy and safe, because of an alliance marriage? How many women would have their sweethearts and spouses back in their arms?

"Why, Lord?" I growl-prayed as I leaned my forehead against the glass. "I ... I want to plan life my way. But ... if this is the only way to help my people ..." I squeezed my eyes shut, "Then ... help me to care for her. I want to be a good husband, despite the fact that she's my enemy. God ... show me how to love my enemy."

2

AURORA

"What?" I stared at Willa, my mother-in-law, my gaze searching hers before turning to my father when I couldn't find what I was looking for. "Surely you're not serious. You're … you're giving me away?"

"For peace, child." Father shrugged, sorrow lining his haggard face, "With Effelwood dead, it is only a matter of time before Findley wins the war. Better to try and settle this peacefully. And besides," he waved his hand at me, "You were married to one of them before."

I sensed Willa stiffen, her gaze on the ground. She had lost much since moving from Findley six years ago. I, too, had suffered much. I had never really loved Alfred, her son, but he had been a good companion, a friend when I had often felt beyond lonely in my own home. Willa had also become a dear confident, the mother I had never known.

"Why me?" I asked, unable to hide the bitterness in my tone, "Why not Helga?"

"Your sister …" Father cleared his throat, his gaze dropping to the ground.

When he didn't continue, Willa turned to me, "She's pregnant, Rory."

I knew my jaw was hanging open in disbelief, "Helga is … with child? With who?"

"With one of the knights." Father's jaw was ticking in and out "They're to wed tonight and be sent to live in the summer home until the child is born."

"You're covering for her again?" I shook my head.

"Don't talk back to me!" Father's brown eyes snapped in anger, "You're going to Findley tomorrow. You will marry Allura's crown prince, and you will be happy!"

I crossed my arms, begging my tears to stay put, "I will go, and I'll do as you have demanded, but not even you can order me to be happy with this, Father."

I turned on my heel and hurried out of the throne room. Once I was far enough away to be sure Father wouldn't stumble upon me, I let my tears trail down my cheeks. I was still grieving, did he not see that? Alfred had only died two years ago. For some, that might seem like plenty of time. But each day I had to face alone, without his crooked smile and curly brown hair, was torture. I knew my family didn't love me, for I had married the enemy. It had not mattered that they were related to royalty or were knights with great acts of valor. No, they were related to the King of Findley, so they were our foes.

Father and Effelwood had never accepted Alfred as part of the court nor as part of the family. But Alfred had cared for me, his brother for Helga, so Father had allowed us to live in the palace. But the plague came, taking Willa's husband and before long, Derek and Alfred were dead as well.

Those were memories best left buried. I sighed, wiping away the tears off my cheeks as I straightened. I didn't know why, but the thought of a new place with new people did sound oddly appealing. Would they accept me, the enemy? Or would I be entering into a marriage much like the life I was praying to escape?

Willa's soft footsteps made me turn my head. She had tears of her own on her cheeks as she grasped my hand in her own, "You do not have to come, child. I can talk your father out of this marriage."

"But … was it not your idea?" I asked softly, tucking a strand of my brown hair behind my ear, "Do you think this will bring peace for both our lands?"

"I do." She whispered, crossing her arms over her thin frame as if that would ward off whatever was troubling her. "I have mourned for both our lands since the day the war started. Ironwolf is a beautiful country, Rory. With the craggy mountains, the red tint in the sky, the sound of the miners singing as they head off to work … it's a different kind of beautiful." She smiled wistfully, "But it wasn't only the land. I fell in love with you girls, too. I always wanted a daughter, and when Derek and Alfred married you and Helga, I had two." She sniffed, squeezing my hands tightly, "Alfred loved you, Aurora of Ironwolf. But I know it wasn't quite the same for you."

I shook my head, "I loved him, truly."

"You cared for him, yes." Willa smiled sadly, "But it was never love."

"You could tell that?" I blushed, my eyes dropping to the ground.

"Aye. And this time, daughter, I want you to find love."

"But I love my people, Willa." I met my mother-in-law's gaze as she caressed my cheek, "If I can stop the bloodshed, to unite our lands …" I shook my head emphatically, "Love does not matter. If both me and the prince of Allura are willing, I want to make this marriage union happen. For our lands and our people."

Willa's light blue eyes flicked back and forth between my dark brown ones, "Are you sure, Aurora?"

"Your people, Willa, will be mine. Just like mine are yours, whether they like it or not." I leaned my forehead against hers. "I want to go with you to your home."

Willa took a steadying breath, "If you are certain, my daughter."

"Aye." I nodded, "I am very certain."

My stomach clenched as I stared up at the large castle that spread out over hilltop. Knights patrolled the walls, their spears catching the sunlight that poured unhindered to the cold, snow covered earth. No billowing, smoky clouds blocked its rays.

"Snow is beautiful." I murmured as I held my hand out the carriage window to catch a flake on my mittened hand. Willa had made them hurriedly in the week before our departure, telling me that it was going to be cold in my new home.

New home, I shivered, but not from the cold. I was to meet the royal family today, and my wedding would be the day after. Nerves made my muscles tense as I fisted my hands inside my gloves.

"You will impress them, Rory." Willa laid her hand on my shoulder, "I promise, the crown prince will be kind."

I swallowed, nodding, but not really believing it. Everyone had thought that about my family to, that they were kind. Oh, how wrong they were.

I rubbed at my shoulder, as the carriage rumbled through the large gates and stopped at two giant doors. Steps, cleared of the snow that was all around us, led up to them and six cloaked figures stood at the top. I swallowed the panic that was keeping the air from my lungs.

"You'll be fine." Willa patted my hand reassuringly as the carriage door opened and she allowed the footman to help her out.

"You're strong." I whispered to myself, "It doesn't matter what they think, only that he marries you and brings peace. Your land needs peace."

Letting out a breath, I took the footman's hand and stepped to the ground. Five of the cloaked figures had all moved down the steps and were greeting my mother-in-law with smiles. The sixth hung back, his arms crossed over his chest and his face hidden in the shadows of his hood.

"Willa!" The low, husky voice of King Willhelm reached me and I straightened my shoulders as I stepped up behind Willa, "I've missed you, sister. You've been gone for far too long."

"Much too long, brother." She kissed his cheek, tears streaming down her own, "You look dreadful."

He chuckled, but it ended in a cough, "Aye. I feel dreadful. But I wish to meet my future daughter-in-law before I return to my room."

I stepped up, gripping my hands behind my back to keep them from trembling. Willa smiled, though sorrow was in her eyes, "This is Princess Aurora of Ironwolf. Aurora, this is King Willhelm of Findley."

The king smiled kindly, his grey eyes sharp despite the sagging of his shoulders and the wrinkles on his face, "It is a pleasure to meet you, my dear. Although, I do wish it could be under different circumstances."

"The pleasure is mine, majesty." I managed, though I thought my heart might beat out of my chest.

"Allow me to introduce my children," He gestured to one of the couples, "This is my middle son, Nicholas, and his wife Della."

Nicholas bowed with a smile that didn't quite reach his eyes as his wife curtsied. Della's smile, however, was followed by a wink, making a blush color my cheeks. Perhaps she would be a friend to me in this strange place.

King Willhelm cleared his throat. He shifted slightly as the next couple approached. The woman was clutching the man's arm, her hazel eyes wide as she stared at me. "My youngest son, Collins, and his wife Sage."

Sage, I swallowed, pasting on a smile I hoped looked real as I bobbed a curtsy. They quickly stepped back, neither of them smiling. I knew why. Sage had killed my brother. As horrible as it was, all I could feel was gratitude, despite the fact that that meant I was here, waiting to meet a fiancé that had been foisted upon me by my father and the Allura king. I forced myself to keep smiling at them, hoping it looked sincere despite my trembling nerves.

"And lastly, my eldest. Benjamin, the crown prince of Allura." The king motioned the lone, solemn figure over. The man moved swiftly, stepping right up in front of me as he lowered his hood. I sucked in a breath as his eyes met mine. They were the palest blue I had ever seen, so much so that they were almost white in color. They were intense, searching my face as if he could decern my thoughts if he looked hard enough. His black hair was pulled back at the nape of his neck, a few pieces hanging by his temples. A light scruff of a beard covered his chin and jaw line, giving him a dangerous air.

I swallowed, realizing I was staring, before dropping into another curtsy. "It's a pleasure to meet you, my prince."

He grunted, holding out his arm to me without a word. I glanced at Willa, but she was already moving toward the doors, arm in arm with King Willhelm.

I blew out a breath, slipping my hand into the crook of Prince Benjamin's arm as he guided me up the steps and into the palace.

It was grander than my home in Ironwolf. Tapestries of Findley's history hung here and there, along with portraits of kings and queens long since dead. Suits of armor stood at intervals, guarding the halls with their battle axes and swords. My grip subconsciously tightened on Benjamin's arm as we passed them, memories of the legions of warriors marching on Olthgath, the capital of Ironwolf, invading my mind.

"Are you all right, m'lady?"

I glanced up, surprised by how low Benjamin's voice was. His eyes were studying me again, and I tried to not squirm under the scrutiny.

"Aye." I wanted to say more, but I clamped my lips together, nodding to reassure him.

He gazed at me a moment more before motioning to another set of wide double doors. "There is to be a feast in honor of your arrival tonight. Then our wedding on the morrow."

I was proud at myself for not flinching at the mention of the wedding. I had just met this stoic man. One look from him made me tremble, and not the swooning weak-in-the-knees type of shaking. He had only said three sentences in my presence. Yet he was to be my husband in twenty-four hours.

"I …" I sighed slightly, "I am simply weary."

"Aye, allow me to show you to your room." He guided me silently down the hall, before pointing to a door, "That shall be our room."

"*Our* room?" I hoped my voice didn't sound as shaky as it felt.

Benjamin stiffened as he stopped before another door. "Aye. And this is your room for tonight."

I nodded, blinking back tears. This had been horribly awkward, and I prayed my marriage would not be the same as this first meeting.

"I was wondering one thing." Benjamin cleared his throat, shifting slightly form foot to foot. It was the most emotion I had seen out of him thus far.

I took a fortifying breath before meeting his gaze, "Aye?"

"Why did you agree to this?"

Out of all the questions he could have asked, I had not been expecting this one. I crossed my arms over my chest, thinking for a long moment, "I want our lands to be at peace. No more death, no more hate. If that means marrying you, a stranger, then it shall be worth it."

He tipped his head to the side. After a moment, he mumbled, "Rest well, Princess," then turned on his heel and retreated back the way we had come.

I hurried into my room, leaning against the door as my back slid down it. The tears I had managed to hold in through the whole meeting finally spilled forth, and I allowed myself to sob before crawling into the large bed to rest my aching head.

WHEN *You* FOUND *Me*

3

BENJAMIN

"She certainly handled herself with grace and poise." Della commented as we sat in the study. Her hand was interlocked with Nicholas' as they sat on the settee before the fireplace. She turned her smile on me, a teasing glint in her eyes, "She didn't appear terrified by that scowl of yours, Benjamin."

I grunted, arms crossed over my chest as I glared at the flames. "We'll see how she handles herself at the banquet tonight."

"I still don't think it's fair to throw the girl to the wolves this early. She has only just arrived."

I glanced at Sage. Out of all my family, I had thought she would have been the most hesitant about this marriage, since she had been the one to kill the Ironwolf prince. But she seemed unaffected by it as Collins wrapped his arm around her. She was scowling at me, as if I was the one deciding to host a banquet for all of parliament. Her glare was almost intimidating.

"It was Father's idea, love." Collins patted her hand, then smiled at me, "And I'm interested to see how she handles tonight as well. She looked almost green when she stepped from the carriage."

"Did she say anything to you as you escorted her to her room?" Nicholas asked.

"Nothing of importance," I growled, annoyance creeping up at the interrogation. "She said she wanted peace, which is the whole reason for this marriage."

Not happiness, not love. Peace. I stared into the flames again, resting my fist against my lips. Could I truly do this? It went against all my instincts. She was the enemy, deserving of death, not my love and mercy. I should allow all her people to die, to fall at the blade of Allura's army.

Yet the pure terror in her gaze as she had stepped from the carriage was seared into my mind. She had carefully schooled her reaction after she had stepped up to Aunt Willa, but before that ...

"Benjamin?" Della's hand landed on my bicep, her brows raised, "Are you all right, brother?"

"Aye." I glanced around the circle, seeing all their puzzled expressions. I must have looked a little terrified myself in that moment. I wasn't one to typically show what I was feeling, and they all knew that.

Della settled back against the settee, her shoulder brushing Nicholas', "I cannot imagine marrying someone I'd just met. It was hard enough coming here for the contest."

"And we had two months to get to know one another before we wed." Nicholas commented, his thumb tracing around Della's knuckles. His blue eyes met mine, his slim brow raised, "It can't be easy marrying someone you met today."

I grunted in reply, crossing my arms across my chest again as Collins piped up.

"It was the same for Sage and me. Two months before our wedding."

"We did go through a life changing ordeal together," Sage scoffed, something I was still unaccustomed to hearing. Most ladies I knew did not snort in polite conversation.

I noticed the dark circles under their eyes, testament to the fact that nightmares still plagued Sage's sleep. Compassion tugged at my heart, and I sucked a breath in through my teeth.

Della leaned forward to look me in the eye. "If you need anything, Benjamin, don't be too proud to ask." Her perceptive gaze studied me, and I fought the need to squirm. Since when did I squirm?

I stood, smoothing my jacket as I did so. I resisted the urge to fidget as I nodded to my family, "Thank you. I must go get …" I swallowed, straightening even more, "My bride."

I could feel all their eyes on me as I turned and strode from the library. It was only once I was in the hall that I let my hands tremble. I reached up, tugging at a strand of hair that was too short to stay confined in my tail. Dropping it almost as quickly, I stepped determinedly down the hall to the door where I had left Aurora a few hours before.

My bride. I swallowed the bile that coated my tongue with a sour taste. *I can do this. I must to do this. For Allura, for my family, for my people.*

With a breath to reinforce my resolve, I raised my hand and knocked. A maid eased open the door, a smile plastered on her face. She curtsied, not meeting my eyes as she slipped out into the hallway, leaving the door ajar.

I watched her retreating form, wishing she would stay to make this less uncomfortable. I sighed, turning to face the girl within.

My eyes widened at the sight. The Princess of Ironwolf stood in the center of her room, her arms crossed over her chest. Her head was held high, her shoulders back. Her dark brown hair flowed around her like a veil, falling nearly to her waist. The dress she had on was unlike anything I had ever seen. Her shoulders were bare, the neckline of the gown cut straight across her chest. Her sleeves were attached to it on the underside, ending at her elbow with the excess fabric billowing behind her. It was a rich purple-red hue, almost the color of wine, and it intensified the deep brown of her eyes.

"Is something wrong, your highness?" Her voice was a whisper, her eyes darting around like she needed to escape.

"Nay." I blinked, my tongue feeling glued to the roof of my mouth, "I am ..." Unsure of where I had been going with the statement, I held my arm out to her, "It's time for dinner."

She bobbed her head gently, stepping up beside me to grip my arm again. It almost felt like her hand was trembling, but I had no idea how to calm her, for I truly didn't know what we were walking into.

For her part, Aurora straightened her shoulders, walking with a graceful float that I had become accustomed to ladies of the courts having. Out of the corner of my eye, I could see her chest rise and fall with measured breaths. She was trying to be poised, and I found my admiration for her grow.

I pulled her to a stop a few feet from the Great Hall doors. I stared at her for a long moment. Perhaps too long, as her eyes began to dart around again.

"Is something the matter, Prince Benjamin?"

"I want peace, too."

That wasn't the speech I had been planning in my head, but when her eyes met mine again, a small smile was on her lips. That smile made my chest tighten and I had to force another breath into my lungs to clear the blurriness from my vision.

"Thank you, your highness. My people are indebted to you." Her brown eyes dropped back to the floor, "I shall do my best to make you happy."

I nodded, again at a loss for words as I offered her my arm. We stepped to the doors and the guards turned to open them together. All the parliament lords and their wives sat at the tables that were normally reserved for the knights and whatever guests may have been visiting. It was a much quieter ensemble than usual, and I resisted the urge to tug on the collar of my jacket.

The table we royals sat at had grown, with Sage and Della having joined my brothers, Father, and me up on the dais. A chair had been added for Aurora now, beside mine at Father's right hand. Her hand tightened its grip again, the only sign I could catch that she was nervous. Did she even realize she did it?

I glanced down at her, "Are you ready?"

She forced a smile, her eyes darting around the room, "I don't have a choice."

Neither do I. I pushed that thought away as I turned and began the long walk down the path that led to our table.

The room was silent. Not a word was spoken as we approached the dais. Aunt Willa sat on Father's left, her smile for the woman at my side alone. We stepped up and around the table. I held out her chair and Aurora sank into it, smoothing her skirt as I eased it up to the table. Straightening my jacket, I slid into my spot, my impassive mask firmly in place.

"Welcome, members of the court!" Father's voice rang out, stronger than it had been in months, "It is with great honor that we welcome Princess Aurora of Ironwolf into our land as the betrothed of Prince Benjamin. May this union bring peace to both our land and theirs."

"Here, here!" Collins cheered, raising his goblet of cider with a grin.

I kept my face as impassive as possible, but the nervous energy coursing through me had me tapping my fingers against my legs as I gazed out over all the members of our Parliament. There was a varying degree of emotions, from genuinely happy smiles, to thin lipped displeasure, to outright disgust – all of it aimed at Aurora. I felt my teeth clench as the servants brought out the food and we all began to eat. I had never been one for social gatherings, and this one, with all the eyes directed at me and Aurora, was threatening to drive me mad.

It will all be over tomorrow. I thought as I chewed a piece of meat, *Although, then I'll have a wife.*

With that line of thinking, I sucked in a sharp breath, causing the meat I'd been chewing to lodge in my throat. I began to cough, taking a large gulp of my wine to keep from choking completely.

Aurora turned to me, eyes wide as my face began to redden. She reached behind me, slapping me hard on the back until I waved her hand away, a blessed breath of air filling my chest.

"Are you all right?" Aurora turned her head, her voice low so only those around us could hear.

I took another sip of my drink, nodding, "Aye. I'm fine."

She nodded once, turning back to her trencher. I watched her for a moment, realizing that she was simply pushing the food around on her plate, barely putting any in her mouth. Her left hand lay in her lap, clenched into a fist. Her gaze kept flicking up to the people below us, and each time her face paled a little more.

"Are you not hungry?" I asked softly, putting another bite of meat in my mouth, although it was significantly smaller than the last.

"I do not have much of an appetite tonight." Her quiet admission made my eyes flick to her, "It's been a long day."

I glanced at my father, who nodded slightly. I was unsure how much he'd heard, but I set my utensils down and stood, "Would you like to go for a walk before retiring for the evening?"

Aurora's eyes swept over the crowd once more before she slowly rose, "Aye. If that is what you wish, my prince."

I bristled at the formality, but there was really no way around it. We had, after all, only met hours ago.

I offered the princess my arm, and her small hand slipped into it once again as we turned and walked out the doors.

The instant they closed behind us, Aurora seemed to relax. But when her eyes met mine, she stiffened again and dropped her gaze to the floor.

Why did I think this was a wise idea, I cursed myself, *We can't even talk to each other. Honestly, what am I supposed to say to a total stranger who tomorrow will be my wife?*

WHEN *You* FOUND *Me*

4

AURORA

I tried to calm my stampeding heart as I felt Benjamin's eyes on me again. He had been gracious enough to rescue from the glares being sent my way at dinner. Although, his coughing attack could have embarrassed him enough for him to want to leave.

"Where are we going?" I shifted, my eyes unwilling flicking back to him again.

"I wanted to show you one of my favorite places in the palace." His voice was completely level and controlled. I couldn't hear any emotion in it at all.

He's so solemn. I thought, my gaze glued to the ground as I tugged on the ends of my hair to make sure it remained over my shoulders. *Why isn't he saying anything? Did I do something wrong?*

"Here we are."

I blinked up at another large set of double doors, stepping back slightly at the thought of another group of people waiting behind this one. Benjamin must have had a similar thought, for he gently tugged me forward, "There will be no one in here."

I felt a small smile tug on the corner of my mouth, "Where are we?"

"The library."

My breath caught as I stared at the gilded doors, my hand trembling slightly. I glanced at Benjamin again, shaking my head, "I don't think I should go in here."

His brows lowered, and he looked quite fierce, "I want to show you."

"All-all right." I complied, suppressing a groan as I followed him through the doors.

It was a magnificent library. It was two stories, with bookcases covering every wall. A large, circular fireplace sat in the center, crackling merrily with chairs all around it. Windows sat on the farthest wall, but large red drapes covered them, blocking out the chill.

The sheer number of books dazzled me, as did the smell of ink, parchment, and leather. I must have sighed as I turned to gaze up at one of the large shelves in awe. Benjamin's voice seemed to rumble across the marble floor, sending a shiver down my back in the process. "Do you have a favorite book, Princess?"

"Nay." I answered too quickly, and Benjamin raised a brow at me, "I … I like the Holy Writ. Willa read it to me after …" I stopped, ducking my head again as I thought of Alfred. What would he think of me, if he could see me now?

If Benjamin noticed my hesitation, he didn't mention it. Instead, he guided me farther into the room. "I love to read. I often retreat here when my position becomes … overwhelming."

So he can talk. I felt the corners of my mouth turn up. I reached up and rubbed my left shoulder, "Do you have a favorite author, m'lord?"

He shook his head, much to my relief. "All storytellers have a special voice, all have a unique tale to tell or a lesson to teach."

I nodded, "Much like the bards. Each have a distinctive song, a melody that only they fully understand."

"Aye. Just like that." Benjamin's mouth ticked up a fraction of an inch as he nodded.

I covered my mouth with the back of my hand, trying to hide the yawn that wanted to spring forth, but of course Benjamin noticed. "Come. You're tired."

"Aye." A blush climbed into my cheeks as we began another silent walk down the halls. As we passed a certain portrait, I paused, pulling Benjamin to a halt next to me.

"Is that … is that Willa?" I asked softly, gazing up at the picture in surprise. An older man and woman sat on two gilded thrones. They were impeccably dressed, a dark navy gown on the woman, a matching coat with golden buttons for the man. He had the dark brown hair of Benjamin, while the woman's hair was a lighter brown. Both had dark, piercing brown eyes.

On the left side of the portrait stood a man who looked so similar to Prince Collins that it had to be King Willhelm. The only thing about him that I could see that was different were his eyes. Instead of the dark brown eyes of his youngest son, King Willhelm's eyes were a dove grey.

But what really interested me was the woman on the right. Willa. She stood straight and tall, with dark brown locks and a dazzling smile. Gone were the lines of age that I had known her to have, and her light blue eyes danced with a joy that had since been snatched away by the cruel hand of sorrow.

"She looks so happy here." I whispered, a tear trailing down my cheek, "She lost so much when she moved to Ironwolf."

"She gained much too." Benjamin stated, his eyes studying me much like I was studying the portrait.

I laughed humorlessly, "I do not see how that balances the scale, my prince."

He didn't reply, simply stepped back onto the red carpet and continued to escort me to my room.

Once he had bid me good night, I stood for a moment, watching him move back down the hall and into the confines of the room that he said would be ours on the morrow.

Ours. A flash of heat swirled through me and I stepped quickly into my room, leaning against the door once again.

"I'm scared." I whispered into my room. "I'm not ready to be a wife again. Especially to a man I barely know."

I stepped toward my vanity, pushing my hair over my shoulder as I rubbed my shoulder again, staring at the angry scar that slashed from the top of my shoulder down past my collarbone. It was a constant reminder of where I came from and who I was. Benjamin knew nothing about me nor my family. I was sure he'd heard tales. Likely, most of them were *less* horrid than the truth. But as I stared at my scar in the mirror, the ugly fact remained glaringly obvious – I was the enemy in this narrative. The scowls and distain of the people in the Great Hall confirmed that.

I leaned my forehead against my cold fingers. A tear slipped down my cheek as I whispered a prayer to the God Willa had introduced me to. A desperate prayer of petition that I wasn't about to make the gravest mistake of my life.

I awoke slowly the next morning, my arm up over my head in my usual way. I stared up at the ceiling of my room, following the intricate patterns carved into it with my eyes. A chill hung in the air, even though I could hear the crackling fire in the grate. The temperature was so different from home. I didn't want to emerge from under my blankets, partly from the cold, and partly because it meant it was time to get ready for my wedding.

I groaned, closing my eyes again as I pictured Benjamin. I should be thankful. I had heard stories about princesses being married to men three times their ages, simply for an alliance. At least this prince was handsome, and close to my own age of twenty-two. But his quiet impassiveness made me nervous, for I liked to know what people were thinking.

Especially here. I thought with a sigh as the door to my room opened and the maid entered.

I glanced at her through half closed eyes. She carried a billowing white gown in her arms, which she hung up on a hook in the wall along with a bright red cape. Another maid entered behind her, handing her a box before leaving again. The first maid set it on the vanity before stepping over to me.

"M'lady?" She laid a gently hand on my shoulder, "My name is Emmy. Princess Della sent me to help you ready this morning."

I wanted to stay in bed all day, to pretend that I was ill and escape the terror of this event. But from Emmy's expression, there would be no escape, no rescue from this day. I rubbed at my shoulder, fear making me feel sick, "Can you please go fetch Willa?"

Emmy raised a brow, but stepped to the door. She whispered to someone on the other side before turning back to me, "Sir Lucius went to fetch her. Why don't we start on your hair while we wait?"

She smiled sweetly at me, not the harsh calculating smile of the people at the dinner last night. I felt the tension lessen slightly in my shoulders, and I nodded. "All right."

I lowered myself onto the stool, crossing my arms over myself as Emmy picked up my brush and began to brush my long tresses.

"How do you manage such long hair?" She asked after a moment.

I shrugged, "I usually wear it down. It hides …" I swallowed, "It is easier to leave it down."

Emmy didn't ask about my hesitation, "Well, it's customary for a bride to wear it down on her wedding day, but if that is what you normally do, why don't we wear it up today?"

I glanced at the dress. The neckline was high, a soft circular shape and if I had the red cloak over it, I wouldn't have to worry about my hair being up. I rubbed my shoulder again, nodding, "Aye, I should like that."

A light knock sounded before the door eased open and Willa stepped in. She smiled at me in the mirror, coming to crouch beside me, "Bridal nerves, Rory?"

Tears sprung into my eyes at my nickname. No one said my name the way Willa did, with such love and tenderness. "I'm … I don't want … I can't handle…"

Willa gripped my hands in her own, "He is a good man, Rory. He will protect you and care for you."

"You said you wanted me to find love."

She nodded, "And I believe that Benjamin has the ability to love fiercely. He simply needs to choose to do so."

"And what if he never chooses that." The tears trailed down my cheeks, "What if my marriage is worse than my mother and father's?"

Willa winced, "I don't think that's possible. You both chose this. And both of you, I know, are stubborn." She laughed at the blush crawling up my neck, "You shall make him fall in love with you, Rory. No matter what happens, fight for love."

I took a deep breath, trying to believe what Willa was saying. I glanced up in the mirror as Emmy patted the last strand of my hair into place. My mouth hung open as I turned, this way and that, to see the little white flowers she had woven throughout. Twists and braids zigzagged across my scalp, forming a lovely updo that took my breath away.

"And the final touch," Emmy smiled, opening the box on the vanity and pulling out a delicate silver crown, "Commissioned by King Willhellm especially for you, m'lady."

The three silver bands were interwoven into a circular braid. A triangle point came down with a tear-drop shaped diamond at the center. Tinier diamonds had been placed here and there along the rest of the crown. Rainbows winked and blinked at me as Emmy raised the circlet above my head and settled it onto my head. The silver stood out in stark contrast to my dark brown locks, and I couldn't help the small smile that tugged onto my lips.

"I've never owned anything so lovely," I whispered, wiping at another blasted tear as it snaked its way down my cheek. "I will have to thank the king."

Emmy shared a look with Willa that I was not able to decern as I stood and walked toward the dress. It was silky, sliding through my fingers with ease. The neckline had tiny pearl beads sewn along it, with snowflake patterns across the bodice. The skirt flared out from a silver belt that would hug my hips once I had it on. It was spellbinding.

Will it be enough? I wondered as both Willa and Emmy helped me into the gown, securing the cloak about my shoulders with a snowflake clasp. Would people see me as the wife of Benjamin today? Or simply a pawn in a greater political coup?

5

BENJAMIN

I adjusted my red velvet coat for the millionth time, trying to keep my emotional mask in place as Collins and Nicholas laughed behind me. My hands were trembling again and it took everything in me not to tug at my hair, which was pulled back from my face with a black ribbon.

"Come on, Ben!" Collins clasped me on the back, "You look as if you're going to a funeral, not your wedding."

"It was easier for you, Collins." I growled as I tugged my shirtsleeve straight under my jacket. "You at least knew who you were marrying."

Collins smiled sympathetically and it made me want to hit something. Hard.

"It will work out," Nicholas promised as he tugged his boots on, "I have a good feeling about her, brother."

Why don't I? I wondered as I took a deep breath. I went to the mantle, pulling a small pine box off of it and shoving it into my pocket. When I turned back around, both Collins and Nicholas had their eyebrows raised.

"That's ... that's the ring you're giving her?" Collins asked slowly.

I nodded, "Aye. And I don't want to talk any more about it." I snapped when Nicholas opened his mouth. He promptly shut it with an audible snap.

I sighed, giving into the urge to tug at a lock of my hair as I stepped toward my window. Another gentle snow was falling, creating a clean slate on the earth. I let the peace that the view provided calm my racing thoughts. It would be fine. It would. I would make it so. I would care for this woman, and make her as happy as I could. Maybe we'd never love each other, but I would do my best to ensure we wouldn't hate one another.

A knock sounded on my door, and Aunt Willa stepped in. "Your bride is waiting for you, Benjamin."

The nerves I had managed to unravel spun back into a twisted knot as I stepped toward the door.

Aunt Willa laid her hand on my arm, halting me, "Try to smile a little, Benjamin. You're scaring her half to death."

"Smile?" I asked, hoping against hope that my brothers couldn't hear this whispered exchange.

"Aye, you know, that shape your mouth makes when you're happy?" Aunt Willa laughed as I scowled, "The opposite of that, my boy."

"I'll ... try." I sighed, reaching up to tug once on my hair before letting my hand fall.

"I know you're frightened as well. But you two ..." She shook her head once, "I have no fear of the future."

Then you're the only one. I swallowed the retort as I stepped out into the hall, my hands fisted at my side as I walked slowly down to Aurora's door.

The tradition of the groom escorting his bride to the cathedral was an old one, but today I wished I could escape there before seeing my bride. In some ways, it would have been easier. In others, it wouldn't.

I knocked quickly, clasping my hands behind my back as Della's maid, Emmy, opened the door with a smile, "Your princess, my prince."

I blinked, words fleeing my mind as I gazed at the woman on the other side of the door. She looked more lovely than she had the night before. Her long hair had been gathered up on top of her head. The red hood of her cloak covered most of it, and I could just make out the sparkling diamond circlet resting on her forehead. The long white gown accented her tiny waist. I could think of no words to say, but I forced a tiny smile onto my lips as I held out my hand.

She studied my face for a long moment, a small smile of her own flicking into place as she stepped up to my side.

"Am I satisfactory, my prince?" She asked softly, her eyes dropping to the ground.

Against the white of the dress, I noticed her freckles. They covered her cheeks, like cinnamon on a cup of warm milk. I smiled in earnest this time, forcing the stiffness out of my shoulders.

"Aye, most satisfactory."

Aurora turned her head up, another ghost of a smile dancing around her lips before she straightened her shoulders. She closed her eyes for a moment, breathing in measured counts before nodding once. "We should be going, yes?"

I nodded, taking her hand in mine. "This is the tradition of arrival to the chapel." I interwound our fingers, a faint heat pushing its way into my cheeks. "We arrive after all the guests, walking up to the priest like so."

Aurora's gaze was locked on our hands, everything about her going completely still. I continued on, unsure if anyone had told her about our customs or not.

"The priest does the ceremony and then we …" Another wave of heat. It was dreadfully hot in her room. "Then we kiss."

If she had been still before, Aurora turned absolutely rigid at that statement. I suppressed a sigh as I continued on, "Then we will return to the palace for a feast and dancing before retiring to our room."

She nodded again, her grip tightening in mine, "Are we going to go now, Prince Benjamin?"

"Please, call me Benjamin."

Her shoulders relaxed slightly, "If that is what you wish."

"Aye, that's what I wish."

Silence settled over us as we began our walk to the church, but I wasn't sure how to break it. The hallways were empty, the only sound coming from the Great Hall as the servants rushed about preparing for the celebration of our marriage.

The closer we got to the castle doors, the tighter Aurora's grip became. I glanced at her out of the corner of my eye as we stepped down the steps into the swirling snowflakes that were dancing on the breeze. Her gaze was straight ahead, her jaw tight as she crossed her free arm over her middle like a shield.

Aunt Willa was right. She is terrified. I pulled Aurora to a stop by the gates, gazing down at her. I needed to say something, but my thoughts grew muddled when her brown eyes looked up at my face.

"Don't be afraid." I snapped my mouth closed, roughing a hand over my face in frustration. Words had never been a strong suit of mine.

Aurora, however, smiled, a small trace of laughter in her eyes, "I'm trying not to be, but it would help if you weren't."

I blinked gazing down at her, "How-"

"I can tell." She pointed at my shoulders, "You're tense. And you're hiding."

"Hiding?" I felt my face pale. How could this woman tell all of that, after only knowing me a day?

"Aye. But we all hide. It's ... human nature." Her voice had dropped, a shiver shaking her slight frame.

"Come." I pulled her forward, heading down the stone streets.

When my brothers had married their wives, the streets had been full of cheering people. People eager to catch a glimpse of their new princesses. As Aurora and I

308

walked down the same road, knights on either side, hardly a person stood along the road. I felt my jaw pop as I tightened it, my temper simmering. Aurora deserved as much celebration as Della and Sage. She was bringing peace, so that the men of Findley and the surrounding lands could come home.

A small hand landed on my shoulder as we stepped up the stairs to the large wooden door of the church.

"Please, do not take an offense for me, Pr-Benjamin." She tucked her hand back under her cloak, her head down, "I am no one of importance. I am simply trying to do what's right for my people. Our people." She tipped her head up, tears shining in her eyes, "I do not care if I am praised or lauded as a hero. I simply … want to be enough to bring peace."

I didn't know how to respond to her admission. Part of me wanted to laugh. As if marrying me would be enough to truly bring peace. I was as worthy of uniting our lands as she was. Yet, another part of me was stabbed by the compassion I'd felt the day before for Sage, making my chest ache. I wanted to ease the sorrow that lined Aurora's face, to take away the fear from her eyes.

Before I could respond, the cathedral doors opened and we began the long walk down the aisle, hand in hand.

6

AURORA

I couldn't breathe. I couldn't move. I could only stare at the dozens of eyes that turned to gaze at me on Prince Benjamin's arm. I shivered, a cold wind pushing us forward, as if God Himself was urging us down the aisle to the altar.

Benjamin tugged on my hand, helping my mind propel my feet forward. I followed behind him as his strode confidently into the church. The glares didn't seem to bother him. Did anything? I tried to not feel fear, as he had commanded, but I couldn't seem to shake the dread that pressed all around.

We stopped before the priest, our hands still tightly entwined as he began the marriage writ. My arm crossed over my chest, hugging all the panic to me. I could not do that here, now. It would do nothing but hurt the little respect that Benjamin might hold for me.

311

Deep breath in. Slowly let it out. It was hard to listen to the priest, as I was focusing all my thoughts on keeping conscious.

I was startled by Benjamin turning, a small box in his hand. He dropped my hand to open it, his steely blue eyes focused as they rose to meet mine. "This ring, I give to thee, as a token of my promise."

He pulled out a thin silver band studded with diamonds. It so perfectly matched the circlet on my head that my eyes flicked to find King Willhelm in the crowd. He smiled at me, winking slightly as Benjamin slid the band onto my finger before claiming my hand in his again.

The priest droned on for a few moments more. Each sentence, every word, made my pulse thunder, for I knew what would happen at the end.

Please hurry and get it over with. I pleaded in my mind, before correcting myself with, *Could this go on forever?*

Of course, it came to an end. The priest smiled, first at me then at Benjamin – my husband – before stretching his hands out over us.

"In the sight of God, and those gathered here, I pronounce you husband and wife!" No one made a sound as the priest nodded at Benjamin. "You may now kiss your wife."

I felt lightheaded as Benjamin turned his knowing eyes to scan my face. He released my hand again, only to settle both of them on my waist. His gaze flicked to my lips before rising to stare into my eyes. I nodded slightly. We had too. If only for those here. They had to know we meant the vows we had said moments before.

Even if he doesn't, I thought, tipping my head back as Benjamin lowered his, *I promise to be faithful and loyal and love him. God help me, I want to love him.*

The kiss was nothing spectacular. It lasted a second, maybe two. But through it, I tried to pour my promise. Benjamin stepped back, a strange look on his face, before his carefully crafted expression of indifference slipped back into place. He clasped my hand, turning toward the crowd. They clapped politely, but I had a feeling that this was very different from his siblings' weddings.

Benjamin guided me down the aisle and back down the street. The crowd behind us chattered and talked, but I was too distracted to care. My eyes gazed up at the looming castle gates, knowing I would be subjected to much more parading before the day was out.

Then there's tonight, I bit the inside of my cheek, deciding not to think about that until I had too.

"Are you all right, Aurora?"

It was the first time he had used my name, and I found that I liked the way it sounded on his tongue. His

313

low timber sent a shiver down my back as I nodded, "I'm simply cold."

Benjamin's arm slipped around my shoulders as he guided me up the steps and into the hall of the castle. He hurried me past the Great Hall and into the library once again. A blazing fire roared in the center of the room, and I stepped toward it with a sigh, holding my fingers toward it.

"This is better." I sighed, feeling Benjamin step up behind me, "But won't we be missed at the feast?"

"We can afford a few moments before we enter." He shrugged, lowering himself into a seat, "It is … common."

I felt heat crawl up my neck at his implication and turned back to the fire, "I have never seen snow before."

I mentally slapped myself for the comment. He wouldn't care about that. Why should he? He was the crown prince and had more important things to worry about then what his alliance wife had and hadn't seen.

"I know that Ironwolf is a warmer climate than here, but you don't have snow?"

At his question, some of the tension eased from my shoulders, "Nay. It's mostly volcanoes and rock. It rarely gets cool, let alone cold." I turned to face him, sinking into a chair a few feet away from him, "My dress from dinner last night was quite warm when I would wear it at home."

I gazed down at the white material of my wedding gown. It made my skin look dark, almost brown compared to it. I knew my freckles were glaringly obvious as well.

"You looked lovely in that gown, but I prefer the one you have on now."

My head snapped up at Benjamin's words. A strange flutter of … something stirred in my stomach at the words.

"Thank you." I bit the inside of my cheek, "You look quite handsome yourself, Benjamin."

His name sounded strange on my lips, although I had used it earlier. His gaze met mine, and my cheeks warmed as he stood and stepped over to me, "Come, it's time for the feast."

The celebration was worse than dinner had been the night before. Then, I had simply been on display from up on the dais. I didn't have to talk or mingle or force a smile.

But now I was on Benjamin's arm, and I had to follow him as he greeted and introduced me to dozens of the lords and ladies of his parliament. My cheek hurt by the time we finally sat down to eat, but my stomach was not hungry. I picked at the pheasant and potatoes on my trencher, smiling politely as even more lords and ladies stepped up to speak with Benjamin.

For his part, Benjamin treated all of the people with the same cool civility that I had been greeted with when I had first arrived. He didn't smile, his lips didn't even attempt to curl. A tiny pang of sadness stabbed my heart. What had Benjamin seen in his life to make him isolate himself so?

I felt a hand land on my shoulder and I startled, my knife clattering against my trencher loudly. A few head turned as I pressed a hand against my burning cheek. Benjamin was at my side. His brows had lowered as he glanced from my face to the knife. A question lay in his eyes, though I wasn't sure what it was.

"Would you do me the honor of dancing with me?" He straightened up, and held out his hand to me.

I nodded, laying my hand in his. My fingers were cold compared to his warm, callused palm, and I winced, wondering if he would comment on it.

But he didn't. He simply guided me into the open space that the ring of tables created, where there was plenty of room to dance. A small group of minstrels stood in the corner and began to play a waltz. Benjamin's other hand settled around my waist and he began to guide me through the steps.

He was easy to follow. I only had to look up into his face to know he wouldn't let me stumble. A grim determination was on his face, like he was marching into war rather than a waltz. A small laugh slipped past my lips, and I quickly pressed them into a thin line.

"Why do you laugh?" He whispered, twirling me under his arm before his hand tightened around my waist again.

"You look as if you're marching into battle." I stared at his chest, not wanting to see the expression on his face, "I found that thought humorous."

He relaxed slightly as he dipped me, a small smile twisting the corners of his mouth, "I suppose being watched as we are makes me feel as if I am on the warpath."

"A battle of opinion?"

"Aye." He spun me in a few more rotations as the music faded.

He stopped in the center of the dance floor, his steel blue eyes staring at me with an unusual intensity in them. Chairs scuffed against the floor as more people joined us, but Benjamin gripped my hand and tugged me toward the door.

Panic gripped my heart as we headed down the hall to his room.

Our room.

I couldn't breathe again. I couldn't move. Was I falling? I felt a strong arm around my waist, sweeping me up, up, up before darkness edged out any awareness at all.

7

BENJAMIN

I felt my chest tighten as I scooped my now unconscious bride up into my arms. She moaned slightly, which relieved some of my panic. It wasn't the first time I'd noticed her moments of fear. I wasn't entirely sure why they happened, but I was determined to find out.

I carried Aurora's slight frame to my room, managing to balance her enough to get the door open. I laid her out on the bed, before stepping back to the door and closing it softly. Turning back toward her, I paused. What would she think, waking in a strange bed, in a different room, with me hovering over her? Would I scare her worse than she already was?

Aurora moaned, her hand fluttering to her forehead as her eyes blinked open. She studied my ceiling first, before sliding down to meet my gaze. I swallowed, clasping my hands behind my back to keep from tugging at my clothing or my hair.

"Are you all right, Aurora?"

"Aye," she groaned, laying her arm across her face, "Did I … faint?"

I took a hesitant step toward her, "I suppose … what was that?"

She didn't answer for a moment, and then I heard a what sounded like a small cry. I took another small step closer, "Aurora? Are you hurt?"

"You're going to think me weak." She rolled to her side, her back to me, "I wanted to be strong."

I reached the side of the bed now, and lowered myself down on to the edge of it. I didn't know what to do, what to say. I'd never had sisters and barely had had a mother. What was I supposed to do with a crying female?

"In my land, I'm considered … worthless."

I sucked in a sharp breath, staring at her back as she continued.

"I didn't want to be worthless here. I wanted to hold my head up and show your people that I can be strong and confident." Another sob slipped out, "But I'm not."

"I think you're very strong, Aurora." I bit my tongue, gazing up at my ceiling. It had been painted a dark blue, with golden stars all across it. The room had once belonged to my mother, and it made me feel closer to her, seeing the stars each night as I fell asleep.

"I passed out because I was afraid."

I turned to look at her, "Afraid of me?"

She rolled to her back, gazing up at me now. Her eyes were glassy again, her nose slightly red. Her cheeks were damp from crying and she wiped at them as she eased herself up.

"Not of you. Of what …" She ducked her head again, a blush blooming in her cheeks, "Of what you might expect from me."

Realization dawned and color climbed up my neck. "No. I expect nothing."

"Truly?" She glanced around my room, "Then why …?"

"Appearances. We have to …" I cleared my throat, shifting uncomfortably as I tried to formulate the end of my sentence.

"I understand." She grasped my hand, "It was much the same for Alfred and me."

Alfred. I had forgotten that she was once married to my cousin. I didn't know what to do with that information, so I motioned for her to follow me as I stepped toward the fire. I added some logs before sinking onto the settee where she had settled herself.

"What was your life like in Olthgath?" I asked, turning so I could watch her face while she spoke. "The way you speak of it makes me think that it was not overly enjoyable."

She crossed her arms across her chest, tugging her cloak closer about her shoulders, "There are some things I remember fondly. I remember helping the cook make cookies, picking flowers in the conservatory, and playing in the nursery with my sister, Helga." A small smile appeared for a moment but just as quickly disappeared, "But then Helga and Effelwood grew closer, and I was the one in the way."

Her hand snaked up to her shoulder, rubbing it as a distant look appeared in her eye, "They … they enjoyed teasing me, but it was cruel teasing."

I stiffened when she didn't continue. "Did they hurt you?"

"I should have been stronger." She dropped her head, her chin nearly hitting her chest.

"What did they do to you, Aurora?"

Her eye grew wide, and I realized I had growled my question. I softened my tone and tried to relax my

322

body. If she had suffered at the hand of her siblings, the last thing she needed was me dredging those memories up again. "Please, I want to help."

"I don't want to talk about it, Benjamin." Her arms tightened around herself and she turned away from me. "What of you? Are you close with your siblings?"

"I'm close with Nicholas." I tried to smile, "We … we both suffered loss when we were very young."

With her back still angled away from me, Aurora reached up and took off her circlet, setting it down on the table beside her, "Who did you lose?"

I felt a lump formed in my throat, the same lump that appeared whenever I talked about my mother. I had no memories of her beside what some of the older servants had told me. Yet, I acutely felt her loss every day.

"My mother. She died when I was a babe from a disease the healers didn't know. Father remarried a year later, and Nicholas' mother died giving birth to him. Then, Father married again, a year after, and that's the woman I remember calling Mother. She had Collins a year after her and Father married."

Aurora had been pulling all the pins out of her hair while I talked, but she paused when I did, turning to face me, "It is hard growing up without a mother. I'm glad you had someone to love you."

A burning began in my eyes, and I stood abruptly, "Would you like something warm to drink? It's cold this evening."

"Is it common for a groom to leave his bride alone in their room on their wedding night?" She raised her brows at me, her tone teasing.

"Nay, but we are not a common couple."

She laughed softly, her gaze dropping to her lap, "Aye, I would like a warm drink."

I nodded, stepping out of the door. I paused, leaning against the wall, trying to gather the emotions that were starting to break loose from the carefully constructed cage I had them in. I fisted my hand against my chest, rubbing it in small circles. Aurora seemed to awaken emotions in me that I had buried long ago. I squeezed my eyes shut. Her voice played in my mind.

They enjoyed teasing me, but it was cruel teasing.

I should have been stronger.

In my land, I'm considered ... worthless.

I growled, reaching back to loosen the ribbon from my hair. She was not worthless. Far from it. She was a beautiful woman, stronger than most I had met. She did not deserve to be treated the way she had from her family, if they had indeed hurt her.

I rubbed at the ache in my chest again before pushing off the wall to go find our warm drinks.

When I returned to the room, this time juggling two mugs of warm milk with cinnamon on the top, I found Aurora curled up on the chair closest to the fire. She had changed out of her wedding gown, which sent a confusing pang of sorrow through me. She had put on a nightgown with a pink satin wrapper cinched tightly about her. She had taken one of the heavy blankets off the back of the chair and had that tucked around her lap as well. She was braiding her hair over her shoulder when I kicked the door closed with my foot.

When the latch clicked shut, she startled, her eyes wide with fright. It was the same look she had had at dinner earlier that evening. Her body tensed as if she was ready to bolt, but when her gaze landed on me, her stiffness slowly softened.

I forced a smile as I padded further into the room, filing away the strange look to puzzle out later.

"Here," I handed her the mug, sinking down into another chair as she sniffed the drink.

"What is this?" She asked, staring at the mug for a moment before turning to glance at me. She seemed more at ease here, away from the crowd of strangers.

"It's milk with a touch of honey and cinnamon." I smiled again, taking a sip, "Cook makes it for me on nights when I have trouble falling asleep."

She sniffed it once more, before raising it to her lips and trying a small taste herself. "This is delicious."

I nodded, "My favorite drink."

"I can see why." Aurora wrapped her fingers around the mug, her eyelids dropping slightly. "It's comforting."

I glanced at my bed then back at her. I didn't want to upset her, but there really was no way around what had to happen.

"Aurora," she stiffened again, and I cleared my throat before continuing on in as soft a tone as I could manage, "I don't want to scare you. I want us to be comfortable with each other, and I don't want to rush you. But-"

"The bed." She stared at it for a long moment, an expression I couldn't decipher on her face. I froze, unsure if saying anything more would push her over the edge, one way or the other.

She finally blinked, "The servants, yes?"

"What about them?"

"They come in early in the morning. If they see one of us not sleeping in the bed then –" She waved her hand in a circle above her head, "Rumors begin. That would then defeat the purpose of our marriage."

"Aye. That is it exactly."

I was impressed by her quick mind. She had clearly voiced what I had been trying to explain, and with much more eloquence than I could have gathered in so short a time.

Her arms were crossed over her middle again, one hand still clutching the mug. "It is a large bed."

"I'll stay on my side. Upon my honor." I motioned to the bed, "Once I'm asleep, I sleep like a rock."

"I trust you, Benjamin," she smiled, "Willa said you would keep me safe, and I believe her. She has yet to lie to me."

Something warm spread through my chest as I stepped up to one of the four posts, "And to ensure that the nosy servants won't seeing us sleeping apart from each other …" I pulled the drapes across the sides of the bed. "That won't bother you, will it?"

Her gaze was on the ceiling again. "There's no top to the canopy."

I followed her gaze, "My father had this room made for him and my mother when they were first married. She loved the stars, so Father had the servants fix the top of the bed so she could still see them, even with the curtains."

I had never told anyone that, and when my gaze found Aurora's, she was smiling again. "That's a lovely tale."

I motioned to her mug, "Are you finished?"

She nodded, setting the mug on the table that held her pins and her crown.

"We shall obtain you a vanity and a wardrobe for your things on the morrow, if you wish."

"I would like that." She stepped hesitantly up to me, "Thank you."

"For what?" I asked, my tongue feeling stuck to the roof of my mouth again as she gazed up at me with her breathtaking dark brown eyes.

"For helping me through this day."

"It's the least I could do."

We stood that way for a long moment, staring at each other. Aurora turned first, her hand covering her mouth as she yawned. She smiled again, a sleepy one, as she padded over to the bed. "Which side do you normally sleep on?"

It took me a moment for my thoughts to come full circle – from chocolate brown eyes to beds.

"The right."

She smiled again as she threw back the blankets and crawled under them, "Well, that's a good thing, since I sleep on the left."

I gave her a small smile in return, before stepping over to my side of our bed. "Good night, Aurora."

"Good night, Benjamin."

8

AURORA

I awoke to the sound of the maid building up the fire. Slowly, the memories of the day before ordered themselves in my mind and I let my eyes slide open. I smiled at the painted stars shining in the morning sun. Benjamin's story from the night before had warmed my heart. Maybe … if his father could love so much, surely there was hope that Benjamin would one day come to care for me.

I turned my head to see him, curled up on his side on the very edge of the bed. I smiled again. If he was startled awake, he would fall right out. But he had kept his word, staying as far from me as possible.

He stirred, his black lashes fluttering as he tried to grasp wakefulness.

I listened for a moment, making certain that I was unable to hear the maid anymore before I spoke. "Good morning."

His lips tugged up into a small smile, "Good morning. Did you sleep well?"

"Aye? And you?"

"Tolerably."

I motioned to the space between us, "You don't have to sleep that close to the edge, my prince."

His brows lowered, "Benjamin, please. And I did not want to frighten you. I've been told I'm a restless sleeper."

"Who told you that?" I laughed softly.

"Nicholas. On a camping trip in the woods."

I curled my arm under my head, "What happened?"

He smirked, edging closer to the me, but with hesitancy, as if I was a forest animal that could be frightened away. "It was a cold night, and we were bundled together in the tent. I was dreaming, I suppose, and rolled over, hitting Nicholas squarely in the face."

I giggled, pulling one of the blankets up to my nose, "Oh dear."

Benjamin nodded, "I gave him a bloody nose, and slept through the whole thing. Imagine my fright when I awoke to blood covered blankets and no little brother."

I laughed harder, covering my mouth with my hand, "Poor Nicholas!"

Benjamin raised his brow, "What about poor Benjamin?"

I shrugged, smirking, "You slept soundly that night."

I felt my eyes widen as he rolled onto his back, laughing. I had never heard a more lovely laugh. His was low, reminding me of the ocean waves rolling across the shores. He turned his face back to me, his eyes dancing as he smiled, "Aye. That's true."

I couldn't seem to get my words to work as I stared back at him. He was relaxed, something I had not witnessed in the two days I'd known him.

Two day, my thoughts reminded me, *you've only known him a short time. There's still a chance he could be like your father and brother.*

With a gasp, I sat up, grabbing my legs as I leaned my forehead against my knees. I forced my breathing to slow, for I refused to pass out again.

"Aurora?" Benjamin's hand landed lightly on my shoulder, "Did I say something wrong?"

I shook my head, my chest burning from lack of air.

He hesitated, I could feel it in his hand on my shoulder, before he slid it down to my back and began rubbing it in slow circles, "I'm here, if you want to talk."

I squeezed my eyes shut, focusing on sucking air into my lungs and Benjamin's hand on my back. I could handle this. He wasn't like my family. Tears leaked out of my eyes and I shuddered, the chill of the room seeping through my light nightgown.

"Are you hungry?" Benjamin's hand never stopped circling around and around as I struggled to pull myself back together.

After a long moment, I sniffed and nodded.

"Then let's get dressed."

I turned my head, my temple resting against my knees. Benjamin leaned against his free hand, one leg propped up to balance himself. His black hair was mused, free from its normal tail. His bare chest … my eyes widened and I turned to push open the curtains. "Aye. Let's."

Another low chuckle followed me as I stepped behind the screen in the far corner of the room. My wedding gown was hanging from one of the hooks, three other dresses beside them. Grabbing the dark blue, I tugged it on. But try as I might, I could not seem to reach all the buttons. The maid was not likely to return this morning, a fact that sent another burst of heat to my face. Would I ever stop blushing over Benjamin?

"Are you almost ready?" Benjamin called and I sighed, stepping around the screen.

"I'm having trouble with the ... buttons." I kept my gaze on the grown, my bare feet cold on the stone. I stepped over to the carpet in front of the fire, still not brave enough to face Benjamin. "Would you ... mind helping?"

I turned my back to him before he could respond. A heartbeat passed before his warm hands nimbly worked their way up my back, securing the buttons as he went.

"Why so many?" He grumbled as he secured the final one, his hands resting on my shoulders.

I brushed my hair over my shoulders, glancing to make sure it hid my scar. "Fashion."

"That is a poor reason."

I laughed nodding in agreement as he turned me around to face him. He wore black trousers and boots. A blue linen shirt that was a shade lighter than my gown was tucked into his waistband. His hair was pulled back again, a few strands at his temples like the first time I'd met him. But unlike this time, a small smile tugged on the corners of his mouth.

"You look lovely, m'lady."

I dropped my gaze, "Thank you."

His hand twitched, like he was thinking about reaching out, but wasn't sure what my response would be. Silence hugged the room, but it had grown more comfortable, as if we were learning about each other even in the stillness.

"Are you ready?" Benjamin cleared his throat, straightening his shoulders and raising his arm to offer it to me. But my eyes landed on his hand, remembering how warm it had felt in mine on the way to the ceremony the day before and of holding it while dancing. I had liked it, the feel of his hand in mine.

I raised my gaze up to Benjamin's, reaching out as I did so to lay my hand atop of his, "Aye. I feel like I could eat today."

He stared at me, moving his hand to clasp his fingers around mine. We stood staring at each other for another long moment, before Benjamin cleared his throat. His expressionless look shuttered off all emotion as he guided me toward the door.

I wanted to ask him about that look, but a part of me knew that we weren't ready for that conversation. Just like I knew he could never know about my family. He would hate me if he knew.

And that thought hurt worse than a thousand arrow heads to the heart.

We stepped through the doors of the Great Hall to the chatter of a couple dozen knights. They were laughing while they ate, the good-natured jests and buzz of a typical morning. A few glanced at Benjamin and me, winking or smiling in turn. It seemed that, if nothing else, we had earned the respect of the men who would no longer be needed on the front lines.

As we approached the king's table, the red headed prince smiled broadly as did the woman by his side.

"You decided to join us in breaking our fast!" The woman tucked a piece of blonde hair behind her ear, "I'm so glad. I have been wanting to talk to you."

I was desperately trying to remember her name. I knew I had met her my first day here, but so much had happened since then. The panic must have shown through, for Benjamin leaned over just a bit and whispered, "Della and Nicholas."

I nodded keeping my eyes on the couple, "I've been looking forward to getting to know Benjamin's family, Princess Della."

"Della is fine." She grinned again, and I felt myself relax. She seemed genuinely happy to have me here, something I was certain would not be true of everyone.

"I would be willing to share my wife's time with you Della." Benjamin motioned to our spots at the table, "But first, let her eat."

"Of course." Della shook her head, smiling at Benjamin, "After you finish, meet us in the study for some coffee."

Coffee? I nodded even though I had never heard of such a thing before. As Benjamin helped me to sit, I looked up at him questioningly, "What is coffee?"

"You've never had coffee before?"

I shook my head, "Is it a food?"

"A drink." He scooped a spoonful of eggs into his mouth, chewing as a thoughtful look clouded his eyes. "I'm not quite sure how to explain it." He stated after he swallowed.

I shrugged a shoulder, "I would like to try it. Is it sweet?"

"More bitter. Though, some people do add cream and sugar."

We lapsed into silence, each focusing on our food. I felt antsy, my left arm crossing over my stomach. What would Benjamin's family think of me, once they got to know me? Would they still accept me? Or would it be glaringly obvious how different I truly was?

The meal ended all too soon, Della gliding over to me with her smile firmly in place, "Are you two ready?"

A shiver stole its way down my spine, everything I had just eaten threating to come back up. But I forced a smile when Benjamin glanced at me. For his sake, I was going be strong and spend time with his family.

"Aye." It was the only word that came out, the rest sticking in my throat as Princess Sage stepped up next to Della. Her smile was also in place, though a more wary look was in her eye.

"Are Sage and Collins joining us as well?" Benjamin asked.

"Aye, I thought it could be a time for all of us to get to know your wife. Is that all right?"

Her question was not a challenge, it was a simple request for Benjamin's approval. His blue eyes flicked to me, his eyebrow barely raising. I nodded once and he turned back to his sisters-in-law, "Aye, for a short while."

Della nodded once, linking arms with Sage. "We'll meet you there!"

A pang of jealousy struck me. How happy and carefree these women seemed. If only the ladies in the court of Olthgath had husbands who loved and cared for them like the Princes of Allura so obviously cared for their wives. A lump formed in my throat, and I dropped my gaze to my lap.

"Are you sure you're ready to do this?"

Benjamin's hand rested on my shoulder, and this time I didn't flinch away. I turned my eyes up to him, blinking back the moisture as I nodded, "Aye. I'll be fine."

His jaw set, a grim determination flicking across his face for a heartbeat, before he rose and intertwined my fingers with his again. "Then I suppose it's time for you to meet my family."

9

BENJAMIN

Aurora's hand tightened in mine as we stepped into the study. The fire was roaring in the grate, warming the room pleasantly. Della was pouring coffee into cups, her graceful movements captivating Nicholas' attention. Sage sat with her hand on Collins knee, his arm draped casually around her shoulder. They all turned to smile at us as we stepped up to claim a settee of our own.

"What do you take in your coffee, Aurora?" Della asked as she handed her a cup of the brown liquid.

Aurora glanced at me, panic in her eyes, and I turned to Della, "Aurora has never tried coffee before."

I felt my wife stiffen, her head dropping to stare at the cup in her hand, her fingers white as she gripped it.

"Oh," Della didn't hesitate, "I'll just fix it how I like it, then. If you don't care for it, I'll get you some tea. All right?"

"Aye, thank you." Aurora huffed a soft breath of relief, her shoulders relaxing at Della's kind words.

I smiled inside as Della took back the cup, stirring in some cream and sugar before handing it to Aurora again. I watched as she raised the cup to her lips, sipping just a bit like she had last night with the milk. However, unlike the milk, her lips twisted up in a grimace and she shook her head.

"I do not think I like coffee."

Collins laughed, "I don't care for it either, Aurora, so you don't need to worry."

She smiled slightly, her shoulders stiffing as she turned toward Sage at Collins' side. I glanced between them, wondering what Aurora would say. Sage had slain her brother. Did that bother her?

"Princess Sage." Aurora whispered, "I feel that I must tell you … I do not hold it against you for slaying my brother."

"I-you don't?" Sage shook her head, "How?"

Aurora shifted in her chair, and I squeezed her hand in my own, wondering about her answer myself. "Effelwood was cruel. Everyone who knew him walked away with a scar, some more real than others."

The end of her sentence only I caught, my brows furrowing in confusion. She reached up laying a hand on her left shoulder, a distant look in her eye, "He killed without reason and hurt those he swore to serve. I-I am thankful his cruelty has ended. I'm only sorry that you're the one who had to do it."

Something pulled at my chest as I stared at her, a powerful emotion that left me lightheaded. I moistened my lips with my tongue feeling the need to fill the silence that hung around the six of us like a suffocating blanket.

"Well." Everyone's gazes snapped from Aurora to me and my cheeks warmed, "I-I-I-"

"Forgive me, but did my eldest brother start a conversation?" I glared at Collins who laughed, "This is a monumental occasion!"

"It was not a fantastic start, though," Nicholas tisked his tongue, making Aurora giggle. I smiled down at her, thankful to see some of her discomfort fading. "He must practice that, don't you agree Collins?"

"Aye, a necessary skill as the future king of Allura."

"Oh, come off it!" I laughed good-naturedly, making all my siblings' eyes double in size.

"Did he just-?" Della shook her head, her eyes flicking between Aurora and me.

"Well, wonders never cease!" Sage laughed along with Collins, her mouth slightly ajar.

"Come," I pulled Aurora to her feet, motioning to Nicholas and Collins, who had miraculously been rendered speechless. "I've had enough of these jesters."

"Where are we going?" Aurora asked once we were in the hallway. She swung our hands slightly, a small skip in her step.

"The library." I stated.

She stopped moving, the smile sliding off of her face. "I ... I don't think that's a good idea."

"I thought you liked the library." I cocked my head to the side, my eyes narrowing, "You said it was magnificent."

"I do. It is. It's just..." She swallowed, her gaze dropping to the floor as she crossed her arms over her chest. "Reading is not something women do."

"Both Della and Sage read." I shook my head in puzzlement, "It is not something that's common, but many noblewomen read."

"Not in Ironwolf." Aurora hid her face in her hands.

"You ... don't know how to read." I shook my head again, this time at my own stupidity.

She sighed, "It was against the law to even let a woman look at a book in Ironwolf."

"But you said you knew the Holy Writ."

Aurora nodded, "Willa has large portions of the Scriptures memorized. She'd often quote it to Helga and me when we would sew together."

She tipped her head back, her eyes narrowing as she began to quote a passage I was unfamiliar with:

The God of my rock; in Him will I trust: He is my shield, and the horn of my salvation, my high tower, and my refuge, my saviour; thou savest me from violence.

"Psalms?" I guessed, pulling her through the library doors, despite her dragging her heels slightly.

Aurora shrugged, "I do not know. She just … had us repeat it. Over and over until we knew it."

I glanced down at her as I sat her by the fire, "Wait here."

I strode through the shelves until I came to a shelf where we had a copy of the Scriptures. Tucking it under my arm, I hurried a little further down until I came to another shelf with some children stories. I added a few to my stack before returning to Aurora's side.

"First, let's find that scripture you were quoting."

She blushed, "You could always ask Willa."

"But where's the adventure in that?" I smiled, and Aurora stared. After a long moment I shifted, her gaze making me uncomfortable, "Is something wrong?"

"I … you have a very nice smile." She dropped her eyes to her lap again, and I shook my head, trying to clear it as I flipped open the Holy Writ.

It took us most of the morning, but we eventually stumbled upon the verse that Aurora had quoted.

"Second Samuel. Chapter twenty-two, verse three." I pointed to it and Aurora leaned in, her eyes scanning the page. I could see the hunger in her, the desire to know what the words said. Anger and sadness swirled inside me at the injustice of what she had suffered. She had been as much a victim of Donogan's cruelty as my people had.

"These are words?" Aurora reached out like she wanted to touch the page, but she pulled back.

Wrapping my arm around her shoulders, I took her hand, "Here. Point and say the words as we go."

She nodded, reading the whole verse. She tried to pull away, but I tightened my grip, moving on to the next verse:

I will call on the Lord, who is worthy to be praised: so shall I be saved from mine enemies.

I stared down at Aurora. She sat so close, her vanilla smell enveloping me. Her shoulder leaned against my chest, her dark brown hair tickling my chin. It was suddenly hard to breathe.

"God's word." Aurora smoothed her hand across the page, not making any move to pull away from me. I didn't even dare breath, afraid the moment would shatter like glass. "Thank you, Benjamin."

"For what?"

She turned to look at me, her face inches from mine. My gaze flicked to her lips but I forced them back to her eyes. Sweet, intoxicating eyes that were brimming with tears.

"Did I do something wrong?"

"Nay." She laughed, shifting away to pull the Holy Writ onto her lap, "You showed me … words."

I smiled, despite the disappointment of no longer having her near. Three days, and the woman already had me wrapped around her finger.

"You're welcome." I held up the other books I'd pulled from the shelf, "These are not Scripture, but they are good for you to start learning with."

"You're going to … teach me? To read?" Her eyes filled with tears again, "It does not bother you?"

I shook my head, "It would be my honor, Aurora of Ironwolf, to teach you to read."

"You are everything Willa told me you were, Benjamin," she smiled through her tears.

"No. I'm not. But I am trying," I bowed my head, embarrassment warming my cheeks.

Her hand landed on mine, "That is all I ask."

I hope that it's enough. I thought, staring down at the laughing bear on the cover of the book I held, *I hope it's enough.*

10

AURORA

A few days after our first reading lesson, I sat in Della's sitting room trying to thread a needle, which was proving to be a challenge. My hands were shaking, partly from cold and partly from nerves.

Della smiled at me kindly, "It's cooler here than in Ironwolf, is it not?"

"Aye." I sighed, letting my hands fall into my lap, "I'm not sure I'll ever become accustomed to it."

"I have lived here my whole life, and I am still unaccustomed to it," Sage laughed.

I smiled as my sisters-in-law began talking about growing up in Allura. I settled back against the cushions, enjoying being included in the cozy atmosphere of womanhood. Was Helga finding this, banished to the summer home with her knight? Did she truly love him, or had one mistake cost her the happiness I was only beginning to discover?

"There they are!" I was shook from my thoughts by Collins waltzing, quite literally, into the sitting room. He grabbed Sage's hand, pulling her to her feet, "Dance with me!" He twirled her into the open entryway, humming a tune as she laughed.

"What has gotten into him?" Della asked as Nicholas scooted around the dancing couple and sat beside her.

"Father decided we will host a Christmas ball." He shrugged, "We used to do it every year when Collins' mother was alive. When she died, so did the tradition. Father thought it was time to bring it back."

I was only half listening, hoping that Benjamin would walk through the door to sit with me like the other two men. But after a few moments, something in me knew he wouldn't be coming. Swallowing the sigh that wanted to escape, I turned back to threading the needle. Managing that, I stabbed it into the materiel with far too much force. I felt the prick against my finger, and I yelped in pain.

Della's brows lowered at my outburst, and she looked about ready to ask me if I was all right, but I couldn't answer that honestly.

"Excuse me." I whispered, turning to escape out the door.

My finger was throbbing, but I barely felt it with the pain that was in my heart. Why did this hurt so much? He was the crown prince. He had more important problems to deal with than the wife he was stuck with. A tear trailed down my cheek, and I batted at it with the back of my hand.

I was staring at the ground, focusing on trying to rein in my thoughts, that I didn't hear the footsteps until I collided with the solid frame. My arms flailed, and I would have fallen but a strong arm caught me at the last moment.

"Aurora?" Benjamin's low tenor rumbled in my ear. "Are you all right?"

A small sob burst out of me, and I flung my arms around his neck. Benjamin stiffened, as if he didn't know what to do for a moment before he wrapped his arms around my waist, holding me tightly. I buried my nose in his neck, trying to staunch my tears.

"What's wrong?"

Of course he thought something was wrong. Normal women didn't go running down the halls crying.

"Nothing." I shook my head as another sob slipped past my lips, "I don't know why I'm crying."

He laughed softly, "Does this happen often?"

"Not often. But it does happen." I tugged him closer, "Please, just hold me."

I blushed at the request, but Benjamin's arms tightening around my waist. "Of course. You only need to ask."

We stood in the quiet hall for a long moment. I could hear his heart beating in a steady rhythm beneath the soft linen of his shirt. He smelled like the sweet scent of the soap the servants used to wash our clothing and his whiskers brushed against my forehead as he looked down at me.

"What's wrong?"

"I …" It sounded so childish now. I squeezed my eyes shut as I whispered, "I missed you."

"I missed you, too." He exhaled, his breath ruffling my hair, "I wanted my meetings to end so I could come find you. Nicholas and Collins beat me to it, I suppose?"

I nodded, "I thought …" I shook my head, "It doesn't matter."

"It does, Aurora. You matter to me."

"Truly?" I leaned back to catch his gaze.

He nodded, "Always."

I smiled, hugging him tighter as he lifted my feet of the ground and slowly spun me in a circle. "Is it true that your father is throwing a Christmas ball?"

"Yes." Benjamin grimaced as he set me back on the ground, interlocking our fingers together as he guided us back to the sitting room, "I do not care for balls all that much."

I smiled up at him, "I can tell."

We stepped into the sitting room to find not just Collins and Sage dancing, but now Nicholas and Della as well.

"Join us!" Collins called, lifting Sage up in a spin before setting her on her feet and promenading away.

"Shall we?" Benjamin bowed, his eyes laughing as he glanced up at me through his dark lashes.

I curtsied, "It would be my pleasure."

His hand settled on my hip, and I remembered our first dance together. I couldn't help but smile. How far we had coming in just a week.

Benjamin whirled me around, nearly colliding with Collins and Sage as they did another wild spin about the room. I smiled as Sage tripped over Collins' feet, both of them tumbling to the ground. She rolled onto her back, giggling as Collins leaned over and kissed her soundly on the lips.

I looked away, feeling as if I had just intruded on a private moment.

"They are not shy about their affections for one another." Benjamin whispered, "Neither, it would seem, are Nicholas and Della."

I turned to where he had nodded. Nicholas had his forehead against his bride's, swaying slowly to some tune she was humming. He pressed his lips against her head, and she smiled, wrapping her arms around his waist to pull him closer.

I tipped my head up to gaze at my husband's face, "Your family is one who loves with abandon. That should be honored."

His hand tightened around my waist. "Do you truly believe that?"

I nodded, "I would not say it if I truly did not believe it."

Benjamin smiled, the light of it stealing my breath, before he gripped my waist in both his hands and spun me into the air. I laughed, my hands resting on his shoulders. He sat me down, his back to the rest of his family, before pressing his lips firmly against my forehead.

11

BENJAMIN

I smiled at the bewildered look on Aurora's face. She stared up at me, her mouth parted slightly. I had truly wanted to kiss her lips, but we hadn't kissed since our wedding day and I didn't want to frighten her.

"I …" She smiled, her eyes sparkling. "I liked that."

I smiled back, bowing as though the song at a ball had ended, "Thank you for my dance."

She curtsied, her smile never slipping, "It was truly my pleasure.

We moved over to the fireplace, all claiming spots much as we had our first morning as husband and wife. Aurora was twisting her wedding band around her finger, tracing the intricately woven silver bands and tapping each diamond.

"That was my mother's ring." I supplied.

Everyone turned from their conversations to look at us. I reached up and tugged at a piece of hair.

"You didn't need to give me such a precious gift." Aurora tipped her head to the side, a loose strand of her own hair brushing against my jaw.

"It was something to show you …" I glanced at the others but continued anyways, "that I'm committed to making this work."

"Benjamin's mother was a commoner." Nicholas piped up, "Father loved her, despite the backlash he got from Parliament, and even his own family. He married her and they were happily wed for five years."

I smiled, thinking about the portrait that hung in Father's room of my mother, "Father tells the story of the day they met often."

I felt Aurora sink closer to me, her head leaning against my shoulder. "Tell it now."

"Yes, Benjamin. I've never heard it." Della leaned against Nicholas, who wrapped his arm around her shoulders.

"They met in the town square," I began, slowly inching my hand toward Aurora's as I spoke. "He had disguised himself, not wanting everyone to know he was the crown prince. He had already bought some sticky buns at the bakery, and was eating one when he happened upon a booth with silk scarves. The girl at the booth was being hassled by a man bigger than Father, but he didn't like the way the man was looking at the innocent girl. He jumped between them, telling the man to go away and leave the girl alone."

I looked up at the ceiling, imagining my father as a young man defending an innocent young lady, as a smile tugged on my lips.

"What happened?" Aurora asked, clasping my hand in hers.

"The man left. Apparently, he didn't find my mother worth a fight with a strange boy. When Father turned to the girl, it was love at first sight. He handed her a sticky bun and joined her in the booth to help her sell the scarves."

"Father is quite the salesman." Nicholas interrupted, "It's one reason he's been such a great king."

I glanced at Aurora. She was proof he was a good salesman, and it was one 'sale' I wasn't upset about.

"Anyhow," I glared at Nicholas, who shrugged, "They sold many scarves, enough that my mother could close the booth and take it all home earlier than normal. Father helped her, and they met like that for nearly a month.

"By then, Father knew he loved her. But he wasn't sure he could marry her. He did research, and found that in Allura, there was no rule about who a royal may marry."

"Truly?" Sage asked, leaning forward, "Well that's helpful."

"There is one now," I supplied, "Because of Father and my mother.

"They were married with much pomp, for the people loved that Father had chosen a common bride for queen. My grandmother was less pleased, especially when the following year her husband died and Father became the king."

"And then you were born the following year." Nicholas nodded, "And she passed not long after that."

Silence settled around us for a moment before Aurora sighed, "Why did you give me her ring then? It must be one of the few things of hers that are left."

I squeezed her hand, "My father fought for the love he had with my mother. And I wanted to show you that I'm willing to fight for you. I want peace, but I also want you to be content and happy."

I blinked, realizing I had said all of that in front of my siblings and not simply my wife.

"I think that is the most words he's ever said in one conversation." Collins stated. Heat flamed in my cheeks and a grin stretched across my brother's face.

"You truly do bring out the best in our stoic brother, Aurora." Nicholas agreed, laughing when Della swatted him across the chest.

Aurora laughed along with him, though a pretty pink had bloomed in her cheeks.

"Are you ready for a reading lesson?" I whispered, smiling when Aurora nodded.

We slipped out of the study without much ado, meandering slowly down the hallway to the library.

"Has it truly only been a week?" Aurora whispered, her free hand reaching out to clasp my bicep as we walked. "It seems longer and shorter, all at once."

I smiled down at her, "I feel the same way."

"I'm thankful it was you, Benjamin." She leaned her head against my arm, and I felt the heat that was becoming more and more common blooming in my stomach.

"And why is that?" I asked as we slipped into the library.

She turned, grasping both my hands in her cold ones, "Because you're … you're…" She rose up on her tiptoes, pressing her lips against my cheek, "You're easy to care for."

It wasn't quite what I had been expecting, but then, I rarely knew what to expect from this woman. Her eyes danced, much as we had earlier, as she gazed up at me.

"I care for you, too." I leaned my forehead against her.

"There's much we still do not know about each other." She paled slightly.

"I don't think that will change anything. I made a vow to love and cherish you, and I will keep that vow." I reached up, running a strand of her hair through my fingers. Aurora stepped back, gasping as if I had slapped her. She gripped the ends of her hair in her hand as she turned and strode toward the fireplace.

I followed slowly, watching as she picked up the Holy Writ and ran her hand over the cover. It was trembling and, as I eased myself beside her, she stiffened.

"Is there a reason you do not want me to touch your hair?" I asked slowly, trying to see her face as she stared down at the book in her lap.

"I …" She swallowed. "I would rather you didn't."

"All right. If that is what you wish."

"All right?" Aurora's head shot up, and she glanced between my eyes before her mouth formed an O of surprise. "You mean that."

"Aye." I nodded, my brows raising, "Why wouldn't I?"

"Let's read." She opened the Scriptures, ignoring my question, "Can we keep reading about Ruth?"

I smiled as she settled beside me, and I decided that the questions swirling in my head could wait until later. Right now, I was going to enjoy this time with my wife.

WHEN *You* FOUND *Me*

12

AURORA

The chimes of the cathedral rang its sixth toll as I rolled to my side, sighing at the empty side of the bed. No matter how early I woke, I found Benjamin gone in the mornings these days. We had been married two weeks, and in another week, it would be the Christmas Ball. Because of that, Benjamin had resumed all his duties as crown prince, which meant going to meetings of parliament, hosting dinners of business matters, and paperwork. So much paperwork.

I rolled onto my stomach, swallowing the tears that wanted to pour again. It wasn't like I hadn't spent time with my husband over the last week. There had been a few evenings we'd slipped down to the library to work on my reading. A slow, tedious job that made me want to confess that my father was right – women weren't made to read.

"Are you all right?"

A yelp slipped out before I could swallow it. I tried to leap to my feet, only to find them tangled in the blankets. I flailed my arms, meeting with air as I tumbled over the edge of the bed. Pain radiated up my arms as my elbows met the ground.

"Aurora!" A strong hand helped me to my feet, blue eyes running over me to assess for injuries, "I didn't mean to frighten you so."

"I am fine, Benjamin. You just startled me. I thought I was alone."

"I am sorry. I-" He paused, his eyes narrowing the way they did when he was puzzling something out. He reached up, tucking my hair behind my back, his eyes on my shoulder, "What is that?"

I blinked, realizing what he was referring to. I grabbed my hair, pulling it back over my shoulder, "Nothing! Nothing at all. I thought you said you wouldn't touch my hair?"

"That scar ..." His eyes had gone hard as he gazed at me, "Who did that to you, Aurora?"

"Why does it have to be *someone*?" I whispered, my eyes on the floor, "It's just a scratch."

Benjamin shook his head, "That was a knife wound. A deep one, too."

I closed my eyes, but that was a mistake. I remembered it all so clearly. It had been right after Alfred had died. I had been crying in the conservatory when Effelwood had found me. He'd laughed at my grief, calling me weak for needing a man at all.

I shook my head, my eyes snapping open. Benjamin had moved closer, the angry look still in his eyes.

"Stay away!" I scrambled to the side, my back bumping up against the wall.

He pulled up, recoiling as if I had slapped him. "I want to help you, Rory."

I groaned at the nickname, my arms encircling myself to ward off the pain. I wanted his help, to let him hold me as I cried. But I couldn't. I had to be strong enough to bear this alone. I turned away from him, shaking my head, "I don't need help, Benjamin. It's over. Done. Nothing you can do can fix it. I-I need to handle this by myself!"

"Isolating yourself doesn't fix it!" He shouted, making me shrink back further, "I should know, Aurora. I've tried it. I want to be there, to help you. But you have to let me."

"I ... I can't." I gasped, "I have to be strong enough."

"For who?" His voice had dropped again, and he took a cautious step toward me, "Who are you being strong for?"

"I …" I swallowed, "I have to be strong for you."

Benjamin's jaw jumped in and out, his teeth grinding together, "Then you'll never be strong enough, Aurora."

He strode out the door, never looking back at me as he slammed it behind him. I listened to his retreating footsteps before I crumpled into a ball and sobbed.

I stayed in the room the whole day. I couldn't bring myself to face Benjamin, let alone the rest of the royal family. I curled up on the settee, a blanket tight about my shoulders, trying to not cry again.

A few hours after the morning meal, a light knock sounded on the door, and I dragged myself over to it. There stood Willa, her brows furrowed and her lips pursed. "What on earth happened between you and Benjamin?"

"Nothing." I wanted to slam the door in her face, my temper simmering from holding so much in.

Willa raised her brows, pushing her way into the room and closing the door. Her eyes strayed up to the ceiling, a small smile on her lips, before she glanced back down at me, "Something happened. Benjamin looks about ready to fall apart. Everyone can tell."

I tried to swallow the lump in my throat as I turned to sit by the fire again. Tears cut off my words, and I pressed a fist to my lips, "He … asked about my scar."

"You haven't told him about it?" Willa sat beside me, rubbing my back like Benjamin had done a few weeks before.

"If he knew, he would hate my family. He would hate me." I shook my head, "I didn't think I'd make him hate me by trying to be strong *for* him."

"He doesn't hate you, Rory!" Willa sighed, "He's hurt, because he wants you to trust him. To let him help you carry your own hurt."

"That's not fair to him," I sniffed, turning back to the flames.

"He's told you things he's never told anyone else, my dear. I'm sure of it."

I looked up at the ceiling, "He told me about the stars."

Willa followed my gaze, smiling sadly, "Aye. They are a constant reminder of her. We all had grown to love his mother so much. When she died, a gaping hole opened in our family."

"What was her name?" I asked, looking over at Willa who had a tear trailing down her cheek.

"Her name was Sophia." Willa smiled, dabbing at her eyes with the sleeve of her gown, "But back to you and Benjamin."

I groaned, "He'll never listen to me now. He was so angry." I shivered, remembering his raised voice and his parting comment.

Then you'll never be strong enough, Aurora.

"I can't do it, Willa." I shook my head, crossing my arms over my chest to hide the tremble in them.

"You can, and I will tell you how."

I half-heartedly listened, amazed at how sneaky my mother-in-law could be.

"And then," she finished, smiling proudly at her scheme, "You'll tell him everything."

"Everything?" I gasped, my chest aching at the thought of telling Benjamin all about my past.

Willa nodded, "Everything."

"Will you help me prepare?" My hands shook as I turned to her.

Willa smoothed my hair behind my ear, ignoring my flinch, "It would be my honor, my dear. You shall always be my daughter, Rory. Never forget that."

I sniffed, embracing her as tears trickled down my cheeks. Willa had come into my life right when I had needed someone the most. She'd accepted me when my own family hadn't, and she had loved me and Helga even at our worst. She had shown us Jesus, and that was something I would never, ever forget.

As I leaned back from her, I pecked her cheek, "You will always be my mama, Willa. Always and forever."

13

BENJAMIN

I had been dreading this moment all day. I stared at the door to my room – our room – wondering if I'd find Aurora in there or not. I roughed a hand over my face, remembering my heated, angry words to her that morning. I had most certainly not been justified in saying such cruel things to her.

Though, the scar had startled me. I had known she was hiding something from me, but when I saw that wound…

The anger simmered in my gut again, wanting to be unleashed at someone or something, but I pushed it down. Now was not the time.

Now is the time to face my wife.

I stepped toward the door, hand trembling as I turned the knob.

The room was dim as I stepped inside. A few candles were lit, and the fire was crackling merrily. I glanced around, not seeing Aurora for a moment. Had she left? I wouldn't have blamed her if she had.

A creak from the vanity in the corner had me turn, and my breath caught in my throat. Aurora's head was down, but her hair was stacked up on top of it. I could see the scar clearly now, as she had on the same dress from her first night here. The scar gleamed white in the candlelight. She didn't say a word, she simply stood there with her arms wrapped around her middle.

"You look lovely." I whispered gruffly.

She shrugged a slim shoulder, "It was Willa's idea."

"Oh."

A strained silence fell over us, suffocatingly heavy. I wanted to go to her, wrap her in my arms and ask her to forgive me, but I couldn't. Because I had meant what I said. She couldn't be strong enough for me, because I wanted to help with the burden. I wanted us to carry our loads together, not separately.

"I need you to listen."

My eyes followed Aurora as she stepped toward the fireplace, her gaze still firmly on the floor in front of her.

"I can listen." I lowered myself into a chair across from her, ignoring the urge to pull on my hair.

"I'm going to tell you …" she swallowed, her chest rising and falling faster than normal, "I'm going to tell you everything."

I stared at her as she folded her hands, her eyes sliding closed.

"I married Alfred out of desperation. When he asked me to marry him, my life in Olthgath was … well, it was hell. I had the bruises and scars to show for it."

My hand balled into a fist, but I remained still and silent as she went on.

"I thought that life would get better if I was married to a kind man with a kind family. I had hoped we'd leave Ironwolf, even move back here. But war broke out between our nations before that could happen. Then Willa's husband died, and she refused to leave her sons."

Aurora's eyes snapped open, her breathing growing shaky as she went on, "One night, after Alfred and I had been married for almost three years, I went for a walk around the hallway before retiring for the evening. I stepped into my room to find my brother standing over Alfred." She batted at some tears trailing down her cheeks. "There was blood. So much blood. Effelwood had a knife in his hand. He said he'd killed both of Willa's sons and told me that if I ever told anyone about what had happened, he would kill Willa, too. Father cleaned up the mess, like he always did, claiming plague had killed Alfred and Derek. But I knew. I knew and couldn't say anything."

My mouth was hanging open, but I didn't have the willpower to close it.

"And then, a few weeks later, I was in the conservatory, letting myself grieve Alfred. He had been a good friend, a good support, even if I hadn't loved him like a wife should." She shook her head, standing on shaky legs to pace. "Effelwood found me, and he laughed. He mocked me and said I was weak for needing a man at all. 'Why do you need a man, little princess? You should be strong enough on your own.' And then, he pulled out his knife and ..." She was shaking like a leaf in a wind storm as her fingers trailed against her scar. I stood and strode to her, wrapping her into my arms. She leaned her forehead against my chest, her sobs coming in great waves. "I was ... terrified. And I ... I wasn't strong enough to get away from him."

"You shouldn't have had too." Tears of my own clouded my vision, and for once I let them, "You should not have had to fear your own family."

"They never gave me a reason to trust them, or to love them." She laughed, but it sounded harsh and cold, "I had to be this perfect woman, above fault despite the fact that my siblings … over and over they messed up and Father would fix it or hide it. I never did anything wrong and yet -" She began crying again and I pulled her over to the settee, settling her in my lap.

I didn't know how to fix her pain, as much as I wanted to. I wanted to take it all away, but I couldn't. I wanted to strike down those who'd hurt her, but that wasn't possible either. All I could do was hold her, and so that's what I did.

"Is that why you hide it?" I whispered once her sobs had tapered off into the occasional hiccup, "Because your father told you too?"

"He said that no one would think me worth marrying if I had a scar like that. Never mind that my brother had given it to me, it was now my problem."

I tightened my hold on her, "Your value isn't determined by how you look or what you know. It's about your heart. And your heart is beautiful, Aurora."

She leaned back, trying to see my face, "I wanted to be strong for you."

"And I told you, you can't do that." She tried to say something else, but I raised a hand, stopping her, "You can't do that because we're a team, Rory. Your hurt is mine, mine is yours. I want to help you, and that means that I want to bare all of your burdens *with* you."

"You don't even know the worst of it, Benjamin." Her lip trembled, and she paused. I stared at her, waiting for her to collect her thoughts enough to speak again, "My father ... he murdered my mother."

I felt myself go completely still. Words vanished, the only thing pounding through my head was one word.

Murdered.

"You know that for a fact?" I finally whispered.

"Aye," She squeezed her eyes shut as she nodded, "He ... he made us watch. Helga, Effelwood, and me."

"How ... how old were you?"

"I was six." Her head dropped to my shoulder, as if she had no strength left in her body, "Mother had done something that displeased Father, and that was why he ..." She swallowed, a tremble shaking her body. "I'll never forget the terror in her eyes, or Helga's screams. That was the day everything changed. My sister and brother became hard, and I tried to be the good girl. Because if my father could kill my mother ..."

"You know I'll never lay a hand on you, Aurora." I shook my head, a lump lodging in my throat, "I'm sorry for the words I spoke in anger this morning."

"I hurt you," she whispered. "I was afraid to trust you."

I ran my hand down her arm, grasping her wrist in my hand to show her the ring, "I come from a family who loves with abandon. You said that yourself." I pressed my lips to her forehead, "I promised two weeks ago, and I promise you again. I will love you till the day I die, Aurora."

She wrapped her arms around my neck, leaning her forehead against mine even as she gasped, "I love you, Benjamin."

I gently laid my hand against Aurora's cheek, cradling her face. I wiped away her tears with the pad of my thumb before leaning in to press my lips against hers. She responded, her lips soft against mine, her body closer than I though possible. Her fingers ran through my hair, making every one of my nerves tingle with life.

She pulled away first, her eyes still closed. "Can we go to bed?"

"If that's what you want." I blinked, confusion in my voice as I tried to collect my thoughts.

"I -" her forehead leaned against mine, her breathing ragged, "Yes, but not the way we have been sleeping."

"Are you sure?" I tightened my arms around her.

"I don't want you that far away tonight or any night ever again."

"Me either, darling," I chuckled, tears clogging my throat.

"I've never had a pet name." Her eyes opened, shining like gemstones in the light of the fire.

I pressed my lips to hers again, and she sighed contentedly as we rose to our feet.

She moved behind the screen to pull on her nightgown, and I leaned against the mantle, my hands shaking as I tugged off my shoes. So much had happened, we had come so far in just a few hours. But Aurora's admission opened up a whole room of questions and obstacles to overcome.

But I know we can face it, God. You are with us.

Aurora's hand landed on my back, and I turned. Her hair was down around her shoulders again, her thin nightdress flowing around her like an angel's robe.

I scooped her up into my arms, my bare feet padding over to the bed where I gently laid her under the covers. I climbed into my side, and Aurora scooted right up to me, her arm wrapping around my middle, her cheek on my shoulder.

"I may have nightmares," she whispered as I brushed her hair behind her ear, "Will that bother you?"

I shook my head, "Whatever happens, we face it together, yes?"

She nodded and I pressed a kiss to her forehead as she snuggled even closer, her breathing leveling out in sleep.

I felt the shaking of the bed first. My eyes flew open and I sat up, trying to focus on the woman at my side.

Aurora had a sheen of perspiration on her forehead as she tossed back and forth. A moan slipped past her lips and tears were running down her cheeks.

"Aurora, darling. You need to wake up." I brushed a hand across her cheek, startling back when her eyes flew open and a scream flew out of her mouth. "Aurora, it's me."

She's pushed herself up against the headboard, her eyes flicking around before she buried her face in her hands and sobbed. I crawled to her, tugging her into my arms right as the door slammed against the wall.

Nicholas and Collins burst in, swords drawn and their hair wild from sleep. I shook my head at them, motioning them back. They stared at me for a long moment, probably surprised to find Aurora in my arms after my mood the day before. But slowly they backed out of the room, the door clicking closed behind them.

"I'm sorry." Aurora repeated over and over, her cold hand laying on my bare chest, "I – he – it was ..."

"It's all right, darling. It's all right." I pressed my lips against her forehead, hoping to reassure her, hoping to calm her. I was not qualified for this job of comforter, but I was trying. Heaven help me, I was trying.

"I woke you up." She groaned, "I must have been loud."

"You were thrashing about."

She groaned again, tears rolling from her chin to my chest. "I'm sorry."

"Aurora." I pulled her up to look at me in the moonlight, "I do not mind. I told you, I'm here for you. Collins and Sage battle the same thing."

"She has nightmares?" Aurora whispered and I nodded.

"Almost nightly, Collins has told me. He is there for her, and I am here for you."

"I hate waking you," she sighed, her body relaxing against me.

I pulled the blankets around us, the chill of the room waning as we shifted so that our heads were on the pillows, "There's no one I'd rather be with, day or night, than you."

Aurora smiled, murmuring something as she snuggled closer, her eyes already sliding closed. I tipped her chin up, letting a soft kiss brush her lips, "Sleep, darling."

She nodded, her breathing already slowing as I wrapped her in my arms, my cheek resting against her head.

"We're going to make it." I whispered, my own eyes sliding closed, "We will be all right."

WHEN *You* FOUND *Me*

14

AURORA

I awoke with warm arms around me, a steady heartbeat thrumming in my ear. I sighed, my eyes slowly opening to see Benjamin, his long black lashes laying against his tan cheeks as he slept. He was relaxed in his sleep, all the tense lines lessening.

I shifted slightly, hoping to stay like this all day. Would that be wrong?

I felt Benjamin shift too, his warm breath tickling my cheek, "Good morning."

I sighed, nestling my nose in the crook of his neck, "Good morning, love."

He chuckled, and it rumbled through his chest like thunder, "Did you sleep after your nightmare?"

"Aye." I shivered and Benjamin pulled the covers around my shoulders.

"Do you want to talk about it?"

I glanced at him. Compassion and love were etched on his face, so intense that tears filled my eyes, "It was … that moment in my bedchambers. Over and over. I tried to get there faster and I just … I'm never fast enough."

Benjamin pulled me closer, his heart beating hard against my temple. "I'm angry for you, Rory. You should never have had to face that. No one should have to."

"But it brought me here." I sniffed, turning so that my back was against his chest and his arms circled my shoulders. His fingers played with my hair, and I relaxed against him. "I wouldn't change that for anything."

"Nothing at all?" He buried his nose in my hair.

I sighed, "Maybe some things. But I would still want to be here, right now, with you."

Benjamin sighed, "Aurora?"

"Yes?"

"Let's stay here today."

"In our room?"

"In bed." His arms tightened and I smiled.

"I think that's a good idea."

He turned me around, his lips brushing my forehead, before I tipped my chin up and let him claim my lips with his.

We were both broken people, in a broken world. But we would make it. We could face the world together, helping each other hold on together. God's grace, something Willa had told me about, would help us through.

Thank you, I thought as our kiss deepened, *Thank you for this amazing gift. This love I thought I'd never find.*

WHEN *You* FOUND *Me*

Epilogue

RORY

Nine months later ...

"Push! Push, m'lady!"

A cry filled the bedchamber and I squeezed the hand in mine tightly.

"Once more!"

"You can do it!"

Sweat poured down my temples, the fire roaring as a pot of water boiled on it. Servants bustled around, quiet chaos fading around me as I focused on what needed to be done. My hand was numb as another broken, ragged cry bounced around and then …

A baby's wail filled the room and I breathed a sigh of relief.

"It's a boy, Princess Della."

I smiled at my sister-in-law as tears streamed down her face. The maids made quick work of cleaning up the sheets and rags as the midwife snipped the umbilical cord and wrapped the little babe in a cloth. After wiping his chubby little face down, she laid him in Della's arms.

"He looks like his daddy," she whispered, her fingers brushing against the red fuzz on the top of her son's head before turning her gaze to meet mine. "Will you go get Nicholas, please?"

"I'm sure he's in the hall." I couldn't help a small chuckle at the thought. Della leaned back against the pillows, the babe nestled to her chest.

I opened the door, and Nicholas turned, his blue eyes wild and his hair looking like he'd ran his hand through it a few dozen times that evening.

"Is Della all right? And the babe?"

"Both are fine. She -"

Nicholas pushed past me, rushing in and climbing up beside his wife. He gazed down at his son, tenderly running his finger down the tiny cheek as he wrapped an arm around Della's shoulder, pressing a kiss to her temple.

I stepped out and closed the door, weariness pressing down on me. Della had labored for only five hours, but the pains had started late in the evening, keeping everyone in the castle awake for hours.

"You look exhausted, Rory." I smiled, my gaze turning to my husband who stood with his back against the wall, his foot propped up behind him. He motioned me toward him, "Come here."

I practically stumbled into his arms, wrapping mine around his waist as I leaned my cheek against his chest.

"A boy or a girl?" he asked after he'd placed a kiss on the top of my head.

"Boy." My eyes were already half shut, my body sagging in weariness. "And both him and Della are fine and resting."

"Which I think you should do, too."

I nodded as Benjamin wrapped his arm about my waist and guided me toward our room.

"When are we planning on having one?" he asked as I slipped out of my sweaty dress and into a clean, cool nightgown.

"One what?" My heart began to beat faster, and I pressed a hand against my abdomen.

"A baby."

"Oh … well," I stepped up to him, "How about in seven to nine months?" I watched his face, waiting.

He raised a brow at me, before his mouth fell open halfway. "Truly?"

I nodded, a tear slipping out of the corner of my eye, "I didn't want to say anything right away, with everything that's happened."

King Willhelm had died a week after the Christmas ball, much to everyone's sorrow. The whole nation had mourned him, but we had also celebrated, for Benjamin had taken the throne with grace and poise despite his grief. Parliament had rallied around him, and they had surprisingly embraced me as his queen. Della had announced she was with child not long after Benjamin's ascension as king, and the castle had been a flurry of activity with all that that entailed.

"A baby?" Benjamin wrapped his arms around me, his words peppered with awe, "A baby, truly?"

I laughed through my tears, "Aye. And I hope he looks just like his daddy."

He tipped my chin up, brushing my lips with his. He moved to my jaw line then buried his nose in my neck. "A baby. Our baby."

He lifted me off my feet, spinning me in a circle.

"Are you happy, m'lord?" I whispered teasingly.

He eased me back from him, "So happy, my lady. You have made me happier than I could have ever imagined. Even if we could never have children," He leaned his forehead against mine, "I would still choose you every time."

I pulled him to me again, kissing him with reckless abandon, "And I choose you. For the rest of my life, I chose you."

I didn't know what lay ahead, and I still struggled with what lay behind. But I had a husband who loved me, and a God who watched over me, and no matter what else happened … that would always be enough.

The End

WHEN *You* FOUND *Me*

ACKNOWLEDGEMENTS

Ah where to begin! So many wonderful people helped me on this journey, and if I tried to name them all, we'd have another book!

First of all, I have to thank my Lord and Savior, Jesus. I couldn't do any of this without Him and the creativity He gifted me. The messages in these pages are from Him alone, and I'm so blessed to be the vessel He used.

To my wonderful family: thank you and I'm so sorry for going off about Benjamin, Nicholas, and Collins like they are real people. I promise, I'm not insane. *twitch twitch* In all seriousness, your love and support mean the world to me, and I couldn't have done any of this without you encouraging me to keep on keeping on!

To my wonderful friend and editor, Kyrsten: Thank you for fangirling even through all my mistakes and typos. Thank you for your encouragement and support. I'm so thankful for your friendship, sweet friend!

To my sister and proof-reader, Abby: Thank you for laughing over hilariously inappropriate typos, for creating aesthetic Pinterest boards, and Spotify playlists for my boys. Thank you for putting up with me and for being willing to read my stories (even if you "hate reading" in general).

To Eve, Alexis, Alissa, Jordan, Anna, Caroline, and Isabella, my wonderful betas: Thank you, thank you, thank you for fangirling and troubleshooting with me! Your support of this family means there may very well be more stories in the future, and I cannot express my gratitude enough!

A big shout out to Hannah Williams and Alissa Zavalianos for letting me pick their brains about self-publishing. They both were a huge help, and I couldn't have done this without you!

And lastly … you! The reader. Thank you for picking up this book, for pressing the *buy now* button, for diving into this world of princes, princesses, and true love. Thank you for making this writer an author and for supporting her dream. You mean so much to me.

ABOUT THE AUTHOR

Anna Augustine has always loved to tell stories that share the love of God through them. When her mom forced her to write a short story for English one year, she discovered how fun the written word can be and has been writing ever since.

She lives with her family of eight in a small, midwestern town with two dogs and a whole lot of crazy. When she's not writing, Anna is either working as a teacher's aide in her local elementary school, taking photos for her bookstagram, or trying to put a dent in her never ending to be read pile.

Follow Me!

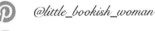 @little_bookish_woman

 Anna Augustine

 @anna_augustine_author